LOVE AND RAGE

Kelsey's Burden Series: Book Five

KAYLIE HUNTER

This book is a work of fiction. All names, characters, places, businesses, incidents, etc., are the imagination of the author, and any resemblance to actual persons or otherwise is coincidental.

Copyright 2017 by Kaylie Hunter

Cover design by Melody Simmons

All rights reserved. No part of this book may be used or reproduced in any manner without the written permission of the author except when utilized in the case of brief quotations embodied in articles or reviews.

Other Titles by Kaylie Hunter:

<u>KELSEY'S BURDEN SERIES:</u>
LAYERED LIES
PAST HAUNTS
FRIENDS AND FOES
BLOOD AND TEARS
LOVE AND RAGE

Chapter One

Six long weeks had passed, and I still didn't have the full use of my left arm. The doctors used a lot of big words to essentially say it was a crapshoot if I'd regain full use of it again. They just kept repeating the same mantras—Be patient—It takes time.

Well, they can all kiss my ass. Time was something I didn't have much of.

And with a bum shoulder, I couldn't carry gear on a raid. I couldn't hold a rifle for long distance shooting. Blocking an attacker in a fight would be a lost cause.

Frustrated, I tried for the fourth time to lift the saddle high enough to settle on StarBright's back. She neighed in protest but stood dutifully in place as I came up short, again, without the strength to raise it higher. As the saddle fell, I stepped back and let it hit the dirt-packed ground.

"What the hell?" Wild Card barked as he ran up beside me and picked up the saddle. "The doctor told you not to lift more than ten pounds!"

He pushed me with his body out of the way and settled the saddle on StarBright's back. After pulling the belly straps, he checked the reins before turning back to me.

"Well?"

"Well, what? I'm not going to sit around and have people wait on me."

"If you don't cut your shoulder some slack, you're going to wreck it for good. And, where the hell are you going this early in the morning?"

"The north ridge needs to be checked. Nicholas has some friends visiting the ranch later this morning. I need to make sure it's clear."

"Well, give me a minute. I'll saddle up and go with you. You shouldn't be out on your own yet."

"You two sound like a bunch of bitching siblings," Wayne chuckled walking up to us.

I placed my left foot in the stirrup and pulled myself up with my right arm. It was harder to do, but I was getting the hang of it. At least it was one thing I no longer needed someone to help me with.

"Hold up, Kelsey," Wayne yelled. "One of us will ride out with you."

I reached over and removed the lead line, freeing StarBright from the fence. Turning her around, I used her body mass to push Wild Card out of the way.

"I'm good," I answered, looking up to face Wayne.

Standing next to him, was Grady Tanner. My chest tightened, and I instinctually raised my bad arm up to cover the burning sensation.

"Kelsey?" Wild Card asked with concern, placing his hand to rest on my hip.

"I'm okay," I said, taking a few deep breaths.

He kept his hand on my hip until I finally nodded and lowered my arm away from my chest.

"Wayne, you're an asshole," I said, turning StarBright once more and giving her a nudge to charge ahead into the field.

"Been called worse," Wayne yelled after me.

"Damn it, Kelsey! Come back here!" Wild Card yelled.

I leaned forward in the saddle, holding the reins in my right hand and gripping the horn in my left and let StarBright run as fast as she wanted. My hat flew back, and my hair clip flew out as my hair whipped around in the wind. This was freedom. The only thing comparable was riding a motorcycle, but I still preferred to ride StarBright.

I lightly tugged the reins, and StarBright veered to the right, toward the north ridge. I sat up in the saddle, and she slowed to a gallop. When I leaned back in the saddle, she slowed to a walk.

"You're the best," I said, patting her on the neck.

She whinnied a reply, and I turned her up the side of the ridge.

My thoughts crashed back to Grady, wondering why he had returned. I had made myself clear that I didn't want him around. I wasn't the same woman I was when we had met. And Grady, he kept pushing me. Invading my space. Trying to get me to tell him about the nightmares. Tell him why I couldn't stand to be in a room with my son or him for long periods of time. How do you explain it? How do you tell someone you are so damaged you know they are better off without you?

It didn't matter anyway. Another war was brewing. A war I would either win and live, or I would die, leaving them all behind.

Turning the final bend in the trail, StarBright climbed the last few feet up the side of the ridge, and I walked her away from the edge and onto the expansive plateau. Sweeping my eyes left to right over the tall grass, from closest to farthest, I searched for any sign of danger. When my natural vision stretched too far into the distance, I pulled my binoculars out and continued looking.

I didn't expect to find anyone. Even before my injury, it would have been near impossible for me to shoot a rifle the distance from the ridge to the ranches. Nor did I know anyone else that could either. But I had called Benny the Barber, a known assassin from Miami. He had assured me there were people for hire shooting a mile mark or better. I looked back at the ranch in the distance. It seemed impossible in my mind, but with the right gun and scope, I supposed it was true.

Confident the field was clear, I ushered StarBright forward. A sharp piercing pain raced up my shoulder, causing me to lean to the left and pull the arm to my chest.

Wild Card was right—I was overdoing it. I needed to be mindful of the weight restrictions. And, I should probably cut Wild Card some slack. He had generously shared his house when I came home from the hospital.

But Wayne was right, we argued like siblings, which made him an easy target for my ever-growing bad temper.

And, Wayne, what the hell was he thinking by bringing Grady to the ranch? Meddling fools.

● ● ●

I worked my shoulder in small circles, massaging it with my right hand. The pain subsiding, I sat upright in the saddle. StarBright misunderstood the movement and stopped. I took a few deep breaths before nudging her forward again.

The morning sun was already drying out the dewy grass, and the breeze kicked everything in its path back and forth. It really was a beautiful day. I nudged StarBright faster, and she easily agreed. At a light run, we skirted the forested areas and made good time crossing the length of the plateau to the back side. I scanned the area with and without my binoculars, not finding anything out of place.

We were now a good three miles from the ranch. Anyone traveling this far would have to access the land from four miles back, thus making it an unlikely target location. But I knew the man wanting me dead had deep pockets and a lot of motivation. If I dropped my guard, he'd kill me for sure.

"Come on, girl," I patted StarBright's neck. "Let's head East. When we get to the bottom, we can take a quick swim."

StarBright trotted along the east path that led to the other side. I continued to scan the area, but as always, nothing. Even my spidey senses were flat, though I wasn't sure if they even worked anymore. They certainly hadn't helped me in the last few battles I had waged.

Slowing StarBright, I turned her to the right, then a quick left to follow the east ridge trail down to the bottom.

A few minutes later, back in the flat grass field below, I released the reins, letting StarBright lead us to the lake in the valley.

The lake was surrounded by Wesley owned ranch land. I wasn't sure which Wesley property the lake actually sat on, or if they all shared a corner of it, but I had never seen anyone other than a Wesley anywhere near it.

I slid off StarBright and let her wander. She wouldn't leave me even if she was startled. I stripped off my t-shirt, and as it snagged on my head, StarBright nosed me in the back, pushing me off balance.

"No fair," I laughed, pulling the shirt the rest of the way off. "You're a sneaky little horse, aren't you?" I teased as I finished stripping off my boots and clothes.

StarBright happily whinnied again as she followed me to the lake's edge. I walked in and drifted into the cool deep water. Dunking under, I let my hair flop back on my back when I came up for air. I turned to see StarBright drinking at the edge before she turned a few feet away to a tall patch of grass to feed.

I stretched my shoulder muscles, then set out to swim a few laps. When my shoulder started aching, I turned and floated on my back.

Dark memories pushed forward in my mind, but I focused on the shade tree's limbs, draped over this section of the lake. The leaves tossed to-and-fro in the light breeze. When I floated away from the tree, I closed my eyes and focused my thoughts on the warm sun as it heated my body. The heat felt good as I drifted in the cool water.

Chapter Two

I was startled when StarBright whinnied. I chuckled to myself, looking up at the sun, realizing it was already late morning. Everyone would worry if I didn't return soon.

"Ok, StarBright. You win. Just let me get dressed, and we'll head back."

I turned to swim to the shore but startled again.

Grady stood leaning against the large oak tree at the lake's edge.

"Is there a reason you're watching me swim nude?"

"If you don't want people to see you, why do it?" Grady grinned.

"Damn, cowboys," I muttered, getting closer to the edge. "Either turn around or leave. I need to get dressed."

Grady turned his back to me.

"We need to talk, Kelsey."

"I've got nothing to say, Grady."

With the exception of my socks and boots, I dragged my clothes onto my wet body. Whistling for StarBright, she happily pranced up to me. I tucked the socks into the boots and then strapped the boots to her saddle.

She turned again, and I chuckled. She had moved so I could climb up on her right side, thus using my good arm.

"You are too damn good to me, girl," I whispered.

After I had pulled myself up, I patted her neck as I leaned forward. Without a word to Grady, I let StarBright race to the ranch house of her choice. She read my mind and took me to Pops' ranch.

Pops, Whiskey, and Sara were in front of the barn when StarBright and I rode up. After I had slid my bare feet into my boots, Pops helped me off the horse. I didn't complain. He didn't offer the help because I was injured. No, he offered it because he was a gentleman, through and through.

"Hey, Whiskey, can you give me a hand with the saddle?" I asked as I unhooked the straps.

"Sure," Whiskey said, effortlessly lifting the saddle and carrying it into the barn.

"Who's following your trail?" Pops asked squinting to see who the rider was.

"Grady," I grumbled, leading StarBright into the barn to brush and towel her coat.

Sara grabbed another brush and pulled her stool over to help. As it turned out, she had no interest in riding the horses, but she loved talking to each of them and brushing them.

"What are you up to today, Little Bug?" I asked.

"Nicholas has some friends over to play," she pouted.

"Did you want to have some friends over too?"

"I don't have any," she whispered.

"What about the neighbor girl?"

"She only wants to ride her horse. And, she doesn't even like computers."

"Hmm. What if you sucker Aunt Charlie into taking you to town to get some new books and some ice cream?"

"Think she will?" Sara grinned.

I pulled my phone out and called Charlie. She happily agreed and said she would be at the house to pick Sara up in ten minutes.

Sara squealed with delight, running to the house as I led StarBright out to the pasture.

"Ice cream?" Whiskey chuckled coming up next to me.

"And new books," I grinned. "Kid is coming down to take her."

"I could use a ride on my bike. I think I'll follow them into town," he said heading for his bike.

"Does he think he's fooling anyone?" Pops chuckled.

"I'll never get upset with him for being over protective of Little Bug. She's too damn important," I grinned.

"She's one of a kind, that's for sure."

Pops looked around and then back at me.

"I sent Grady to Wild Card's ranch. What are you going to do about that problem?"

"Snitch some leftover breakfast from Hattie, and then hide in the barn the rest of the day," I answered as I walked to the house. "Did you expect anything less from me?"

"Not at all, baby girl," he chuckled. "I'm heading out to move the cattle. Reggie's supposed to meet me out there to give me a hand."

"Need me to help?"

"No. You go rest that shoulder you wrenched up again. You're not fooling anyone either."

I stuck my tongue out at Pops before kicking the mud off the bottom of my boots and heading inside.

"You better take those damn boots off, Sunshine," Hattie hollered from the kitchen.

I grinned and kicked the boots off, stacking them by the front door.

"Good Morning, Hattie," I said, stepping into the kitchen and grabbing a cup of coffee.

"Good Morning, Sunshine," Hattie grinned. "You're late. Did you go up to the north ridge this morning?"

"StarBright and –," I started to say, as I turned around.

Sitting at the breakfast bar with his own cup of coffee, Grady sat grinning at me.

"What the hell are you doing here?"

"Kelsey Harrison, mind your manners," Hattie scolded.

I glared at Grady as I sat, two stools away.

"Yes, I went to the north ridge this morning. Everything was clear," I answered Hattie's original question.

"It always is, dear," Hattie said, setting a plate of eggs and fruit in front of me.

"Well, someday, it might not be," I grumbled.

Grady chuckled and continued to eat his own breakfast.

"Pops told you to head to Wild Card's place."

"He did, but before I left, Hattie came out and offered me breakfast," Grady grinned.

I glanced up at Hattie, and she smirked as she put the bread away.

"How did you find me at the lake?" I asked him.

"Hattie told me that after you search the ridge, you go to the lake to take a swim."

"And, you thought you'd sneak out and spy on me, did you?"

"It was my suggestion," Hattie interrupted. "I told him he should grab a swimsuit and meet you out there. It was a beautiful morning for a swim."

Hattie refilled Grady's coffee cup but wouldn't look up to face me.

"Hattie, I swim the lake in the nude," I said, sipping my coffee.

The look on her face was priceless. She huffed and puffed and looked back and forth between us, all the while her face getting redder and redder.

"I, I, I didn't know… Why on earth would you skinny dip?!" she yelled. "Oh, Dear. *Sara*!"

Sara came running down the narrow stairs. "Is Aunt Charlie here already?" she asked.

"Just got here," Charlie said walking in. "What's all the yelling about?"

"You girls need to pick Kelsey up a swimsuit when you're in town. She's been skinny dipping in the lake!"

"She's always skinny dipped in the lake," Reggie said coming into the kitchen with Jackson. "She has suits, just refuses to wear them. We just stay away from the lake when she swims."

"Except Wild Card," Jackson chuckled.

"He hasn't snuck out there to watch her since she put manure in his boots as a punishment," Reggie laughed.

"Y'all are nuts," Anne said as she walked down the stairs, shaking her head. "Come on Sara. Whiskey is giving me a ride on his bike while we follow you and Charlie into town."

Sara, Charlie, and Anne left just as quickly as they had arrived. I turned to Reggie and cocked an eyebrow at him.

"That's the look you give me when I forget something," he grinned.

"Pops is out in the field moving the cattle and said you were going to meet him to help," I glared.

"Shit," Reggie said, running out the door.

"Which field?" Jackson grinned, walking backward toward the door.

"Far west pasture."

"Come on, Grady. Give us a hand," Jackson called as he walked out.

"Well, ladies, it's been interesting," Grady grinned and sauntered out.

"What is he doing here?" I asked Hattie.

"I called and asked him to come. I told him we were short on security. I gave Ryan the week off," Hattie answered as she washed Grady's plate in the sink.

"*You what?*"

"Well, truthfully I called Bones first, but he laughed at me and told me he was busy. He suggested I call Grady. I wasn't sure it would help at all but had to try something, so I went ahead and called. And honestly, I was mighty disappointed Bones dismissed me so quickly. I mean, I know things between the two of you didn't turn out the way he wanted, but –,"

"*Hattie!*" I yelled interrupting her babbling.

"Okay, fine," she said, tossing the dish towel on the counter. "Let me have it."

"Why? Just tell me why you would go behind my back and do something like this," I asked.

"Because I see it! I see week by week you get stronger and stronger—and angrier. You're angry at the whole damn world right now, and it scares me."

Hattie fidgeted with the salt and pepper shakers as she looked down at the counter.

"You're the one that's always kept it together. You planned. You carried us through all the scary shit. But, you're not yourself right now. I don't know what's going to happen if you keep going the way you are."

"I can tell you what's going to happen, Hattie. You only needed to ask," I said, standing up and stepping away from the breakfast bar. "I'm going to hunt the bastard down and kill him."

I walked away, moving down the hall to the front door. I felt my pulse thumping in my neck as I tried to calm myself. My hands were shaking as I thought of the man I was hunting, the man who was hunting me.

Grady stood just inside the door, listening, watching me. I grabbed my boots and continued outside.

"I thought you left," I said when he followed me out.

"I forgot my hat," he said, watching me.

"You better go get it then."

I leaned over and put on my socks before putting on my boots. By the time Grady returned, I had jumped in

Pops' truck and was driving down the long dirt driveway toward the main gates.

Chapter Three

Son of a bitch—I thought, hitting the steering wheel.

I was too hard on Hattie. She was only trying to help me, but damn it, I hated it when people interfered.

I pulled out onto the road and drove to the next driveway which was Wild Card's ranch.

Pulling up in front of the house, I let the truck idle and just sat there. Within minutes, Wild Card came out and leaned into the passenger window.

"Staying or going?" he grinned over at me.

"I could use a drinking partner," I shrugged.

He grinned and got in the truck.

"Nicholas safe?" I asked.

"Wayne and Ryan are both with him," Wild Card nodded.

"I thought Ryan was on vacation this week," I said following the turnaround and driving back to the main road.

"Hattie's a wonderful woman, an excellent cook, and has a great sense of humor," Wild Card grinned. "But it would be a cold day in hell before any of us let her call the shots for security assignments."

"Thanks."

I relaxed my grip on the steering wheel and rolled my head a little to each side, trying to loosen the muscles in my neck.

"You want to talk about it?"

"No," I said shaking my head. "I want to get rip-roaring drunk."

"You're long overdue."

I put the heavy pedal to the floor in the old pickup, and she chugged at a reasonable clip down the long straight road.

"Nothing too classy for you," Wild Card grinned getting out of the truck.

"What's wrong with the Rockin' Roost?" I laughed, standing in the littered gravel parking lot.

"It's fine. Just as well, anyway. You forgot your purse, so for once I get to pay."

I snorted and pulled Pops truck seat up. Reaching under the driver's seat, I pulled out a leather pouch filled with twenties.

"What the hell?"

"I have cash hidden in all the ranch vehicles. Even the tractor," I grinned.

I stuffed a couple hundred dollars in my back pocket and followed Wild Card inside. I wasn't paying much attention, though, so when he abruptly stopped, I slammed into him.

Standing in front of us, the bartender was holding a shotgun on a guy, who was pointing a gun back at him. Off to the side, another guy pointed a gun at two local cops, who also had their guns out. We'd walked into a standoff.

All of them nervously glanced at us before refocusing on their targets.

"Shit! What the hell does a girl have to do to get a day off? I just wanted to get drunk," I complained walking the rest of the way into the bar and stepping behind the counter.

"Whiskey, vodka or beer?" I asked Wild Card.

"Better start with tequila shots," Wild Card answered slowly walking up to the bar and pulling out a stool.

"I don't know," I said, coming around the corner of the bar with a bottle of tequila and vodka. "The tequila looks tainted."

I held up the tequila bottle to inspect it as I set the vodka bottle down on the bar-top.

"What do you think?" I asked the guy holding the gun on the bartender. "Think it's still good?"

I held the bottle out for him to look. When his eyes focused on the bottle, I watched them widen as I flipped the bottle upside down, swinging it into the side of his head.

He swayed, taking a step back, but stayed upright.

Slamming his arm onto the back of a stool, he dropped his gun and cradled his arm. Before he could think to pick his gun up, I pulled my Glock and held it tight against his forehead.

The other gunman was still pointing his gun at the cops but was now watching me.

"Let's play a game," I said to the other gunman. "Let's see if I can shoot your buddy here, and then shoot you, all before you get a round out of the chamber."

"That's not really a fair game," Wild Card chuckled, as he leaned over the bar and grabbed some drinking glasses. "He's probably never shot anyone before. How many people have you killed now?"

"I have no idea," I said, puzzled by the question. "I left a lot of dead bodies in Louisiana."

"Exactly. Maybe you should give him a demonstration of your shooting abilities before he decides if he wants to play."

I looked at the gunman, and he nodded.

"Okay, sounds fair. What should I shoot?"

Wild Card threw one of the glasses up in the air, toward the front of the bar. I turned and shot the glass, before re-aiming my gun back at the original bad guy's head.

The other gunman looked at me and then where the glass had been shot mid-air. He set his gun on the floor and stretched his arms upward as far as he could reach.

The two cops tackled him and cuffed him before coming over and cuffing the first gunman.

"You're right. The tequila looked bad," Wild Card laughed.

After holstering my Glock, I picked up the gun on the floor in front of me and set it on the bar top near Wild Card. I looked back to see the cops were leading the bad guys out of the bar in cuffs. Unfortunately, before they had tackled their guy, they had set their weapons on a nearby table which they had forgotten to retrieve. They had also left the other bad guy's gun sitting on the floor.

Collecting all three guns, I added them to the pile in front of Wild Card.

I poured two fingers of vodka in each of our glasses and then went behind the bar again to search for the cranberry juice. Not having any luck, I looked up at the bartender who was staring at me, still holding the shotgun.

"If you're not too busy, mind helping me find the cranberry juice?"

He set the shotgun down and pulled the cranberry juice from the lower cooler.

"Chilled even," I grinned, as I added a dash to our glasses.

"You're my favorite ex-wife," Wild Card said, clinking our glasses.

"Yeah. You lucked out," I laughed.

"I had told the owner the tequila looked funny," the bartender said.

Wild Card and I looked up at the bartender and tilted our heads. The young man was completely serious. I looked back at Wild Card, and we downed our drinks.

Chapter Four

We were three sheets to the wind when the Chief of police came into the bar.

"I should've known it was Kelsey Wesley," he said.

"Kelsey Harrison," I corrected him. "I never changed my name."

"I suppose you've both drank too much to give me a statement about the robbery?"

"I don't think you want our statements," I grinned. "Might be easier on your ulcer if you just use whatever story your rookies gave you."

"Rookies," Wild Card chuckled, leaning his head on the bar.

"Those *rookies* are two of my most seasoned officers," the Chief said.

"Well, if it makes you feel any better, they're smarter than Billy here—," I said, pointing to Billy, the bartender.

He looked at me confused, but shrugged and set down a beer for the Chief.

The Chief sighed and uncapped his beer. He took a long swig before pulling out his phone and calling someone.

"Your truck is at The Rockin' Roost if you're looking for it," he said into the phone. "Yup, I'll stay and have a cold one until someone gets here."

There was a pause in the conversation, and I sat there openly watching and listening to his call.

"No, they're together. I haven't arrested them yet. Cooper's wife stopped an armed robbery, so I sort of owe them." The Chief glared at me. "I know, life's a bitch."

He hung up, and I looked at Wild Card, but his forehead was leaning on the bar top as he laughed.

"You called Pops on us?" I asked the Chief.

"Hell, yes. I need all the help I can get when you're in town. What's with the guns on the bar?"

"Two are from your bad guys, and the other two are your deputies'."

"You're shitting me."

"Afraid not. I figured they'd have noticed by now," I shrugged.

Wild Card laughed so hard he fell off the stool and onto the floor.

The Chief and I both looked down at him but then turned away, ignoring him completely.

"So how long will you be in Texas this time?" he asked.

"Until I'm healed up. Got a bum shoulder."

"Take a fall off a horse?"

"Nope," I said, stealing Wild Card's full drink and replacing it with my empty. "I was held captive and tortured for five months, followed by being arrested and having guards beat the shit out of me. I'm not sure who exactly injured what."

The Chief looked at me and realized I was telling the truth.

"It's all good, Chief," I assured him. "Barkeep!"

"Who me?" Billy the bartender asked.

Chief rolled his eyes.

"Another bottle, please."

The best and worst experiences in a person's life can happen in ho-dunk bars. On the one hand, they were known for frequent fights and persons of low moral standing. On the other hand, when word spreads that you are partying it up, everyone comes out to join you, as was the case for the Rockin' Roost on this very average weekday.

Anne, Whiskey, Grady, Reggie, Jackson, and Pops had all appeared at some point at the bar and were working hard to catch up on alcohol consumption. The Chief was long gone, and a few of the regulars had started filing in.

The jukebox was turned up, and Wild Card had pulled me onto the six-foot by six-foot designated dancing space to spin me around for a few songs. I was escaping to the safety of the bar when my phone vibrated in my back pocket. I answered it, walking toward the door where it was quieter.

"Kelsey," I giggled into the phone.

"Find a sober driver and get to Pops'," Charlie ordered over the line. "The security team spotted someone behind the barn. I have everyone locked in the house while they search."

I had never sobered so fast in my life.

I turned back to the bar and looked straight at Grady as I answered Charlie. "We're ten minutes out. Be safe."

"Security breach at Pops' house!" I yelled loud enough to be heard over the music.

Tossing the cash from my back pocket onto the bar top, I wheeled around at full speed out the front door.

"Keys!" Grady yelled, running beside me across the gravel lot toward Pops' truck.

I tossed him the keys as I ran to the passenger side. Wild Card pushed me through the open door to the middle of the seat and climbed in behind me. Grady climbed in the driver's seat and fired up the pickup.

Within seconds we were flying down the old country road at top speed.

I heard tires squeal behind us, and Wild Card turned to look.

"Jackson's driving Reggie's SUV. It looks like Anne's driving her SUV. Is that smart?"

"You don't get between a mama bear and her cub," I answered. "We'll be lucky if she doesn't pass us."

Fortunately, it was a short enough drive she didn't get the chance. Grady hit the driveway at full speed sliding sideways, only straightening out when we were halfway down the drive.

"Shit, you drive as crazy as Kelsey," Wild Card yelled.

Grady hit the brakes when we were alongside the front of the house. We were out of the truck before it fully stopped.

"Don't enter!" I warned Wild Card away from the door.

I glanced around.

Everyone froze in place, and I scanned the yard, listening. It was quiet, too quiet.

"Kid, are you safe in there?" I yelled from the front porch.

"Rainbows and Sunshine," she called out the safety phrase.

"We're coming in. Don't shoot us," I yelled back before turning the handle and entering.

Sweeping my gun ahead of me, checking the rooms as I went, I worked my way into the main room. In the dining room, I found Charlie, Sara, Nicholas, and Hattie crouched down in the corner behind the heavy oak table that had been flipped on its side.

"Grady and Wild Card, search upstairs. Whiskey and Jackson, take the downstairs bedrooms." I turned back to see who else was around. "Pops and Anne, get behind the table with Charlie."

Anne and Pops climbed around the table and Pops loaded one of the shotguns leaning against the wall. Anne already had her Glock, but checked the clip again, before pulling Sara and Nicholas in to hug and kiss them.

Everyone returned within minutes, reporting the house was clear.

"Charlie, where did you last see our security team?"

"Two teams of two went out to search. One team to the front of the property and one team out behind the barn. I haven't heard from them since."

"Jackson and Reggie, stay in the house. The rest of us will search the property. Wild Card, turn on the breakers to the yard lights."

After Wild Card had stepped into the laundry room to turn on the breakers to the yard lights, we moved back onto the front porch.

At least a dozen high beam halogen lights lit up a good quarter of a mile around us.

"What are you sensing?" Wild Card asked, stepping up behind me.

"Nothing, but I haven't tested my spidey senses since everything happened. I've been wondering if they're broke."

"Well, mine aren't, and I'm not sensing anything," Grady whispered.

"So, why is it so damn quiet?" Whiskey asked.

Whiskey was right. It was quiet. Too quiet.

"No!" I yelled, running for the barn. "*No!*"

My arms weren't strong enough to pull the heavy barn door open, so Grady pushed me out of the way and did it for me.

I spotted Ryan on the floor of the barn, just inside the door. I crouched down, gun raised in front of me and checked his pulse.

"He's alive," I whispered before stepping over him and moving forward.

The second stall door was partially open. It was StarBright's stall. My hands trembled, my gun shaking, as I stepped forward. Grady gently grabbed my wrist, forcing me to lower my gun, as he stepped in front of me, entering first.

"Wayne's alive," he whispered.

Someone turned on the barn light.

I stepped forward, behind Grady, and looked inside the stall. I started to tremble so violently I felt myself ricocheting off the barn post I was standing next to.

Grady grabbed me by my upper arms.

"Look away," he ordered.

He shook me with a bit of force.

"Look away, damn it."

I looked up at him through blurred vision.

"Your family is inside, and we still have two security guards to find. I need you to pull it together."

I nodded and took a few deep breaths.

He was right. This wasn't the time.

"We need to see if the other security guards are in any of the other stalls," I whispered.

"You watch the barn doors. Whiskey and I will check the stalls," Grady said, shoving me toward the front of the barn.

I moved to one side of the barn door, and Wild Card moved to the other. We had a full view of the front yard, but nothing moved.

Whiskey returned a few minutes later and told me the other two guards weren't in the stalls. I motioned for him to move to the ladder. He nodded before slowly climbing up to the loft to search. When he was done searching the one side, he climbed down and then up the other ladder to check the other loft. Returning a few minutes later, he nodded to let me know both lofts were clear.

"Where's Grady?" I asked.

We heard something being dragged across the wooden slat floor. The sound was coming from the tack room in the back. Wild Card and I grinned at each other.

"I completely forgot I had a stash in the barn," I whispered.

"Good thing Grady is good at finding your hidden supplies," Wild Card laughed.

"Weapons?" Whiskey asked as Grady jogged up to join us.

"And, fucking flak jackets," Grady grinned.

He grabbed me by the back of my head, pulling me into his body, and kissed me. Releasing me just as quickly, he tossed a jacket over my head.

"Crazy war nut," he laughed as he strapped a jacket on himself.

Wild Card secured his jacket before moving over and securing mine for me. I saw Grady look at him questioningly.

"She still can't move her left arm very well," Wild Card answered the silent question.

"You should have stayed in the house then," Grady grumbled.

"Bullshit," Whiskey snapped. "I'd choose an injured Kelsey to cover my back before anyone else, any day of the week."

Whiskey made a move to step out of the barn, but I pulled him back.

He looked at me, and I shook my head.

"Spidey senses are working just fucking fine," I whispered as I motioned for him to step behind the support post.

I turned to Grady and motioned for him to climb the ladder across the way, and I started to climb the one near me. Each on our own side of the loft, I motioned to the side window and then pointed downward. We moved over to our assigned windows and slid the wooden latches over, swinging the windows open at the same time.

Looking down, two men approached each side of the barn doors. They were only a few feet away from stepping into Whiskey and Wild Card's firing range.

Grady whistled, and both men looked up in surprise.

I shot my guy in his gun hand, and Grady shot his man with a kill shot.

"Why didn't you kill him?" Grady yelled over to me.

"I don't know who they are. What if they are neighbors trying to help?"

"Well then—I'm fucked," Grady yelled.

Wild Card stepped out and secured the man I had shot.

"Relax, Grady," Wild Card laughed. "These guys aren't local."

Grady ran a hand down the front of his face.

"I'm really glad to hear that, brother," he sighed, heading down the ladder on his side.

"Whiskey, drag our visitor into the back of the barn and convince him to start talking," I called out from my upper perch.

Whiskey grabbed the man by his injured hand and dragged him screaming into the barn.

"Wild Card, get a sniper rifle from my hidden stash and come up here. There's a good visual of the entire yard."

"Do you see anything?" Grady asked as Wild Card went to get a rifle.

"Two bodies, halfway up the drive and about fifteen feet off to the right. I think they're our missing security guards, but we'll need coverage to cross in the open to check."

My phone vibrated in my back pocket, and I holstered my gun to check it.

"Hello," I answered while scanning the yard.

"Pops called," the Chief said. "He said to get ambulances ready but to not let them cross onto the properties until you gave the all clear."

"Stay back. We have two good guys down, two bad guys down and two missing guys. We have heavy firepower pointing in multiple directions."

"Anything I can do?"

"We have guards stationed at the other ranches. Swing by and tell them we are on red alert. Have them check the barns. The horses here are dead."

"Shit. Call me back when you can."

Disconnecting, I tucked the phone back into my pocket. Trading the phone for my Glock, I turned the safety back to off.

"How bad is your arm?" Grady whispered.

"About thirty percent," I answered honestly, stepping away from the window so Wild Card could set up the rifle.

• • •

"Damn. Perfect sniper nest," he grinned. "Get going. I don't like that Wayne and Ryan have been unconscious for so long."

"On it," I said holstering my gun again so I could use my right arm to go down the ladder.

"This sucks," I grumbled to myself.

"I'm sure it does, but Whiskey was right. Even injured, you'd be my first choice going into a shit storm," Grady whispered as we both stepped out of the barn.

We moved twenty paces forward before we turned and started moving outward away from each other to clear the sides of the barn. Once we were out far enough to have a clear visual, we kept our backs to each other and continued moving forward while we scanned our own 180-degree side. When we started down the driveway, we naturally moved in, closer to each other.

"Why did you come back?" I whispered.

"Because Hattie asked me to."

"Bullshit."

"Okay. Because you need me."

"No, I don't Grady. Any one of the guys could be helping me right now."

"Yeah," he whispered. "But who's helping you cope with all the other shit?"

"I've got it handled."

"Bullshit. You're a ticking time bomb."

The only noise was the sound of my boots in the gravel as we made our way down the drive. I couldn't hear Grady's movements but I sensed where he was.

"Turn toward the road, and I'll turn toward the house. We need to move into the brush," I whispered.

"You know for sure these are our guys?"

"No, but if they even breathe wrong, Wild Card has a perfect shot."

We both turned into our new positions and started moving into the brush. When we were about five feet away, I signaled to Wild Card.

"They're our guys. I'm going to check to see if they're alive."

Grady moved around to cover me, and I checked the guards. The first one was knocked out cold, and I found a dart stuck in his arm.

"Tranq gun," I whispered, pulling the dart out.

I checked the second guy and found the same.

"They're both sleeping on the job," I whispered. "Keep covering me for a second."

I holstered my gun and called Whiskey.

"Anything?"

"Swears it was just the two of them. They used tranquilizer guns on the guards at the gate and then snuck into the barn. When the horses started going nuts, Wayne and Ryan came out. They hit them with tranquilizers too. Wayne wasn't going down, so they hit him in the head with a shovel."

"Okay, I'm calling the Chief to send the ambulances in. Warn Wild Card and clean up anything incriminating."

"Got it."

The Chief answered on the first ring. "The other barns are good. You ready for us?"

"We cleared the property. We have four drugged security guards who will need rides to the hospital. You have a green light to enter."

Chapter Five

Grady helped the deputies load the guards from the gate into a squad car while Wild Card helped the two ambulances load Ryan and Wayne.

"You should ride with Wayne," I told Grady.

He turned and pulled me close to him, our faces only inches apart. "Don't do anything stupid until I get back," he ordered.

He kissed me briefly before turning to jump in the ambulance. Wild Card slammed the doors closed.

"He's got your number," the Chief laughed.

"Shut up," I snapped before jogging toward the house.

From the porch, I called out 'rainbows and sunshine,' and Reggie opened the door.

"All clear," I yelled down the hall as I jogged toward the dining room.

Nicholas dove over the table and wrapped his arms around me. He was shaking and crying.

"I'm so sorry, Nick. I wish I knew how to stop all this," I said while holding him tight and kissing the top of his head.

"Whiskey?" Anne asked, holding Sara.

"He's fine. He'll be inside in a minute," I nodded.

"Pops, the horses—," I started to say. My voice cracked, and I tucked my face into Nicholas's hair, smelling his shampoo.

Nothing else needed to be said. Pops, Reggie, and Jackson walked out of the house in silence. I picked

Nicholas up and carried him over to the couch and sat with him clinging tightly to me.

"You okay, Hattie?" I asked as she was picking up some of the chairs.

"Right as rain, Sunshine," Hattie smiled back. "Don't you worry about us. Charlie kept us safe."

Whiskey came in and lifted Sara into his arms and wrapped an arm around Anne, who smiled up at him. He sat next to me on the couch and pulled Anne down next to him on the other side.

Charlie helped Hattie pick up the overturned furniture. I felt like I should be helping too, but my son needed me more. I kissed the top of his head again and stroked his back.

I wasn't sure how long we sat in silence, but it must have been a good length of time because Grady walked back through the door.

"Wayne and Ryan?" I asked.

"All four of them are fine. Casey, Ryan, and Bobby are expected to sleep until morning. Wayne's jacket partially blocked his dart, but the gash on the back of his head was enough for the hospital to admit him. He's awake, though, and bitching up a storm."

"I thought we were taking the night off tonight and getting drunk?" Whiskey grinned at me.

"Someone messed up the schedule," I grinned back.

"It's not funny!" Nicholas yelled at Whiskey.

We all sighed. I looked down at my son and kissed the top of his head.

• • •

"No, Nick, it's not funny, but sometimes it feels better to laugh than cry," I said.

"It's all your fault," he yelled at me. "Why can't you be a normal mom? If you were a normal mom, the bad people would leave us alone!"

"You're stupid!" Sara yelled from Whiskey's lap.

"Am not!"

"Are too!"

"Enough!" Hattie yelled. "You two stop your bickering right now."

Hattie dragged a dining room chair over near the couch.

"Kelsey, I have to apologize to you," she said with tears building in her eyes.

"What are you talking about? You don't owe me an apology."

"Yes. Yes, I do. And, not because I interfered and called Grady. I knew you'd be pissed and yet, I'm still glad I did it. But because of the other things I said. About you being angry."

"I am angry," I shrugged.

"And, you have every right to be. What I'm sorry about is doubting you. Doubting that you'd figure this out and be okay. After everything we've been through, I should've trusted you. I'm sorry."

"And, I'm sorry I was a bitch to you," I smirked.

"You were mean to Hattie?" Sara asked.

"Very mean," I nodded.

"I think you need a spanking," Grady said, wiggling his eyebrows.

I rolled my eyes and looked back down at Nicholas. "You okay?"

"You shouldn't have gone outside," Nicholas pouted. "It wasn't safe."

"I was perfectly fine."

"But you're a girl," Nicholas said. "You should have let the men handle it."

"Nicholas Harrison, I love you," Charlie said. "But that is the stupidest thing I've ever heard you say."

"Charlie—"

"No, he's old enough," she said stopping me. "Your mother saved me when she was only a teenager. Then she became a cop to help others. She adopted you because you needed someone to protect you. That's what your mom does. She protects people. Being a girl has nothing to do with it."

"She saved Sara and me too," Anne said.

"And, your Aunt Lisa," Hattie added.

"She saved my ass the day I met you," Grady said. "I was shot, and she ordered me to play dead. Then she pulled a sniper rifle out and shot the bad guy."

Nicholas was quiet but looked up at Grady.

"I'm not lying buddy. If there's someone you want by your side when the bad guys come, it's your mom."

"Here, here," Whiskey said.

"But I just want a normal mom," Nicholas pouted.

"Nick, a normal mom wouldn't have been able to get you away from Nola when you were just a baby. A normal mom wouldn't have been able to hunt her down and come find you," Charlie said.

"But she can be normal now. Nola's gone."

"I don't know how to be normal anymore, Nicholas. I'm sorry," I said, kissing his hair.

"But you could try."

"I can't right now," I said. "The man I made angry is going to keep coming after me until I stop him."

"But what if you get hurt?"

"If I get hurt, your Aunt Charlie, Aunt Anne, and Hattie will take care of you."

"But what if they don't want me?" he whispered.

"Nick," Anne said. "You're family. You're stuck with us whether you like it or not."

I kissed Nick on the head one last time before sliding him off my lap and over to Charlie.

"You two go get into some pajamas while I help with the rest of the cleaning up. You can camp out in the living room tonight, and if you brush your teeth really well, then you can watch a movie."

"But we haven't eaten dinner yet," Sara said.

I looked up at the clock and then looked back at Hattie.

"They haven't," she sighed. "I was getting ready to make baked macaroni and cheese when all hell broke loose."

"Pizza it is then," I said, walking toward the front door as the kids cheered.

The deputies from this morning were on the front porch when I stepped outside.

"I have an emergency," I told them. "I need seven large pizzas within the next twenty minutes, or I'm never going to get the kids to sleep tonight."

I handed one of them some cash.

"Run the lights and make it snappy."

Both deputies took off running down the stairs and jumped into their cruiser. Turning the lights and siren on, they left at high speed.

"What happened?" the Chief asked, running across the yard.

"Nothing. Your deputies are idiots," I grinned. "I told them to go on an emergency pizza run. And, they did."

"Damn it, Kelsey. Messing with them is not funny."

"Yes, it is," Pops chuckled, walking up to the steps. "Baby girl, you need to come to the barn with me."

"Pops, I don't think I can," I admitted.

"You'll be fine. Come on," he encouraged by grabbing my arm and pulling me along.

Grady walked up on the other side of me and intertwined our fingers. I squeezed his hand tightly and allowed Pops to lead me out to the well-lit barn.

Halfway there, I heard a horse whinny. I knew that horse. I ran the rest of the way to the barn.

Stepping inside, StarBright's head popped out of her stall, and she whinnied again.

"She's fine," Reggie said, placing a hand on my shoulder as I reached up to pet her.

"They're all fine," Jackson said.

"But all the blood?" I asked.

"Best we can figure, she was raising holy hell when the men came into the barn," Wild Card said. "One of them must have tried to kill her, but running a knife through a horse isn't easy. We're figuring about the same time, Ryan and Wayne showed up. The intruders must have sedated the rest of the horses after they shot Ryan and Wayne."

"The cut on the side of her neck isn't deep," the local vet said. "I didn't even need to stitch it."

"I want security on the barns," I said aloud but was focused on StarBright as she nuzzled into me.

"I already called Donovan," Wild Card said. "Told him we were four guys down and needed an additional six full-time to cover the barns. This is getting expensive though."

"She can afford it," Grady grinned, reaching past me to pet StarBright. "And, if she couldn't, I'd pay for it myself."

Chapter Six

By the time I had checked each of the horses, the deputies had returned and were sitting in the porch rocking chairs eating slices of pizza. I nodded a greeting and walked into the house.

"There better be some pepperoni pizza left," I called out.

Sara and Nick sat side by side on the floor atop a pile of pillows and blankets in the living room, with grinning faces, smeared with pizza sauce. Charlie was on the couch, bogarting an entire box to herself, and everyone else was sitting at the now upright dining room table. I slid into a chair, and Hattie passed me a plate with two gooey slices.

"I changed my mind," the Chief said. "You can send the deputies out for emergency pizza any time you want."

"At least they got something right today," I grinned.

"It's not my fault. No one qualified wants to work in a town where the most exciting thing that happens is a bar fight," the Chief grumbled.

Pops, Hattie and I looked at each other and laughed.

"Well, except when you're in town," the Chief added with a grin.

"Just trying to keep you on your toes, Chief. And, if I were you, I'd ask Wild Card to sign up."

"Really?"

"Sure. He loves this town, but he's bored. Pops has the cattle. Reggie has his horses. Wild Card doesn't have anything to do when he's home."

"Kelsey's right," Pops nodded. "You should corner him and ask him."

"I just might do that," the Chief nodded.

"Until then, you got two really great pizza delivery boys," Hattie laughed.

"Hardy-harr-harr," the Chief grumbled, rolling his eyes.

I looked into the living room and saw Sara and Nicholas whispering to each other. Charlie was sitting right behind them grinning, listening to what they were saying. I was about to ask what was going on when the rest of the guys came in and started rifling through the pizza boxes.

When I looked in the living room again, Charlie was sitting on the floor in-between Sara and Nicholas and all three of them were leaned forward watching the large screen TV. The volume was low so I couldn't hear anything, and the angle of the TV was such that I couldn't get a clear view. I got up and walked over.

"What the hell, Kid?" I asked Charlie. "You can't let them see this!"

I made a move to get to the TV, but Grady stopped me.

"What is this?" Grady chuckled.

"The video of the shooting at the store last winter," Sara said. "Nicholas didn't believe me that Aunt Kelsey's a badass, so I pulled the video to show him."

"Language, little bug!"

"Rewind it so we can all watch," Grady grinned, pulling me down on the couch with him.

I shook my head but didn't stop them. It was probably breaking every parenting rule in the world to see real life violence like this video, but Nick had been surrounded by real life violence for years. And, he needed to understand I could handle myself.

Sara reset the video to the beginning, and Charlie turned up the volume. The video started with us all standing behind the register counters checking our guns and picking on Tyler for leaving his truck in the front of the store to be shot up. When the biker gang started shooting out the front windows, we all ducked down. Then all hell broke loose.

I cringed watching Whiskey get shot and go down. Then cringed again as I watched Wild Card spin me around and take the bullet meant for me.

Grady tightened his arm around me.

The next part was straight out of a movie, it was so unbelievable. I watched myself like some out-of-body experience, jump the counter and dual wield my Glocks, walking straight into the middle of the biker gang. I never stopped shooting. Reggie, Jackson, Tech and James followed me over the insanity line, and in a V-formation, we shot any bad guy that moved.

I jumped up and grabbed the remote, shutting the video off.

"See," Sara said to Nicholas.

"Mom, are you crazy?" Nicholas asked.

"Maybe just a little," I smirked. "But that was a special day."

"That was one of my all-time top five days," Reggie grinned.

"You're all nuts," the Chief said, shaking his head and walking out.

It took two more hours to get the kids to settle down enough to sleep. Anne and Whiskey were curled up on the floor with them, camping out for the night.

Charlie, who hadn't moved more than a room away from the kids since the security breach, was sleeping on the couch next to them. Reggie and Jackson both slept in the matching recliners. Everyone else was quietly talking at the dining room table. I filled up a travel cup of coffee, kissed Pops on the cheek, and walked out of the house. I was taking the night shift in the barn to watch the horses.

I walked a wide perimeter around the barn and then entered and inspected each stall, room, and loft. Confident all was well, I took Copper out of her stall to brush her down.

She wasn't named Copper because of her coat color. No, she was a mostly white horse. But she used to be a police horse. When she was retired, Reggie bought her for the kids to ride.

Copper whinnied in pleasure as I stroked the soft brush down her coat. She was still a little dopey from the tranquilizer, but alert enough that her ears pinned back when the barn door opened.

Knowing it was only Grady, I continued to brush her.

"They've got some amazing horses," Grady said, stroking Copper's forehead.

"That's Reggie's doing. He's good at finding horses for various purposes. Pops' horse used to be a rodeo legend," I nodded. "Now he's one of the best cowpoke horses I've ever seen."

Grady cleaned out Copper's stall and added fresh hay before I moved her back inside.

I was thinking about which horse to brush next when Grady came up and started removing the straps on the flak jacket I was still wearing.

"I'm assuming you're only wearing this because you didn't want to tell anyone you couldn't get out of it?"

"The stupid Velcro straps are too long, and my arm is completely done for the day," I sighed.

"You need to learn to ask for help," he chuckled, pulling the jacket off me.

"Yeah, sure," I smirked.

"So, what's the status on your shoulder," he asked while gently rubbing the surrounding muscles.

"I fractured the socket. It's healing, but not fast enough."

"Thus, the bickering this morning between you and Wild Card because you were trying to lift a sixty-pound saddle five feet into the air?"

"Maybe," I answered, leaning my head back and closing my eyes.

The shoulder rub felt like perfection.

I was momentarily disappointed when he stepped away. But grinned when he kicked a bale of hay out and had me sit on one end while he sat on the other end behind me. He pulled my shirt out from inside my jeans and reached around to unbutton it. I didn't stop him. For one, I had a tank top on underneath. For two, I was completely comfortable with anything Grady did to me.

Sliding my shirt off my good arm, followed by sliding it carefully down my bad, Grady tossed the shirt onto another bale of hay. He started rubbing the muscles again, and I closed my eyes.

"That feels so much better than when the physical therapist does it."

"This physical therapist—a girl, right?"

"No," I chuckled. "Katie hired him based on his looks, but I wasn't interested. Charlie might have hooked up with him though."

"You need a new physical therapist," he grumbled.

"Hmm," was all I managed to vocalize as the rhythm of his movements were soothing the throbbing pain more than any heat pack or cold pack ever had.

He started rubbing down my neck and down my back. It took me several minutes to realize he could feel my scars through my tank top. I stood abruptly.

"Oh, no, you don't," he followed me, turning me toward him. "I don't care about the scars. And, neither should you."

He pulled me in by my hips, tucking me into his body. I could see the desire in his eyes before he leaned closer and kissed me. It was a fierce kiss. His tongue searched and plunged, and my entire body tightened as I pulled our bodies tighter together with my right arm.

● ● ●

His hands stroked and searched me from my head to my thighs, squeezing my ass along the way. My body heated. My breathing became labored.

And, then I remembered why I sent Grady away in the first place.

Pushing with my good arm and stepping away from Grady, I tried to clear my head.

"Kelsey—,"

"NO! Damn-it," I said, dragging a hand through my hair. "Weeks ago, I told you to leave me alone. To not come back."

"Quit hiding from this shit," Grady yelled, turning me around and forcing me to face him again.

I tried to push away, to distance myself, but he moved us back along the wall and pinned his arms on both sides of me.

"You're not scared when I touch you, so what is it? Why do you keep pushing me away?"

I looked toward the barn doors, trying to focus on anything but Grady.

"Look at me," he ordered, gently turning my chin to face him. "What are you running from?"

"You!"

"Why?"

"Because I can't do this!' I yelled, frustrated. "I can't be normal. I'm covered in scars. I have a madman trying to kill me. And if I survive—then what? Grady, I can't have kids. They took that away from me. I can't settle down and have a big family. Hell, I can barely manage to stay in the same room with my own son for more than a half-an-hour. Don't you see? I'm damaged! They broke me!"

"You are not damaged. You are not broken. You're just scared," Grady whispered stroking my cheek. "And, I don't care if you can have kids. None of that matters."

"It matters to me," I admitted, looking up at him as the tears slid past.

"I know," he said, brushing the back of his hand on my cheek to wipe them away. "But I'm here. Let me help."

I leaned my head onto his chest and continued to cry. He wrapped his arms around me and picked me up, carrying me into the tack room.

Using his foot, he kicked the cot out from the sidewall into the center of the room. Laying down on the cot, Grady pulled me on top of him. Feeling safe, protected, I cried until I fell asleep in his arms. And, for the first time in a very long time, I slept in peace.

Chapter Seven

"I should have known," Jackson chuckled from above us.

Startled, I scrambled off of Grady, and off the cot. Grady chuckled as he moved his arms behind his head and stretched his back, not bothering to get up.

"Shit, it's morning," I said, looking out the window. "I'm a shitty night-guard."

"I stayed awake until the new guys Donovan sent showed up. You needed some sleep," Grady yawned.

Grady reached out for my hand, but I stepped away.

He sighed and got up. Stalking toward me, he positioned himself between me and the door.

"We're not doing this again. Whether you like it or not, I'm here. I'm staying. And, you and me—it's real."

He kissed me briefly before turning and walking out of the tack room.

Jackson grinned, still standing in the middle of the room.

"Shut up," I said, as I stomped past him.

"I didn't say anything," he laughed as he followed me out.

Pops was in the barn, cleaning stalls. Jackson and I both grabbed pitchforks and helped with the last two stalls. After feeding the horses and petting StarBright, I stepped outside into the bright sun.

"The other barns?" I asked, yelling back inside.

"This is the last one. We started at Reggie's this morning," Jackson said stepping out of the barn.

"Okay, I'm going to make a quick circuit of the north ridge," I said, turning my attention to the far distant property.

My hand started to shake, and the hair on the back of my neck stood up.

"Reggie is already up there," Pops said. "He went to the ridge while we finished the horses."

Wild Card walked up carrying two cups of coffee. When he went to hand me one of the cups, he saw my face.

"What is it?" he asked, throwing both the cups into the side yard.

"Reggie's in trouble. Who's covering security here?" I asked as I ran back into the barn.

Pops started saddling StarBright as Wild Card, Jackson, and Grady started saddling their own horses.

"We have a full team on the property, and Wayne's inside with the kids," Wild Card said.

"Pops, raise the red flag. Lock down the house," I ordered, jumping on StarBright's back. "Wild Card and Jackson — take the east trail. I'll take the west. Eyes open and safeties off."

I didn't wait for them, but pointed StarBright to the west entrance of the ridge and leaned down to let her run.

She covered the distance in record time. I could hear another horse approaching as I led her up the narrow incline, but kept my focus on the trail.

• • •

Nearing the top of the ridge, I pulled my Glock from its holster and thumbed the safety off. I was regretting bringing StarBright. She would be exposed when we crested the top of the ridge. I was willing to put my own life on the line, but couldn't stand the thought of her being hurt.

I nudged her faster the last few feet. At the top of the ridge, I turned her into a small grove of pines. I scanned the area with all my senses. I could see Copper about a quarter mile down the ridge, dancing nervously too close to an unmoving Reggie. He was laying on the rocky surface, face down. One wrong move and the horse could crush him. I held my position despite desperately wanting to go to him.

Grady pulled up over the edge of the trail and followed my lead into the grove.

"He moving?"

"No, but if he's pinned down, he may be playing possum."

"I'm familiar with that game," Grady whispered. "Where's the threat?"

"Somewhere in the trees on the other side of the prairie," I whispered, scanning the tree line in the distance.

StarBright shifted her weight between her feet, eager to move forward.

"Call Wild Card. I'll follow the trees and come in from this side, and he can come in from the other side. You and

Jackson hold back and when you hear shooting, get Reggie out of here."

"Be safe," he nodded as he pulled his phone.

I turned StarBright deeper into the trees.

Twigs crackled beneath us as I directed StarBright through the thick forest. I hoped we were far enough away from the shooter, so he wouldn't hear us.

I nudged StarBright to move faster as we weaved around the west side to the back of the prairie. I opted to travel further to the north. My best chance was to sneak up behind the sniper. Wild Card would have a shorter distance to travel since the ridge and prairie were narrower on the east side. I hoped he decided to turn further into the woods as well. My gut was telling me whoever was out there, was a professional.

Deep enough into the forest, I slid off StarBright. I grabbed a handful of oats from a side pouch, feeding them to her and calming her down to get her to stay. When she settled, I moved by foot southeast, to what I hoped would be behind my enemy.

About halfway to my target, I spotted a palomino tied to a tree. The gunman wouldn't think much of hearing a horse in the woods, with his own being here. I unhooked the girth strap and slid the saddle to the ground before untying the horse and slapping his rump, leading him in StarBright's direction. The palomino would follow her scent and stay with her unless someone changed his course.

I continued forward, careful to remain silent as I maneuvered around the trees. Fifty yards in, I found him.

A few feet inside the tree line, the sniper lay in the brush with a rifle. The rifle rested in a low standing tripod, pointed directly at Reggie who lay in the far-off distance.

I moved to the left and settled next to a big oak tree, sighting my Glock. I had a perfect shot. Unfortunately, if his finger was on the trigger, he could still let off a round and hit Reggie. I held my position.

From my far left, a whistle pierced the air.

My eyes never left my Glock's sight, and as the sniper rolled back away from his rifle, I fired.

The bullet purposely landed an inch outside his right ear, blowing chunks of dirt and bark to ricochet around his head. I had his full attention. He slowly raised his hands in surrender as I moved forward. Stepping over tree limbs and walking through the dry brush, I held my sight on him the entire distance. His eyes never wavered as I approached.

From the left, I could hear Wild Card approaching.

"Why didn't you take the kill shot? Surely, you weren't worried he was another neighbor," Wild Card called out.

"Nope," I said, holstering my gun.

While Wild Card held his gun pointed at our prisoner, I removed the rifle from the tripod. Taking a step behind the sniper, I slammed the butt of the gun into the back of his head. He slumped over, half rolling into a patch of briars.

"But, I wouldn't mind asking him a few questions," I grinned.

Wild Card nodded while he pulled his phone out to call Jackson on speaker.

"Reggie's okay," Jackson answered. "The bullet grazed his ribs, spinning him off the saddle. He was playing possum like Kelsey said."

"Good thing. He was inside the crosshairs the entire time," Wild Card said.

"I'm taking Reggie down. You two good?"

"Kelsey is. I'm not. She got to shoot somebody, again. The only thing I got to do was whistle," Wild Card complained.

"Maybe next time, big brother," Reggie laughed.

"Take it easy heading down. We'll be there as soon as we can."

"Grady's heading your way. Reggie can ride, so we'll be okay."

"Copy that," Wild Card said hanging up.

Chapter Eight

"Did Grady give you any grief when you split off from him?" Wild Card asked while searching the sniper and removing his other weapons.

I found some rope and passed it to him to tie the sniper's hands. It would have to do until we got back to the ranch.

"None," I said shaking my head. "Grady's not like that."

"I know. I just wasn't sure if you noticed," Wild Card grinned. "Never thought I would see the day."

"The day for what?"

"When someone actually figured you out. He somehow manages to protect you and trust you to protect yourself at the same time."

I smirked but didn't say anything. Grady did understand me, in ways no one else ever came close.

Grady entered through the center tree line. He was riding a spooked Copper. I stroked the horse's neck to calm her, and she nuzzled into me.

"Where are the rest the of horses?" Grady asked.

"There's a palomino about 50 yards back. I sent him in the direction of where I left StarBright," I said. "I could whistle, but I'd have to go back for the other saddle, anyway. I dumped it in the woods."

Wild Card whistled for his horse. "You guys go ahead. I'll keep the prisoner entertained until you get back."

Riding double in the saddle, we quickly made it back to where I had dumped the saddle. I whistled for StarBright, and she led the palomino to us a few minutes later. Grady strapped the saddle on the palomino as I tried to calm a still nervous Copper.

"Settle down old girl," I coaxed, petting her coat.

She leaned into me, and I could feel her tremble.

"I think I better ride her out. She might be jumpy on the trail down."

"You sure? If she starts acting up, your shoulder might not be strong enough to control her."

This was the Grady I was falling for. He knew my limits and was letting me know I was passing them, but still letting me make my own decision.

"I hear you're pretty good with horses. Can you take her?"

"Won't be a problem. I'd feel better if you were on StarBright," he nodded, bringing me her reins.

I didn't say anything as I hooked the palomino's reins to StarBright's saddle and climbed up on StarBright's back. Grady stroked Copper's neck a few times before climbing onto her back and turning toward the prairie.

"Took you long enough," Wild Card complained. He was leaned back with his Glock resting on his chest, and his feet crossed, propped up on the unconscious sniper. "I was about to start a camp fire."

"We'll roast marshmallows later. Get off your ass and load him on the palomino," I said.

"You sure the horse won't throw him?" Wild Card asked, lifting the guy's upper body and dragging him over.

"Do I care?"

Grady snorted and got off Copper to help load the prisoner on the palomino's back. They weaved the girth strap through the man's tied hands so if he did fall, the horse would drag him along. It was my turn to snort as I loaded the remaining gear into StarBright's saddlebags.

"Hurry up," I called, once again sitting in the saddle and turning my horse out into the prairie. "I'm hungry."

"Yes, ma'am," Grady said, following behind me.

Halfway down the ridge, Copper started fighting the decent. Grady was leading her down the ridge behind me.

"Hold StarBright back, so Copper can't bolt," Grady ordered.

Grady's order made sense, but I wasn't willing to risk StarBright if Copper pushed the issue. At the next switchback, I slid off StarBright's back and slapped her rump to send her home.

Copper was ready to charge down the trail, but I stepped in front of her and pulled her lead tight and downward.

Focusing her on me, I walked backward down the trail, urging her on.

"If she spooks again, she'll knock you off the ridge," Grady whispered.

"Not my Copper," I purred at the horse, rubbing her forehead. "Just a bit further my girl."

She whinnied and shook her head, but settled into a nice pace following me the rest of the way down the trail.

"You should have stayed on StarBright," Grady said when we reached the lower field.

"She couldn't risk StarBright," Wild Card said as he exited the trail, pulling the palomino behind him. "Kelsey would take a bullet for that horse and the rest of us would too, just to save her the heartache if something happened to her."

I held my good arm out, and Grady helped swing me up in the saddle behind him. He set the horse in the direction of Pops' ranch. Wild Card turned off toward his own ranch with the palomino. The security guards would help him secure the prisoner.

I tipped my head back, closing my eyes and absorbing the morning sun on my skin.

"You love it out here," Grady said, tilting his head back toward me.

"I feel free here."

"When everything settles, will you live in Texas?"

"I don't know. Charlie wants to go back to Florida. Anne and Whiskey are ready to go back to Michigan. No matter where I live, my family gets split up."

"What does Nicholas want?"

"I've been too afraid to ask."

"Because you know he'll want to stay in Texas?"

"Maybe," I sighed.

A horse neighed in the distance, and I heard fast hooves moving our way. I leaned around Grady as he pulled Copper's reins to a stop.

"Something's up," I said, sliding off Copper and waiting for StarBright to pull up alongside me.

Her coat was wet with sweat, and her eyes were peeled back. She neighed again, as I climbed up, forgetting about my injured arm. Shooting pain lanced up my shoulder. Using my right arm, I pulled my left arm closer to my body.

"You okay?"

I nodded but still waited for the pain to subside before I grabbed the reins.

With a shake of the reins, I leaned forward and gave StarBright the lead to run.

StarBright led us to the far west field where Pops cattle were feeding. I saw the cougar before StarBright pulled up to a stop. It was 50 yards out.

Pulling the rifle from the saddlebag, I passed it to Grady as he pulled up beside me. I knew my arm wouldn't be able to hold it steady.

Grady slid off Copper's back and handed me the reins, stepping a few feet away to take aim.

The shot rang out, and StarBright stayed steady, but Copper spooked again, going up on her hind legs. With only one arm useful, the drag from Copper's reins pulled me off StarBright's back. I tightened my hold with my right hand, trying to pull her closer.

"Settle down girl. Settle. Come on," I cooed.

"She's going to bolt," Grady whispered.

I let go of the reins as Copper reared back on her hind legs. StarBright, moving in between Copper and me, reared back to protect me.

Copper turned and fled in the opposite direction.

"Damn, I love your horse," Grady chuckled, walking up and kissing me.

"Did you get the cougar?" I laughed, pushing away from him.

"Of course."

Chapter Nine

Grady sat behind me as we rode back. The saddle wasn't big enough which left me sitting half on top of his lap. I was trying desperately to think of anything but the feel of his rock-hard erection. He rested a hand on my upper thigh, his strong thick fingers stroking the inner skin in a rhythmic pattern. I was dizzy from the sensations drumming through my body.

When we reached the barn, he lifted me effortlessly off StarBright's back and nudged me over to a nearby bale of hay to sit. He ran a hand down my cheek, down my neck, as he stared at me. Shaking his head, he abruptly turned back to StarBright to remove her saddle.

We were silent as I watched him work. His biceps flexed as he moved the brush down her shiny coat. His jeans gripped his muscles as he leaned over to work her legs. He glanced back only once, and I saw the heat in the quick glance. My nipples tightened and my breaths shortened. I wanted him. As much as I tried to fight it, I wanted him. And, he knew it.

After settling StarBright in her stall, Grady turned and focused on me. He watched my eyes as he walked the length of the barn toward me. Reaching me, he lifted me, carrying me into the tack room. I wrapped my legs around him as he leaned my back into the wall.

"I need you," he whispered, before trailing warm wet kisses down my neck.

"Then take me," I answered, as I lifted his jaw and kissed him.

Throwing my right arm around him, my fingers weaved into his thick hair as I deepened the kiss. Unable to lift my left arm I used my hand to pull his shirt from his jeans and run my fingers on his hot skin, just above his waistline.

"Fuck," Grady grumbled, as he grabbed my ass tighter and moved me over to the tack table. "This wasn't how I imagined it, but I can't wait."

Grady pulled my boots before attacking the button on my jeans. I was just as frantically pulling at his belt with my left hand as I stripped his shirt over his head with the right. I stroked his heated skin along his shoulders, chest, and abs as he stripped my jeans and underwear down my legs.

He kissed me deeply, as he moved me forward on the edge of the table, leaned me back and slowly entered me.

My head spun as I felt him stretching and flexing inside me. My body responded by gripping him tighter. With one arm around my waist and his other hand tangled in my hair, Grady pulled out and rocked back into me, over and over. Gaining speed as we continued to kiss.

Gripping my hair firmly, he pulled my head back as he used his other hand to lift my shirt. He sucked my nipple into his mouth as he rocked harder and harder, driving me to the edge of release.

Moving my right hand back into his thick hair, I pulled him tight to my breasts and held on as best I could. He lifted me, pulling me further off the table, so only my upper back leaned against it. He gripped my ass tight, his fingers embedding themselves into my flesh as he slammed into me. I screamed my release as my insides convulsed around him.

"Fuck yes," Grady moaned, his lips leaving my nipple and moving to my neck.

I felt his own release pulsating hot liquid as he leaned over me.

Grady shifted my weight back to the center of the table. We were both breathing hard.

"Did I hurt you," Grady asked, his hand stroking the side of my face.

"No," I laughed. "No, you didn't hurt me."

I sat up and kissed him briefly before letting him see my smile.

"Good," he grinned back, fondling my breast and kissing my neck. "Because I plan on doing that again."

"I'm not sure how many more wild romps I can take on the tack table."

"I'm sure we can find a few more locations. In fact, I think we might need to go for a swim in the lake later."

"It will have to be much later," I said, pushing him back so I could jump down. "I'm starving, and I have a prisoner to interrogate."

Grady playfully tried to stop me from dressing, but in the end, he grabbed his shirt and began to redress.

I walked out of the tack room and saw Ryan leaning against the horse stalls, grinning.

"Did you need something?"

"I was told to let you know lunch is ready," Ryan smirked. "But I didn't want to interrupt."

"Sure, you didn't," Grady laughed, walking out of the tack room. "We'll be there in a minute."

Grady wrapped an arm around my waist as I watched Ryan walk out of the barn.

"I should be embarrassed, right? Or he should?"

"Ryan likes to watch, so don't plan on him being embarrassed," Grady grinned.

My blood ran cold, and my head spun.

Grady grabbed for me as I started to sway. Moving me over to a bale of hay, he sat me down next to him but didn't lessen his hold on me.

"Kelsey," Grady whispered, holding my face in his hands. "Hey, it's okay."

My vision centered on Grady. I shook my damaged thoughts away.

"Shit, sorry," I said, trying to pull a full breath of air into my lungs.

"I shouldn't have said that. I wasn't thinking," Grady said, pushing my hair away from my face.

"Not your fault." I took several deep breaths.

"Ryan isn't like that. He'd never allow a woman to be hurt. He's only into the consensual shit," Grady said.

"Yeah-yeah. It's all good," I said, trying to shake off the memories.

"Look at me, Kel," Grady whispered.

I couldn't face him. One minute I was my old self again, and the next I'm sitting on a bale of hay as cold shivers racked my body.

"Kel, you have to look at me."

Tears threatened. My lower lip trembled. I forced myself to look up at Grady.

"I'm here. I'll help you, but you've got to let that shit out. You can't keep trying to hide it."

I buried my face in his shoulder and let the tears flow.

Wrapping his arms around me, he lifted me up onto his lap. His hands rubbed up and down my back comforting me.

It took me a good ten minutes before I was able to stop crying and wipe my face.

"Sorry."

"For what? Being human?" Grady sighed, stroking my hair out of my face again. "You should've seen how messed up I was after the service. And, I didn't get through it on my own Kel. I had a lot of help. Ryan, Wayne, Wild Card, Bones—they were all there for me. You have to learn to lean on others."

"I don't know how."

"Then I'll teach you," Grady whispered, cupping my face again and kissing me gently.

I clung to him, welcoming his touch. When Grady touched me, the darkness, the memories, faded to the background. Needing them to vanish, I leaned into him and kissed him back.

He stripped my clothes from my body as he leaned me back onto the bale of hay. Every move was slow, purposeful. Every touch was gentle, comforting, real. His kisses were tender. He watched me intently as I climaxed before following me with his own release.

Chapter Ten

"Mom, why do you have hay in your hair?" Nicholas asked, pulling some straw out of my hair.

I choked on the burger I was chewing, and Pops thumped me on my back while he laughed.

Wayne, who had apparently already been released from the hospital, grinned as he took a big bite of his burger.

I looked up at Grady as he pulled another piece of straw out of my hair. He shrugged before turning to Nicholas.

"I was marking my territory," Grady answered Nicholas with a smirk.

"What does that mean?" Sara asked.

"If you two nosy kids must know, I was kissing Kelsey in the barn and quite pleased I kissed her so dizzy she didn't know she had straw in her hair," he laughed.

"Ewww. Gross," Nicholas said, completely done with the conversation.

He ran off to the back of the house.

"I bet you were doing more than just kissing," Sara said.

Grady spit up his coffee and started coughing.

"Sara, will you check to see if the washer is done yet," Hattie asked, distracting Sara with a mission.

Sara ran down the hall to the laundry room.

I tossed my napkin to Grady to use to clean the coffee as Pops and Wayne leaned forward, faces down, laughing.

My phone rang. It was the gate guard announcing a visitor. I verified the guest and gave permission for him to enter. Turning to Hattie, I thought about how to word the announcement.

"Whatever it is, Sunshine, spit it out," Hattie insisted clearing her and Pops' plates.

"Henry's here," I blurted.

Hattie froze in place for a brief moment, before relaxing her shoulders and walking toward the kitchen.

"Well, isn't that nice. It will be good to have a visitor."

"Reginald Wesley!" Jackson yelled as Reggie fled into the living room. "Get your ass back in bed and let Charlie fix your wound!"

"No way. She scares me."

"It's just a scratch. Quit being a baby," Charlie walked out saying.

"It's a bullet wound. I'm in pain here."

"*Whatever.* Kelsey has had a hundred of those bullet grazes. It barely needs a band-aid," Charlie said.

"I think it needs stitches. What do you think Kelsey? It's my first bullet wound you know," Reggie said, holding the towel out for me to see the flesh burn along his ribs.

Sara came back into the room and looked at the wound too. She smirked at me. She'd had worse cuts from wiping out on her bike.

"I have just the thing for that. Hang on a second," I said, getting up from the table and moving into one of the back bedrooms.

I came back out with a tranquilizer gun and shot Reggie in the leg.

"Now you've been shot twice!" I grinned at Reggie.

He looked down at the dart in his leg, then back up at me and grinned.

He fell backward, and Jackson caught him before he hit the floor.

"Patch him up," I said to Charlie.

Jackson chuckled and dragged Reggie down the hall.

"Well some things never change," Henry grinned from the entranceway.

"Hey, Henry. Welcome," I smiled.

Pops walked up beside me, sipping his coffee and looking down at the dart gun.

"Can I have that?" he asked.

I passed him the gun and went back to the table to eat my burger.

"Thank you," Jackson sighed, coming out to the dining room. "He's sleeping like a baby. How long will he be out for?"

"I have no idea," I shrugged. "I didn't read the instructions."

Everyone, including myself, looked at the dart gun sitting in front of Pops.

"Looks to be a canine dart," Grady said. "If so, I would guess about an hour."

"So, we'll have to listen to him all afternoon?" Wayne groaned.

"I have the shots Doc gave me in Florida. We can give him one of those after he eats."

"Why didn't you give him one of those to start with?" Sara asked.

"Because it was more fun to shoot him," I admitted.

She covered her giggles with her little hands as I pulled her up onto my lap. Nicholas came up to my other side, but I couldn't reach around Sara with my right arm to pick him up. Grady scooped him up onto his lap before it became an issue. Nicholas was content because Grady still had homemade fries on his plate to snitch.

I had been half watching Hattie fuss over Henry as she flitted around fetching him lunch and coffee while keeping a watchful eye on Pops who scowled into his own cup. I ducked my smirk behind Sara's hair.

"So, Henry, what brings you to Texas?" Grady asked, winking at me.

"I was missing my Hattie of course," Henry grinned. "Now, don't get me wrong, Kelsey, I've been busy stocking clothes for the store when the reconstruction is done, but it was time for a vacation. And, I couldn't think of anywhere I'd rather be than where I could visit with Miss Hattie."

Hattie blushed and swatted Henry on the shoulder with a towel.

Pops extended his hand over the dart gun.

"Pops, you and Jackson need to head out to the west range," I said. "Grady shot a cougar earlier. Copper ran off, so we didn't have a way to haul the cougar out."

"Mighty appreciative, Grady. Been seeing signs of one about."

"Sure thing. StarBright took us straight to it, so it wasn't an issue."

"Love that horse," Jackson grinned, heading for the door. "I'll get the truck, Pops. Put away the dart gun before Kelsey takes it away from you."

Pops threw a glare at Jackson's back but carried the dart gun to his bedroom.

I grinned at Henry, who looked a bit perplexed.

"You have cougars running around here? Is it safe for Sara and Hattie? Maybe they should come back home."

"We take good care of our women and children around here," Pops snapped, returning from the back hallway. "Don't you worry your pretty little head about it."

Pops stomped out the front door, slamming the screen shut behind him.

Hattie stood in the kitchen and looked up at me with huge eyes.

I, of course, snorted.

"I didn't mean no offense," Henry said, looking back at the door.

"Don't sweat it, Henry. So, how long are you visiting for?"

"Can only spare a couple days. Was hoping to rope Hattie into riding back with me," he grinned, wagging his eyebrows at Hattie.

"You are sweet, Henry. But, I can't leave right now. Thank you for the offer though," she smiled, touching his shoulder.

Henry looked up at her grinning.

"Well, then," Grady said, reading a message on his phone. "We have a meeting at Wild Card's house," he said.

"Can I go too?" Charlie asked returning from her nursing duties. "I need a break from the munchkins," she teased, tickling them.

"I'll watch the kids," Hattie nodded. "And, Anne and Whiskey will be around."

"I'm still on house duty too," Wayne said, lifting his coffee. He had a bandage on his forehead but otherwise appeared to be back to normal.

"Let's go, then," I said, clearing my plate. "Henry, we can move your stuff to Reggie's house later. Best if you sleep there as Pops' house is already crowded."

I grabbed Grady's plate on my way by, but my left shoulder cinched up. Grady snared the plate before it fell. He picked up a few empty glasses, acting as if nothing happened.

I walked into the kitchen and after setting my plate down leaned my head against the refrigerator.

"Give yourself a break," Grady said, kissing the side of my neck and wrapping his arms around me.

I leaned back into his embrace and sighed.

"It was a plate! It barely weighs anything!"

"And, I've watched you over work your shoulder at least a dozen times. You are supposed to be resting it."

"I'm frustrated."

"I know," he chuckled, vibrating my back. "But right now, we need your brain, not your shoulder. Let's get to Wild Card's barn, and you can feel more useful."

"You just want to get me in another barn," I smirked, turning to face him.

"The thought crossed my mind."

"Uh-hmm!" was Hattie's version of announcing her presence as she walked into the kitchen with more plates.

"Sorry, Hattie," I grinned.

"No, she's not," Grady chuckled.

I swatted him with my good arm before heading to the front door. He followed me out, but when I opened up Pops truck to get behind the wheel, he stepped up beside me and slid me across the bench seat.

"I'm capable of driving."

"For the rest of the day, you're going to give that shoulder a break. There's no reason for you to be wrenching it while driving this old pickup on rutted roads."

"Fine."

"Don't pretend to be mad. It just makes me want to find a place to park and spank your bottom side."

Grady drove down the long drive and turned left toward Wild Card's house. I looked over at him and grinned. I couldn't help it. The thought of Grady spanking me sent all kinds of tingles throughout my body.

"For security purposes, we better check out this two-track lane," Grady grinned, turning right and up a two-track trail to the vacant property across the road.

At the top of the hill, he turned the truck to the left behind a large shade tree.

I was already sliding a leg over him before he had the truck in park.

"You are amazing," he grinned, before kissing me and pulling me tight against him.

He quickly stripped the buttons on the front of my shirt and pulled my tank top up. He broke our kiss, to pull a hard nipple into his mouth. I moaned at how good it felt and started to strip his belt as he unsnapped my jeans.

"I need you," I moaned, feeling like the clothes would take forever to strip off.

Grady moved us to the passenger side, stripping my boots and jeans at the same time.

Finally freeing him from his jeans, I stroked his hot length. I was wet with anticipation. He lifted me, sliding himself into me as we both leaned our heads back and enjoyed the internal caress.

I tightened, clenching against him as he raised and lowered me again.

"Fuck yes. Milk me, baby," he moaned, pulling my tank top up again to suck the other nipple.

He continued to lift and lower me in slow strokes, controlling the movement. My body heated, and the pressure built.

"More," I moaned.

Grady slid forward in the seat, slouching back and throwing me forward into him.

"Take the reins, Sweetheart," he whispered as one of his hands slid to my bare ass and the other kneaded my breast.

I spread my knees further and rode him hard and fast. My clit dragged through his pubic hair, wetting it in hot streaks. We went over the edge together.

"Hot damn," Grady panted, kissing me briefly. "You deserve a medal."

I couldn't talk. I was breathing too fast. I dipped my forehead to rest on his chest.

"We should get dressed before someone reports us for trespassing," he chuckled, pulling my tank top down.

I moved beside him on the bench seat and pulled on my panties and jeans. I finally caught my breath by the time I was putting my socks on.

"No one would be called out to this property. I know the owner," I grinned.

Grady looked at me and laughed, understanding my meaning.

"How long have you owned it?"

"A couple years," I shrugged. "I bought it back when Wild Card and I were married, but he doesn't know."

"Who does know?"

"Only Pops. He sneaks his cattle over here every year just to hear the boys yell that he's going to get thrown in jail for trespassing."

"Those Wesley men," Grady chuckled shaking his head.

He opened the passenger door of the truck and stepped out. I finished pulling my boots on and followed him. Walking hand in hand, we climbed the hillside. The tall grass floated with the breeze as we looked down at the long stretch of land in the lower valley.

"It's beautiful, isn't it?"

"You're beautiful," Grady said, pulling me in front of him, my back to his chest. He wrapped his arms around me, one hand stroking my abs. "You ever going to tell them?"

"That I own the land?"

"No, that you plan on moving back to Michigan."

"I haven't decided what I want," I sighed, leaning my head back on his shoulder.

"Oh, it's what you want. But you also want this."

"I can't choose between them."

"You don't have to figure it out today," he said, pulling me back to the truck. "We're late. And, I need a shower."

Chapter Eleven

Wearing fresh clothes and my hair still wet from my shower, I walked into the dining room. Charlie, Wild Card and Ryan were sitting around the table, waiting for me. Grady leaned against the nearby wall, grinning. He also had wet hair and fresh clothes on. He must have used Wild Card's private shower after I kicked him out of the main house bathroom.

"There's something everyone needs to see," I said, leading everyone out of the house and out to the barn.

The breath I was holding slowly expelled when Grady reached out and grasped my hand. I nodded entering the barn and leading them up the stairs to the bunkhouse loft.

"Why are we going to the loft?" Wild Card asked.

"Because I turned it into a War Room," I answered, opening the door.

I waited as everyone filed past me into the room. The setup was similar to the other War Rooms I had in Michigan and Miami. TV monitors were mounted along one wall. A large table was covered in laptops and piles of folders and papers. Another wall was covered with surveillance photos.

"How in the hell did you do all this without me seeing you?" Wild Card asked as he looked around.

Grady grinned and pulled out a chair.

"You only come into the barn to clean the stalls and feed your horse," I shrugged.

Charlie had answered a text message before she studied the surveillance photos on the wall.

"Who's this?" she asked.

"The guy who sent a professional sniper to our doorstep," I sighed, sitting next to Grady at the table. "I'm only going to be able to cover this once, so help me get everyone on a conference line."

Charlie set up a teleconference line with Tech, Katie, and Donovan. Their faces appeared on the wall mounted screen.

I called Bones, and Grady helped me set up another screen and link the two connections.

"Well, look at that glow. Is somebody getting laid?" Katie teased me.

"Hey, Katie. Are you gaining weight?" I asked.

She jumped back to look at herself, and everyone laughed.

"Bitch," she laughed, sitting back down next to Tech in the Michigan War Room.

"Right back at you, babe," I winked.

"So, what's on the agenda?" Tech asked.

"Yeah, I've been out of the loop. When did you get another War Room?" Donovan asked.

"I set it up in secret. We're in Wild Card's barn. What I'm about to share doesn't go out of our circle. No cops. No Feds."

"You call the shots on this one," Charlie nodded. "So? Who's the man that you're afraid of?"

"*Was* afraid of, Kid. I won't live in fear of him anymore."

Jackson, Whiskey, and Anne entered the room and looked around for a brief moment before they joined us at the table.

"The kids?" I asked Anne.

"Pops, Wayne, and three other guards are with them. Hattie put on a movie to keep them distracted."

"Something happen?" Bones asked, raising an eyebrow on his screen.

"We had a close call last night and again this morning. Everyone is okay, but we need to talk about a possible relocation."

"We'll tighten up security," Wild Card said, shaking his head.

"The horses could have been killed," I reminded him.

"But they weren't," Grady said, putting his arms around me. "And, if you move Nicholas and hide him away, it will be no different from how he lived with Nola. At least here, he can run around and play like other boys."

"I agree. The kids are safer here," Anne said. "But we can't keep waiting to be blind-sided. We need to go after whoever is trying to kill you."

"I know. I've been trying to get my shit together so I could leave, but this damn shoulder isn't cooperating."

"Then you be the brains and let us be the muscle. Just, tell us what's going on," Jackson said.

"I will. I don't have a choice. I can't beat this guy alone."

Grady rubbed my back, comforting me.

I took a deep breath before blurting out some truths.

"The man trying to kill me was one of the first men Nola brought to torture me. But, he was worse than the others. Like Nola, his excitement was centered around my pain—both physical and mental. If truth be told, it was him, not Nola, who finally broke me. He made me wish I was dead."

Charlie got up and walked up behind me, placing a hand on my shoulder, offering me her strength. I placed my hand on top of hers and continued on.

"First, he watched me being tortured. Then he tortured me himself. But he sensed there was more he could do. And, one night, he found my breaking point. He tortured a young woman, barely out of her teens, and made me watch. I lost it."

Charlie leaned over and wrapped her arms around me. Grady rubbed my thigh. My hands shook as I looked up at everyone, but only saw flashes of memories.

"And, once he saw my reaction, he found more women. More victims to torture."

"Shh… It's over. It's over," Charlie whispered, holding me tighter as my body trembled.

"No, it's not. He's still out there. It's not over until he can't hurt anyone else. He's sick and twisted and—untouchable."

"No one is untouchable," Wild Card said.

"Yeah, he kind of is," Bones sighed.

Everyone turned to the screen Bones was on.

"So, Bones knows who he is?" Charlie asked.

Bones nodded, "Jonathan Vaughn."

"Jonathan lives in Pittsburgh. Bones is there under the pretense of learning the family business while he keeps tabs on Jonathan for me," I said.

"To what end?" Grady asked. "If you know who he is and where he is, why don't we just kill him?"

"Yeah," Donovan said. "I like that plan."

"Because," Bones said, "He's running for governor."

The room was silent.

Bones was looking anywhere but at his computer monitor while everyone else watched me.

"No wonder this guy has you rattled," Grady said, pulling me over and onto his lap.

I think he needed to feel me close. Charlie looked in shock as she returned to her chair. I knew what they were thinking. I had had months to come to terms with the dangers of going after such a public target. If any one of us were caught trying to go after him, we could spend the rest of our lives in prison.

"Holy shit," Katie said. "Super big fish."

"The media would never let the story drop," Tech said.

"Especially not this guy," Bones said. "He's rich, charismatic, and resourceful, which would be bad enough but he's also the leading candidate."

"If we kill him, we'd have every Federal agency in the country hunting for us," I said.

"So, then we need the Feds, right?" Wild Card asked.

"They'll never get enough evidence on him to make it stick. He has too many powerful friends and enough money to have a good lawyer spin any story they wanted,"

I said, sliding off Grady's lap and walking over to the surveillance photos.

"So, what's the plan, boss?" Katie smirked. "You wouldn't be looping us in if you didn't have one."

I grinned at Katie on the screen before leaning folder to slide a stack of folders closer to me. I opened up the first one and started pulling out papers.

"I've been digging into his financial accounts and companies the best I can. I'll send what I have, but Tech, I need you to carefully, and I mean very carefully, dig deeper."

"On it," Tech grinned.

"Kid, work research on his family," I said, sliding another folder down the table to her. "He has a wife and two daughters. In every picture, his eldest daughter looks scared out of her mind. Find out why."

"He better not have touched her," Charlie grumbled.

"Bones is working the social connections. He's starting to get invited to the same parties and around the same rich cronies as Jonathan."

"Well, makes a hell of a lot more sense than the BS story you fed me about *wanting to spend time with family*," Tech laughed.

"It was all I could think of," Bones chuckled.

"Why did you tell Bones and not anyone else?" Grady asked.

"I told Bones I needed someone to watch Jonathan. I'm sure he assumed why, but I didn't offer an explanation. Bones' family is wealthy, influential, and lives in Jonathan's backyard so to speak. That access gives him the best cover to get close to Jonathan. No one would be surprised if Bones started hob-knobbing at the country club."

Grady nodded but still looked uncertain.

"Grady, I'm not a threat man," Bones said. "Kelsey and I straightened out our shit."

Grady nodded again but didn't say anything.

"I'm currently digging into Jonathan's criminal history and connections," I said, changing the subject. "It's dark and personal. I need some loose strings tugged to see if we can get more information, but I'm too visible. I'm also not too keen on sticking my head out of the gopher hole just yet. I'm hoping someone can sneak out to check a few leads."

Grady, Wild Card, Ryan and Jackson all nodded.

"How did you get illegal dirt on him?" Donovan asked.

"I stole Nola's purse when I escaped. Inside it was a small ledger book with names and contact information. I've been analyzing the information, and a lot of it leads back to Jonathan from what I can tell."

"Anything you want me to dig into?" Tech asked.

"He uses the same call service number Nola used when we were trying to track her down. It didn't help us find Nola, but maybe you could have Carl do a bit of hacking and see if he can find anything."

"I'll get him started. He's been bored and driving us nuts. He rewired the microwave yesterday so it would play Baby's Got Back when you run it. Hattie's going to be pissed when she gets home."

"Katie–get Hattie a new microwave," I chuckled. "Bones, do you have anything new?"

"I got word that Rebecca was having dinner with someone I don't approve of, so I crashed her date," he smirked. "She's pissed, but low and behold, Jonathan was dining at the same restaurant with some of his friends. He seemed very distracted by some phone calls and at one point stepped down the hallway to talk."

"You control freak. You crashed your sister's date?" I laughed.

"Not important," he grinned. "I went to the restroom and was able to hear part of his call. He wasn't happy. Something about a plan going badly."

"That would be a raid on the ranch. Wayne was hit with a shovel, and my horse was cut, but everyone's fine."

"Shit."

"Did you hear anything else?"

"No, but we need to get ears on him. I can't get close enough."

"I'm not pulling the Feds in on this. And, with his security team, it would be near impossible to bug him or his phone. For the moment, we keep going as we are."

"You're the boss," Bones nodded.

"I think you would mingle better if you had a date other than your mother or sister to some of these functions. Do you have any objections to me sending Bridget your way?"

One of Bones' eyebrows rose an inch higher than the other. "I wouldn't mind Bridget keeping me company, but this isn't exactly a laid-back crowd that would understand a club girl being at their fancy parties."

"You're an idiot," Katie said, rolling her eyes.

Tech laughed so hard, he had to step away from the computer.

"What? Why am I an idiot?" Bones asked.

"It doesn't matter," Anne said. "Katie, get Bridget looped in and see if she is willing to meet up with Bones."

"Any immediate questions?" I asked.

"What's the plan with the guy tied up downstairs in the tack room?" Wild Card asked.

"I talk to him, alone."

"No," Grady said.

"I agree. That's not a good idea," Anne said.

"I don't really care. I need answers, and I have a better chance getting them if I go in alone."

"Questions, answers, research—How does any of this help?" Jackson asked. "How does researching the crap out of this guy solve anything?"

"We gather the intel and wait. When we are ready to strike, we hit him from every angle: family, money, reputation, freedom. When he is stripped of everything, then I decide what to do with him. But whether I send him to prison or send him to hell, he'll be penniless, powerless, and alone."

"How long have you been planning this?" Charlie asked in a whisper barely loud enough to hear.

"Since the day I escaped."

Chapter Twelve

After getting everyone started on research projects, and then spending the next fifteen minutes arguing with them as to why I needed to question the sniper by myself, I finally walked down the loft stairs to the tack room.

I should consider myself lucky. They finally agreed to Jackson being the only one to accompany me. At least I knew he'd stand back and allow me to fly solo instead of jumping off the handle and beating the tar out of the guy.

Opening the door, I found the sniper was tied to a support beam. Someone had been nice enough to bandage the side of his head before binding an old rag around his head to function as a gag. Having been sleeping, when the door opened, he was instantly on alert, his gaze locked on me. I knew exactly what he was thinking because I had been in his shoes not so long ago. He was looking for an escape, a weakness he could exploit. But there was no escape.

I pulled a burner phone from my pocket and pointed it at him, taking a picture. He tried to turn away, but he was tied too snuggly to the post to move more than an inch. I sent the picture to Benny the Barber, no message, just the picture. Within a minute, I had a reply.

Sniper. Goes by Leo. Works high-risk jobs. No one will miss him if he disappears.

I handed the phone to Jackson so he could read the message. He nodded, handing it back before leaning against the far wall to wait and watch.

"So, Leo? Is that your real name or a nickname?"

He just glared at me.

"That's okay. I don't really care. What I found interesting is that no one will miss you if you disappear. Now, that's valuable information."

He flinched but kept his eyes trained on me as I walked up to him.

I pulled the edge of his shirt collar over to inspect a tattoo. A Marines insignia, interesting. Jackson stiffened when he saw it.

Sliding a switch blade out of the inside of my boot, I cut open the sleeve on his right arm. An anchor tattoo. Ripping the sleeve lower, I found his service dates tattooed on the inside of his forearm. He served two tours.

I stepped back and looked at him again. His anger had faded, and he was looking at me with curiosity more than anything else.

I texted Benny again.
What the fuck aren't you telling me?

It took a few more minutes than the last message for Benny to reply, but when it came through, I knew it was true.

Ex-military. Came back a little messed up. Believes his kills are to protect his country. Takes jobs from government and those pretending to be the government.

I set the phone on the tack table and opened the folder I had brought down with me.

"Pam Tate. Twenty years old. Senior at Colorado State University." I turned and held a photo of the young woman out for Leo to see. "I watched your client cut her body to pieces while she screamed for help. When she finally passed out, he left her alive to bleed out in front of me."

I stepped closer, holding the photo inches from his face.

"She regained consciousness before she died. She begged me to save her. I was chained to a cement wall and helpless."

Leo shifted his eyes from the photo back to me. He was trying to read me. I picked up the next picture.

"Karen Pierson. Eighteen years old. Your client raped her with foreign objects. He punctured her organs from the inside. I watched as she died a slow painful death. He whistled softly while he sat in a chair only a few feet away from her, watching her face writhe in pain."

Leo looked several times from me to the photo of the young girl wearing her college sweatshirt laughing with her friends.

"Hey, Kelsey—" a voice startled me from the doorway.

I wheeled around to the door. There stood both the police deputies. I looked at Jackson and then at Leo, before trying to mask my surprise and address the deputies. From where they stood, they couldn't see Leo.

"Hi. What are you two doing here?" I asked as I walked toward them, trying to lead them back into the main barn area.

"The Chief wanted us to check in with you and see if you needed any extra security tonight," one of the deputies grinned.

The other deputy was smiling too, but looked around the corner and saw Leo tied to the post. Jackson had blindfolded him and was rubbing Leo's bare arms and chest. *Oh, boy!*

"No, we're good here. We actually are in the middle of something though and could use some privacy if you know what I mean."

"So, you're into all that kinky stuff?" the deputies asked.

"The kinkier, the better," I grinned, steering them away from the room. "What can I say? I was raised up North."

"Yeah, makes sense," the deputy nodded. "Well, we'll be off then. Give us a call if you need anything."

The second deputy seemed a bit too interested, and a little excited, trying to look back to see what Jackson was doing to Leo, but the first deputy reached back and jerked his arm to get him to follow.

When they walked out of the barn, they were both whispering and laughing.

"Oh, My Holy!" Anne squealed from the stairway. "What the hell is going on in there?"

I turned back to Leo and Jackson. Jackson had stripped Leo's jeans to his knees. Leo was wearing red, white, and blue themed boxer shorts. Jackson held his hands out to his sides and laughed.

"Bravo."

"Homophobes really don't want to know what goes on in gay relationships," Jackson grinned.

"Well, they were pretty easily convinced all Yankees are sexual deviants, that's for sure."

"It's all the snow," Jackson laughed. "We imagine all kinds of crazy things when we think of being cooped up inside for months."

"We're not cooped up. We can drive just fine in the snow," I said, rolling my eyes.

"I don't want to know what is going on," Anne said, shaking her head. "I'll send one of the guys outside to stand watch of the barn until you're finished."

Anne jogged back up the stairs, and a few minutes later, we could hear everyone laughing. Wild Card and Grady came down and peeked into the room. They continued laughing until they saw the service tattoos. Then both of them froze.

"I'm almost there. Just give me a few more minutes," I said to them before turning back to Leo and removing his blindfold.

He looked frantically at the door, but his shoulders sank in defeat when he saw it wasn't the deputies standing there.

"Now, where were we? Oh, yes. Your Client. See I have other victims I could show you. But I think, just maybe, the one that will send you over the edge is this one."

I picked up the last photo in the pile. I felt my eyes pool but took a deep breath to shake it off. I turned the photo to Leo. He glanced at it and then glanced back at me.

"Do you want to know what he did to this little girl? Do you want to know what I saw? What keeps me up at night? The nightmare that plays on a loop in my head when I close my eyes? Do you want to know?"

Leo looked at the picture again. He took his time, seeing the girl, absorbing the happy grin as she stood in her pretty pink dress with a corsage on her wrist and her Daddy's arm around her.

Leo looked back at me and shook his head before dropping his focus to the floor.

"For hours, he taunted her, scaring her, before he ever touched her. She clung to my bare leg, trembling so hard the chains on my wrists rattled. And, when she became numb to him, that's when he hurt her. That's when he got his knife out."

Leo shook his head rapidly back and forth.

I ripped the gag off of him, and he muttered, "No—Stop—Don't tell me."

"You work for a monster."

"I didn't know. He told me you were selling government secrets to North Korea. He gave me pictures. Showed me documents."

"He lied," Jackson said. "Your clients are telling each other how to work you. How to use your blind patriotism to do their bidding."

Jackson rolled up the sleeve of his shirt and turned his inner forearm to Leo, showing him the Army tattoo with his service dates.

Leo stared at the tattoo, completely transfixed. Jackson looked at me, and I nodded to let him finish talking to Leo.

"I need clients, victims, dates, and locations," I said to Jackson before I walked past Grady and Wild Card.

We wouldn't be killing or torturing anyone tonight. Leo was broken long before we tied him up.

Leo's full name turned out to be Raymond Leo Sacket, but he always went by Leo. After the service, he was recruited by the government as an assassin, mostly with the CIA. Donovan was running the victims' profiles and trying to help Leo find out who on the list was truly deserving of a death sentence and who was a victim of greed and power.

Prior to coming after me, the only jobs Jonathan Vaughn had hired him for were to kill the DA in Miami and the harbor cop in Louisiana. I admitted to Leo the world wouldn't miss either one of them.

Around three a.m. I convinced everyone it was time to get some sleep. Anne and Whiskey had left hours earlier and promised to keep the kids at Pops' house for the night. Charlie and Wild Card decided to walk to Pops' house and crash there, still nervous of another attack. Reggie came and picked up Jackson, Ryan, and Leo to go to their ranch.

Grady followed me across Wild Card's porch and into the house.

"We have the whole house to ourselves, and I'm too tired to do anything about it," Grady sighed as we dragged ourselves down the hallway.

"I hear you," I yawned.

I glanced at the couch I had been sleeping on the last few weeks and then at the two bedroom doors. One was set up as my son's temporary bedroom, and the other was my ex-husband's. I shuffled into Wild Card's bedroom and threw myself on the bed face first.

Grady chuckled and pulled my boots off before undressing himself and climbing into the other side of the bed.

"Come on," he coaxed, pulling me over beside him.

He pulled the covers out from under me as I rolled away and then over the top of me as I rolled back toward him. I didn't care that I was still fully dressed. I was lights out within seconds, snuggled up against him.

Chapter Thirteen

It was early dawn when I woke to Grady's hands stripping me of my clothes. My jeans and socks were somewhere under the covers, tangled within the blankets. He had my outer shirt unbuttoned, and his hand slipped under my tank top as he fondled a breast.

"Hmm," I moaned rolling to give him more access.

"That's my girl," Grady chuckled, as he lifted my tank top and sucked on a nipple.

I felt his hard-on pressing into my leg. My hand lowered, slipping between our bodies so I could stroke him.

He responded with a deep moan that vibrated my breast and made my other nipple stiffen.

"You like that, huh?" I grinned.

He moved up my body and kissed me. Sucking my lip, before dragging me in for a deeper kiss. His hand moved down my body and slipped inside my underwear. It was my turn to moan as his fingers parted my folds, sliding up and down my sex.

"You like that, huh?" Grady chuckled.

"More please," I moaned.

Grady leaned in to kiss me again as two of his fingers slipped inside of me, and his thumb stroked my clit.

"No, Nicholas—Wait!" I heard Charlie yell just before the bedroom door flew open.

"What are you doing to my Mom!" Nicholas yelled at Grady. "Get off her!"

Nicholas ran over and proceeded to push Grady away. Luckily the blankets covered us. Grady quickly slipped his hand out of my panties and went to roll back, when he stopped abruptly.

"Kel? You need to let go of me," Grady grinned.

"Oh!" I had completely forgotten I was still grasping his penis under the blanket. I immediately released him.

Grady wriggled under the blankets, putting on his boxers as I attempted to talk to Nicholas.

"Nick, you need to knock first, so you don't startle people. You about gave me a heart attack," I said.

"You stay away from my mother!" he yelled at Grady.

Standing, Grady leaned over and briefly kissed me. "I'm going to go make coffee."

"Go Away! Don't touch her! We don't want you here." Nicholas yelled.

"That's enough," I scolded. "I understand that you are confused, and maybe a bit scared, but you will not talk to Grady like that."

Charlie patted Grady on the shoulder, offering her support as he walked out.

Nicholas looked down at the floor, still angry, but no longer yelling. Sitting up, I pulled him to me and wrapped my arms around him. After a few minutes, he reciprocated the hug.

"I love you. And, your feelings matter. But, I also care about Grady, and it hurts me when you treat him badly."

"If you care about him, why did you send him away last time? He was mean to you, wasn't he?"

"No, he wasn't," Charlie said, walking into the room and flopping onto the end of the bed. "You know if he was mean to her, none of us would have let him come back."

"Nick, I was scared and confused. Grady tried to help me, but I didn't want anyone's help. It's not his fault."

Nicholas snuggled into me but didn't say anything. I knew he'd have to mull over his thoughts and feelings before he could decide for himself.

"I need to talk to both of you," I said, stroking Nicholas's hair back.

"You're leaving again," Nicholas sighed.

"Yes."

"Why?" Charlie asked. "It's not safe."

"The ranches are the safest place for the kids," Grady said, coming back in with three cups of coffee. "But, if Kelsey stays here, they'll keep trying to get to her. The kids can be better protected if she's somewhere else."

"I can't go with you," Charlie said, looking up at me before glancing at Nicholas who remained quiet in my lap.

"No. You have a much more important job, Charlie. You have to be with this munchkin until I can come back."

I tickled Nicholas, but he swatted my hand away and fled the room.

"Shit."

"Let me talk to him," Grady said, handing us our cups before jogging after Nicholas.

"That a good idea?" Charlie asked me after Grady left the room.

"Yeah. Nicholas likes Grady. He just doesn't trust either one of us will ever stick around long enough to raise him."

"From his perspective, I get it," Charlie nodded.

"Me too."

Charlie leaned over the bed to look down the empty hall. "Well I don't hear any yelling. That's a good sign," Charlie grinned taking a sip of her coffee.

I nodded and took a sip of my own. "Damn. Grady makes good coffee."

"Wasn't Grady," Charlie laughed, getting up to leave. "Nick and I were making you coffee when he heard moaning and ran in to see if you were okay. I didn't have time to stop him."

"It's been awhile since I've had to lock the bedroom door," I grinned.

"Bet you won't forget next time," she giggled as she walked down the hall.

After showering quickly in Wild Card's private bathroom, I crossed over to Nicholas's room where we shared the dresser to store our clothes. I dressed in a pair of comfortable shorts and a v-neck t-shirt. In the closet, I found my favorite pair of slip on tennis shoes.

Heading to the kitchen for a coffee refill, I found Henry sitting alone at the kitchen table.

"Hey, Henry," I grinned. "You need to talk to me?"

"No, no. Just up with the birds and wasn't sure if it was too early to go see Hattie. I want to ask if she'd like to go to the flea market with me today. Heard there's a good one about 10 miles from here."

"I'm sure she'd like that. And, around here, everyone gets up early. She's probably serving the third round of breakfast about now."

"I should go over then? I don't want to upset your father-in-law."

I stumbled for a second when he called Pops my father-in-law but then realized everyone, including Hattie, called him Pops. Henry would sound ridiculous calling him Pops, though.

"Call him Greg, if you don't want to call him Pops," I grinned. "Give me a minute to gather my bag, and you can give me a ride."

"Be a pleasure, Miss Kelsey. A real pleasure," Henry grinned.

When we arrived at Pops' house, everyone on all three ranches was either sitting around drinking coffee or filling up a plate from the buffet style breakfast Hattie had set up. Hattie stopped talking with Pops and rushed over to serve Henry.

Pops glared. I snorted.

I filled my plate and found an open spot next to Grady. He winked at me while he ate his breakfast.

Nicholas sat on his lap sharing the oversized plate of food. Next to Grady was Whiskey with Sara perched on his lap. I grinned and shoveled a forkful of syrup-soaked pancakes into my mouth before looking about the room.

The pancakes stuck in my throat when I realized Leo was sitting across the table from me.

"Swallow," Grady whispered, leaning toward me. "Stay calm."

I managed to swallow the pancakes, half choking to do so, and rinsing them down with the coffee Hattie sat in front of me.

"Thank you, Hattie."

"You are very welcome, Sunshine."

"Is someone going to explain to me why Leo is sitting at the table?"

The room went silent.

"Mind your manners, Kelsey. Leo is a guest," Hattie scolded.

"Leo is the sniper who shot Reggie yesterday."

"Oh, dear," Hattie said, looking over at Leo. "I didn't realize. Ok, proceed then."

"Kelsey—," Reggie started.

"Oh, Hell-No!" I glared at Reggie. "Don't you dare tell me I'm being unreasonable. My son and my niece are sitting at this table. He was hired to kill me. And now because y'all have this military bond shit going, you trust him enough to risk their lives? Hell-No!"

"I won't hurt them," Leo said.

"And, I'd like to believe you, but I won't risk their safety to find out you're lying."

"I'll take him," Ryan said from the end of the table.

Everyone turned to look at him.

"You're right. It was stupid of Jackson and Reggie to believe him just because he says he didn't know. I have to go home for a few weeks, and he can come with me. I'll call Jackson twice a day to confirm Leo's with me and behaving. If Jackson doesn't hear from me, he can sound the alarm."

"And, what? You're going to cuff him to your truck to get him to go with you?"

"I'll go," Leo nodded. "You're right—you have no reason to trust me. They should've never brought me over here. The smart move would have been to kill me."

"It's still a possibility," Grady said in a low tone not looking up from the table. "If you don't do exactly as Ryan says, when he says it, I'll come after you myself."

Nicholas snagged the bacon from between Grady's fingers while he wasn't paying attention. Grady retaliated by tickling him.

Ryan nodded at Leo toward the door, and they both took their plates out to the front porch to finish eating. Wild Card moved over to the hallway to lean against the wall and drink his coffee. He'd have a full view of the doorway from where he stood.

Pops walked back to the table, carrying a fresh cup of coffee and cuffed Reggie and Jackson upside the back of their heads as he walked by. He sat down across from me and grinned as both Reggie and Jackson pouted.

"Kelsey, you're finally wearing shorts?" Charlie grinned, changing the subject.

"Figured since we caught a sniper yesterday, I could take the day off from riding up to the ridge. Besides, I'm tired of trying to hide my scars," I shrugged.

"It's going to be hot out today. Smart thinking," Pops nodded.

"You going to move the cattle to the property across the road? The lower valley offers more shade," I asked.

"Don't encourage him," Wild Card grumbled. "One of these days, he's going to get arrested for trespassing."

"Doubtful," Hattie grinned, sitting down at the table between Pops and Henry.

"Shit," Reggie laughed, finally looking up and spotting my grin. "Kelsey owns the property."

"Only took a few years to figure it out. Good for you," Pops grinned.

Grady laughed. Wild Card and Jackson looked surprised.

"You knew too?" Jackson asked Grady.

"Found out yesterday. Beautiful chunk of land. Private too," Grady winked at me.

Henry cleared his throat and set down his fork. "While everyone is working on the ranch today, I was hoping to steal Hattie away. There's a flea market I thought we'd check out."

"Oh? Sounds lovely," Hattie grinned.

"The boys can move the cattle without me. It's best if I go with you to the market, so you don't get lost. Being Northerners and all," Pops said.

"Really?" I laughed. "You? At a flea market? You know that involves all-day shopping, right?"

"It's what a proper host would do," Pops said.

"Yes, that sounds reasonably respectful," Hattie sighed. "What a fun day this will be."

Hattie looked ready to panic as she glanced between Henry and Pops and then looked at me like I was expected to throw her a lifeline.

"The Kids!" I said a little too loudly. "I mean, why don't you take the kids with you? They haven't been able to get away from the ranch much. You can take Wayne and Jackson along for security. I'm sure the kids would love the flea market."

"Please! I want to go," Sara pleaded.

"Anne and I can go as well," Whiskey nodded.

Anne grinned over at him and kissed him on the cheek. I swear, Whiskey blushed a bit behind his newly grown beard.

"What's a flea market?" Nicholas asked.

"You can buy crafts and used stuff there," Pops answered. "We can look for a larger saddle for you to use on Copper."

"Yes, I think the kids going is an excellent idea," Hattie sighed with relief.

"Sure. The more the merrier," Henry nodded, looking puzzled. "Why don't they ride with Greg and the security guards. You and I can take my car. We can follow them there since Greg knows the roads."

Everyone looked down at the table, trying not to laugh, as Hattie wrung her hands.

"The RV is fueled and ready," Wild Card grinned. "Everyone can ride together."

"Mighty fine idea. It'd be good to run the engine," Pops nodded in agreement. "We haven't had much use for it over the last few years."

Hattie let out a huge breath and left the table in a rush. I glanced at Wild Card as he loudly slurped his coffee and sent a wink in my direction.

Chapter Fourteen

The things you do for family, I laughed to myself.

I carried another bucket of dirty water out and dumped it into the grass. Pops had ordered the kids and me to clean the RV while Wild Card, Reggie, and Jackson moved the cattle over to my property. Henry and Pops both stayed in the kitchen, insisting on helping Hattie make picnic lunches for everyone.

Grady was assigned to change the oil on the RV and was currently showing off his tight jeans from the undercarriage.

"I can feel you watching me," he laughed from somewhere below the beast.

"I don't know what you're talking about," I grinned.

"I'll take a rain check on those thoughts," Grady answered.

I hurried back into the RV before I distracted Grady from his chores.

"Mom," Nicholas said from up in one of the drop-down bunks where he was supposed to be putting fresh bedding on. "Are we going to live here?"

"In Texas or in the RV?" I laughed.

"In Texas," he said, rolling his eyes. "Is that why you bought the property across the street? Because we are going to live here?"

"I own a lot of properties, Nicholas."

"Are we rich?" he asked.

"No," I laughed. "You are dirt poor. Your Aunt Charlie and I are rich."

"How come I'm not rich?"

"Because you work too slow," Charlie answered from the lower bunk.

"Aunt Charlie? If you're rich, why wouldn't you buy me the Xbox I asked for?"

"Because you haven't earned it," Charlie answered. "Your mother worked her butt off to provide for us when we were growing up. And, when either of us wanted something extra, we had to work even harder to earn it. When you show me you've earned an Xbox, then maybe you'll get an Xbox."

"What do I have to do?"

"Show respect to others, work hard, and help out with chores without being asked," Grady answered, stepping into the RV.

He had grease on his nose, and I wiped it with my cleaning rag.

"You should be proud of your mom and Aunt for raising you to be a good man," Grady said to Nicholas as he winked at me. "Now are you going to finish your chores or are you going to keep lollygagging?"

Nicholas hurriedly finished making the bed, before jumping down and grabbing the furniture polish and rag to wipe down the cupboards. I laughed and went back to washing the countertop.

We finished cleaning the RV at the same time the boys came back from moving the cattle. Pops, Hattie, and

Henry came out with the picnic lunches. Pops proudly carried the bags, as Henry followed, insisting he should drive since he was used to driving the freight truck. Pops, of course, countered, saying it was his vehicle and he knew how to drive it. Henry winked at me before conceding that Pops was right and it would give him more time to catch up with Hattie, anyway.

Pops stomped into the RV.

Sara giggled as she grabbed Hattie's hand, dragging her inside.

I stopped Nicholas as he went to hurry in after them.

"I know, I know. No begging for things I haven't earned. No back-talk. No yelling. Be on my best behavior."

"Well, as long as you know," I grinned, leaning over to give him a sloppy kiss on the cheek.

He ran into the RV laughing, wiping my spit off his face. Whiskey, Anne, and Wayne followed him in, all grinning.

Jackson turned to me, ready to board the RV, "Anything, in particular, to watch out for today?"

"No. We should have a few days off. Jonathan still expects Leo will kill me, so he won't send anyone else for a few days."

"Perfect!" Reggie grinned. "You can look for a new afghan for the living room. I'm thinking a blend of sunrise cream and celestial blue, but if you can't find celestial, I'd settle for queen blue."

"How did I not know you were gay for all these years?" Wild Card chuckled.

Jackson rolled his eyes, kissed Reggie on the cheek and boarded the RV.

As the RV pulled out, I turned to everyone else, and my smile instantly disappeared.

"Kid, what's wrong?" I asked, running up to Charlie.

"Nothing. Not a damn thing," she grinned, with tears streaming down her face. "It's just been so long since I've seen you and Nicholas together like that."

I wrapped her in a hug, and then Reggie wrapped his arms around both of us, holding us close.

"Alright, girly moment over," Wild Card laughed. "It's almost nine, and we have to call Tech and Katie."

"Where's Leo?" I asked, stepping away and wiping the happy tears.

"Leo is with Ryan and Ryan is packing his gear at my house. You can talk to them before they leave. And, for the record, I agree it was stupid to have him come to breakfast," Wild Card said, glaring at Reggie.

"What? That was all Jackson. I warned him Kelsey would be pissed," Reggie said.

"Does everyone throw Jackson under the bus?" Grady laughed.

"Yes," we all admitted.

Arriving back at Wild Card's ranch, I walked up to the house as Ryan and Leo were walking out carrying Ryan's bags.

"You know he could turn on you?" I said to Ryan.

Ryan nodded and continued to the truck to load the bags.

"I get it," Leo said.

"No, you don't. But if you cross me or anyone associated with me, you will," I said, before walking away.

In the War Room, everyone was deep in research. We had an open conference call with Tech, Katie, and Carl in Michigan. Tech and Katie were researching the business finances and media releases. Carl was hacking the phone messaging service. Even if no one was talking, I felt closer to them.

I had sent Tech and Katie back to Michigan after I was released from the hospital. Jonathan wasn't a threat to them like Nola had been. He wouldn't hurt my family or friends unless he had to, in order to get to me.

I had tried to send Anne and Hattie home as well, but they refused to leave until I was better. And, Whiskey had stayed to be closer to Anne and Sara. Most days it felt like I had ripped apart our family, but not today. I watched the screen as Tech and Katie argued over a laptop and Carl looked over to see if anyone was watching before hunkering down to hide what he was doing on his laptop with a small grin on his face.

"Carl?" I laughed.

"Yes, Kelsey?" he looked over at the monitor.

"Whatever you are doing, stop it," I grinned.

Tech jumped over to Carl's laptop and started cussing. He took control of the laptop and started typing at warp speed.

"We don't need ten gallons of blue moon ice cream, Carl," Tech said shaking his head. "And, if we did, we'd pay for it, not steal it by faking a payment order with the manufacturer."

"But I like blue moon ice cream. And, so do Kelsey and Sara."

"I'll pick some up later today for you," Lisa laughed, walking into the room with Donovan.

Donovan released his arm around Lisa and carried their baby girl, Abigail, over to the monitor.

"She's getting so big," I grinned, walking up closer to the screen. "And, those little fingers."

"And, she has her Aunt Kelsey's temper," Lisa laughed, stepping over to pull the pink blanket back from Abigail's chin. "She woke me up at least a hundred times last night."

"And, you loved every minute of it," I grinned.

"I did," Lisa grinned back. "But I wish you were all here to enjoy it with me."

"Me too, Lisa," I nodded.

"Me too," Katie grinned. "I got stuck having to change a dirty diaper yesterday. Would've never happened if Anne or Hattie were here."

"You didn't change the diaper," Tech said, rolling his eyes. "You freaked out saying babies were disgusting, and then I changed the diaper."

"Same thing," Katie shrugged.

"Kelsey," Charlie called out, pulling my attention. "I'm not getting anywhere with Jonathan's daughter."

Charlie had been researching social media accounts of the eldest daughter to see if we could get a better understanding of the girl and if she was suffering from trauma.

"I'm not surprised," I said. "Her social media is probably managed by Jonathan's campaign team."

"Bridget flew out this morning," Katie said. "If she can help Bones get closer to the family, then she'll have access to the daughter."

"It might be our only angle," I nodded. "How about the criminal links? Where are we?"

"Three of Jonathan's companies appear to be shell corporations," Tech said.

"One of them was linked to a group in New Orleans," Wild Card nodded. "The other partners have rap sheets, but all minor stuff. I think it's worth checking out."

"Can you go?" I asked Wild Card.

"I'll leave after lunch," Wild Card nodded.

"You shouldn't go alone."

"Jackson and Wayne are needed to run security on the ranches. And, Grady needs to stay with you."

"I can take care of myself."

"You're the one with a target on your back, so you need the extra security," Grady said, giving me a scolding look.

"I'll be fine," Wild Card said. "If it turns into anything more than surveillance, I'll call for backup."

Wild Card kissed me on the forehead and walked out.

"I could go," Reggie said, looking at the door Wild Card had exited. "How come nobody thinks of me?"

"No offense Reggie, but recon really isn't your thing," I grinned. "Besides, I was hoping you'd be willing to go on a different a road trip."

"When do I leave?"

"I need you to drive out early today with one of the SUV's and head to Las Vegas. Grady and I will leave after dinner and meet up with you. I need to say goodbye to Nick and Hattie before I go."

Grady reached over and rubbed a hand down my back.

"Sounds good," Reggie grinned. "Jackson's going to be so jealous."

Reggie hurried out of the room. Grady shook his head and turned back to the laptop he was working on.

"Do we have anything else?" I asked Tech.

"Katie and I have been working on the other companies. Some are legit, some are dirty, and some have very questionable books. Katie thinks we should get a professional to help us. She reached out to Cameron, and he gave her a couple names of some corporate attorneys."

"Get someone hired," I nodded to Katie. "If possible find someone who likes to get their hands dirty with hostile takeovers. We need a shark. And, then get him or her up to speed. I'll be in Pittsburgh by this weekend, and they should meet me there."

"You want me to book you a rental somewhere?"

"No need," Grady said. "I called a buddy who has a townhouse in Pittsburgh. We'll have the place to ourselves for as long as we want it. He's overseas, so he's not using it."

"I need to draw Jonathan's attention away from Texas," I told Katie. "Grady and I will fly to Las Vegas, and then we can meet up with Reggie and drive from there. Jonathan will think I went underground."

"Smart," Charlie nodded. "But what if he catches you in Vegas before you slip away?"

"He still thinks Leo is on my trail. He won't have time to switch gears that fast."

"If Leo didn't betray us, you mean," Grady said.

"Right. If Leo reached out to Jonathan, then it could get tricky, but it's worth the risk. And, it's easy lose a tail in the crowds in Vegas, so even if they are waiting for us, I'm confident we can slip away."

"I'll book suites at the Bellagio Hotel to steer them away," Katie said. "They'll focus on the hotel rather than the airport thinking you will be an easier target there. They'll be scrambling to find you when you don't show up."

"And the student becomes the master," I grinned at Katie.

"This scheming stuff is a lot of fun once you get the hang of it," Katie grinned.

"Like trying to convince Tech that babies were disgusting, and you didn't know how to change a diaper?" Lisa asked. "When you were the one who taught me?"

"Seriously?" Tech glared over at Katie. "You played me?"

"Like a fiddle, Babe," Katie said leaning over to kiss him.

Chapter Fifteen

Wild Card was on his way to New Orleans and promised to check in on a burner phone sometime tomorrow. Clothes and supplies were loaded with Reggie in the SUV and on their way to Vegas. Grady and I would be flying out of El Paso on tonight's red-eye to meet up with him. The only thing we would carry with us for the flight over was an overnight bag and a couple hundred dollars.

Closing our research down early afternoon, we relocated back to Pops house where Charlie and I started digging out food to cook for dinner. Grady relaxed in a recliner, eventually falling asleep.

"He's exhausted," I grinned over at Charlie.

"He's been worried," Charlie nodded. "He called every day after you sent him away. I doubt he's been sleeping much."

I nodded but didn't say anything. I knew he had been calling. And, not just Charlie. He'd been checking in with everyone. I had been trying to ignore it at the time. Hoping he'd give up. I was glad now he hadn't. I needed him. I needed his strength. His belief that I could overcome all of this.

"I hope Hattie didn't have a different plan for these steaks," I said as I slid the last bag of marinating steaks into the refrigerator.

"I think Hattie's going to be so frazzled from a day of Pops and Henry fighting for her attention, she'll be hitting the wine hard when she returns."

"She has her hands full," I laughed, moving over to help scrub the potatoes. "I wonder which one she'll choose."

"Why does there have to be a choice?"

"Because Hattie's not you. She doesn't shut men out of her life by having a revolving door policy. She needs a man who makes her laugh and makes her feel safe. Someone who'll stand by her side."

"Which one do you think she'll pick?"

"One lives in Texas and the other lives in Michigan," I shrugged. "She might pick where the man lives, rather than the right man for her."

"She won't leave you," Charlie said shaking her head. "She can't. You mean too much to her."

"I don't like the thought of her not being around either, Kid."

"So, where do you want to live, when this is all over?"

"I don't know," I answered honestly, looking over the breakfast bar into the living room. Grady was still sleeping, arms tucked behind his head, stretched out in the recliner. "There's a lot I haven't figured out yet."

I had the charcoal filled in the oversized grill and was about to add the lighter fluid when Grady came out and took it away from me.

"I got it," he grinned.

I didn't argue. I lacked the patience of getting the coals hot without using half the bottle of lighter fluid.

"They should be back soon," I said while looking down the long driveway.

"What's wrong?" Grady asked, pulling me to lean against him.

"What if I'm making a mistake by letting everyone help me? What if they get hurt?"

"They won't. But even if they did, they wouldn't blame you. Just like you wouldn't blame anyone else if you got hurt while trying to protect one of them."

"I'd blame me. I don't know if I could handle the guilt."

"You're doing the right thing," Grady said, kissing the back of my head. "The kids will be safe. And with our help, you have a good chance of taking this guy down. We'll figure it out."

"Wild Card and Reggie are out there alone. And, I sent them."

"Wild Card volunteers for much more dangerous missions on a regular basis. If you hadn't given him an assignment, he would have called Donovan for a security gig. He was getting bored."

"And Reggie?"

"Reggie right now is driving like a bat out of hell to get to Vegas, so he has time to gamble before he has to pick us up at the airport. The only danger he's in at the moment is the possibility of a speeding ticket."

"Reggie sucks at gambling. I hope he remembers to put gas in the car before he hits a casino and loses all his money."

"He's in one of your SUV's and your bags are in the back. He'll raid your extra funds if he needs to."

"True," I nodded, grinning up at Grady. "Thank you."

"For what?"

"Being here with me."

"Always," he grinned down at me before giving me a brief kiss.

We heard the RV coming down the long drive. A few minutes later, Jackson was the first one to come barreling out, carrying what appeared to be a knitted blanket of blues and creams.

"Tell me this is celestial blue," Jackson said. "Please!"

"Like I'd know?" I laughed.

"Alright, where is he?" Jackson sighed. "I've been stressing over this damn blanket long enough."

"He's not here," I shook my head.

"We needed him to drive to Vegas," Grady explained. "Kelsey and I will meet up with him later tonight. You, Charlie, and Wayne will be in charge of security while we are gone."

"So, he gets to gamble in Vegas, and I'm stuck babysitting? Damn it. He doesn't deserve the blanket," Jackson grumbled, shoving the blanket into Grady's arms before storming into the house.

"He's mad?" Grady asked.

"Jealous," I grinned. "Jackson rubs it in when he gets to go somewhere, and Reggie has to stay behind for the horses. Reggie's going to have bragging rights."

"It's like living with a bunch of damn teenagers," Pops chuckled, making his way over to us. "I'll take the blanket, though. I need a new one."

"You just want to rub it in Reggie's face that you got his blanket," I smirked.

"Maybe," Pops grinned, kissing me on the cheek and snatching the blanket out of Grady's hands.

"They're all nuts," Anne said as she walked passed us toward the house.

Whiskey winked as he followed Anne.

Hattie and the kids came over and started emptying bags to show me everything they bought. Henry and Wayne joined Grady at the grill to watch the coals turn white. When Hattie handed me a bag, I peeked inside. Swimsuits. Every size and color imaginable. When I looked up at her, she winked at me.

"Looks like after dinner, we are all going to the lake for a swim," I grinned.

The kids, excited by the plan, went tearing into the house to tell the others, nearly knocking Charlie over who was carrying out trays of steaks to cook. Grady and Wayne took the steaks from her, and she moved over to sort out the swimsuits until she found one she liked. She came back a few minutes later wearing the skimpy bikini top with a pair of cut off shorts that didn't leave much to the imagination.

"Girl, you got too much self-confidence," Hattie chuckled.

"Nice way of putting it Hattie," I laughed.

"You're just jealous," Charlie said, sticking her tongue out at me. "You're too top heavy to get away with the look."

"Or maybe she's capable of behaving with a bit more modesty in front of her elders and the children," Pops barked, walking out of the house and tossing a t-shirt at Charlie. "Button up or go back to Reggie's. There's nobody around interested in what you're selling, girl."

"It wasn't offending me," Wayne chuckled, winking at Charlie as she slid the t-shirt over her head.

We ate outside at the picnic tables and then walked to the lake after everyone changed and grabbed towels. Henry and Pops were driving Hattie nuts, so I told them I needed to talk to Hattie alone. Everyone except Grady moved on ahead of us. Grady stayed back far enough to give us privacy but close enough to get to us if danger struck.

"So, you're leaving," Hattie sighed. "When?"

"Tonight, when we get back from the lake. It's safer for the kids if I'm not here."

"But you're not going somewhere to hide, are you?"

"No," I shook my head.

I looped my arm through Hattie's, and we strolled together through the tall grass.

"Do the others know? Are you letting them help you?"

"Yes. I told them everything. Jackson and Charlie will stay here and run security for you and the kids. Wild Card,

Reggie, and Grady are helping me. And, the rest of our family is doing what they can too."

"Kelsey, just don't disappear. We can't go through that again," Hattie stumbled, and I tightened my hold around her, pulling her in for a hug.

"I won't disappear. Promise," I whispered, holding her as she cried.

Hattie nodded and stepped back to wipe her tears. "Then you do what you have to do and then come home."

"And where is home, Hattie?" I asked.

"Wherever you are, Sunshine," Hattie grinned. "It's the only thing I know for sure."

She looked up ahead, and we watched Pops and Henry both scrambling in the field to pick flowers.

"Dear Lord, those two need to stop," Hattie said, shaking her head. "All day it was like a testosterone competition."

"Who won?"

"Neither. They both made fools of themselves," she grinned, looping our arms again and walking toward the lake.

I moved into the deeper water and started swimming laps. I was only a few laps in when Grady swam out and stopped me.

"Enough," he grinned at me, water running off his nose.

He pulled me toward him, and I wrapped my legs around him.

"I think there's a shade tree over around the bend that would hide us from everyone," he grinned, as he stroked my ass under the water.

"With the kids out here?" I grinned back. "Not happening."

"I know," Grady chuckled. "But I was hoping for at least a rain check."

He leaned down and kissed the end of my nose.

"How's your shoulder?"

"Better today," I nodded. "Hasn't hurt as much."

"Good," he said, turning us. He swam backward toward the shoreline, towing me along with him. "Nicholas has been watching you all evening."

"I know," I nodded, looking up at the shoreline where Jackson was trying to get Nicholas's attention, but he was watching me instead. "He's scared. I don't know what to say to him to make him feel better. I don't want to make him promises I'm not sure I can keep."

"Tell him the truth then. Trying to hide what's happening just scares him more."

I nodded and wrapped my arms around Grady's shoulders, holding him close as he swam us to the water's edge.

After toweling off and throwing on a t-shirt, I reached out a silent hand to Nicholas. He refused the hand but walked beside me toward the house.

"I need you to listen to me. It will be hard, but it's important. Will you promise to hear me out?"

Nicholas looked away but nodded.

"I'm leaving with Grady tonight. We are going to fly out and meet up with Reggie. The bad guys will think I'm in Vegas, which means you and Sara will be safe. Once we lose them, Reggie and Grady will help me go after the man trying to hurt me. He's really scary, but I have a plan. I'm going to try to end this, so we don't have to hide anymore."

Nicholas remained quiet looking away from me, but he reached his hand up to hold mine.

"I need you to know, if anything happens to me, your Aunt Charlie will make sure you are taken care of. Don't ever worry about being alone. You have a home here and one in Michigan. You will always be safe. You will always be loved. And, I will come back to you as soon as I can."

"You're not coming back. You'll be dead," Nicholas whispered.

"Nick," I lowered myself to my knees and turned him to face me. "I love you. I will always love you. I'm taking every precaution I can think of to go after this guy. I want to come home and to watch you grow up. I want to watch you laugh and play with your friends. I want to see you go off to school and soccer games. I want to see you become the man I know you'll be. A man I know I will be so proud of."

"It's not safe," Nicholas cried, clinging to me. "Let's just hide. We can hide from the bad man. We'll run away and never come back. Just you and me."

"No, Nick. That's no way to live. For either of us," I whispered into his ear, holding him as his body trembled in my arms. "You have to be brave. Have faith. I'll find a way."

"I don't want to lose you."

"I don't want that either," I said, pulling him back and looking at his tear-streaked face. "But I don't want either of us living in fear. I don't want to be crippled by it. And, I can't let this man keep hurting people. He needs to be stopped."

"Why does it have to be you? Why can't Grady go after him?"

"This man has a lot of dangerous friends. Grady, Reggie and everyone else could end up in prison trying to help me. Is that what you want? For Grady to go to prison for the rest of his life?"

"No," Nick groaned, wiping the tears from his face.

"It's going to be okay, one way or another. You will be safe, loved, happy. That's all that matters to me. You have to promise me you will always remember how much I love you."

"I know, I know," he said pulling away.

"Oh, I don't think you do," I grinned through my own tears, pulling him in and giving him raspberry kisses all along the side of his face as he squealed and tried to fight me off.

"Gross, Mom!" he laughed.

"Yeah, gross Mom!" Grady laughed, walking over to join us. He tossed Nick up into the air before throwing him on top of his shoulder to carry like a sack of grain.

Nick laughed, and Sara ran over circling around them as everyone else joined us for the walk back. Charlie snagged me by the elbow and steered me away from the group.

When I heard their voices drift away, I looked up at her tear stained face. She swallowed me in her arms, crushing herself to me.

"You're breaking my heart, Kelsey," Charlie cried. "I don't know if I can let you go again."

"You have to, Kid. He needs you. He needs to know he'll have you if I don't make it back."

"But you need to make it back. I can't do it alone."

"You're not alone, Kid. You have plenty of people around to help. They're your family too."

"But I still need you."

"Kid," I said, pulling away and looking at her. "I'm proud of you. I'm proud of the woman you've become and proud to call you family."

She looked down, unable to face me. I swung an arm around her shoulder and started to lead us back to the house again.

"I'll find a way out of this. Just take care of him until then."

She nodded and tucked her head on my shoulder.

Pops was waiting at the edge of the lawn and pulled Charlie in for a hug. "I got this," Pops nodded. "You get going, baby girl."

Pops had tears in his eyes, but stood proud and strong, holding Charlie up and shielding her tears from the rest of the group gathering on the porch.

Grady stepped out of the house carrying our overnight bags and nodded at me. He walked over to the car and got in.

"I'll be home soon," I promised everyone, unable to say any more goodbyes.

I hurried to the passenger side, sliding quickly inside the car.

"Drive. Please, drive," I whispered to Grady.

After turning us around and pulling out into the driveway, Grady reached a hand over to my leg.

"Hey," Grady said, rubbing my leg. "Talk to me."

"I don't know if I can do this. I don't know if I'm strong enough this time."

"Babe, you are plenty strong enough. You're the strongest person I've ever met."

I leaned over the center console and tucked into Grady's shoulder. He wrapped his arm around me and held me as he drove us to the airport.

Chapter Sixteen

The flight was long enough to take a nap and short enough that by the time I was getting restless, we were preparing to land. When we exited the plane, I texted Reggie to pick us up.

Following the signs and bypassing the luggage pickup, we were about to walk out of the airport when a slot machine started blaring, and I heard a familiar voice exclaiming he'd won.

I turned, and Grady followed.

"He didn't," Grady said, shaking his head.

"Oh, yes, he did."

Sure enough, Reggie was gathering his winnings from the quarter machine as a small crowd cheered him on. The machine was still dropping quarters when I grabbed Reggie by the elbow and dragged him away. Grady took the bucket of quarters from Reggie and handed them off to an elderly couple as we walked by.

"But, I won," Reggie complained, looking back at the machine that was disappearing from his sight.

"Where's the SUV?" I asked, steering him out the door.

"In the parking garage," Reggie said, pulling out the parking pass.

"Damn it, Reggie."

"What? Why are you mad?" he asked.

"There's a contract on Kelsey's head," Grady said, pulling Reggie's other elbow at a quicker pace. "And now we have to cross through a parking garage and get into an unattended vehicle that may have been tampered with."

Grady shoved Reggie toward the parking garage entrance.

"Shit," Reggie said, jogging ahead of us and scanning the parking garage. "When you say it that way…"

"It's fine," I said. "Let's move quickly, though. I don't like being this exposed when we literally announced we were coming here."

"Yeah. I get it," Reggie said, continuing to jog ahead of us, searching for anyone crouched between the cars.

When the SUV was in sight, he hit the unlock button, and we all cringed. When nothing happened, he hit the engine start button, and we all visibly cringed again.

"Wait here," Reggie said, running up to the SUV.

He jumped in, reversing out of the parking space. He continued to back up a good distance away from us before putting the SUV in drive and accelerating. When he was near us, he slammed on the brakes and rolled down the window.

"I think we're good," he said, breathing heavy and sweat trickling down his forehead. "Appears to be bomb free and the brakes work."

Grady shook his head and grabbed my carry-on bag. I slid into the front passenger seat as Grady took the back seat, digging into the bags in the back to get our guns out.

"Whew," Reggie breathed out. "That was intense."

Reggie pulled out of the parking garage and turned right into traffic.

"And yet, completely unnecessary if you wouldn't have felt the need to gamble instead of waiting like I asked you to!"

"But we're in Vegas, Baby!" Reggie grinned.

"We picked up a tail," Grady said, peering out the back window.

Reggie had just stopped for a red light, and we were in the inside lane. I unhooked Reggie's seatbelt, sliding over him to squeeze between him and the driver's door.

"I've got the brakes—move," I ordered.

Reggie bailed to the passenger seat.

"Buckle up, everyone."

When the light turned green, I hit the gas and sped past the other vehicles, cutting in front of them as I banked a hard right onto a side road. Cars honked and slammed on their brakes. Reggie grabbed the oh-shit bar since he had failed to get his seatbelt on in time. I made another right turn, and then a quick left into another parking garage, quickly pulling the ticket out of the machine to get the gate up.

Pulling ahead about twenty feet, I put the SUV in park while switching the lights from automatic to manual to shut them off.

"What are we doing?" Reggie asked, trying to right himself in the seat.

From where we sat, we had a clear view of both the streets I had turned onto.

"What kind of car are they driving?" I asked Grady.

"That one!" Grady pointed.

A dark blue SUV drove past but never turned onto the second street.

"Works for me," I said turning the SUV around.

I cut across the small drive between entrance and exit and swung into the exit lane. Feeding the parking pass into the machine, it showed a balance of $4.70 due. I glared over at Reggie, and he dug a $10 bill from his pocket, handing it to me. I put the money in the machine and drove away without collecting the change.

"Hey," Reggie said, looking back at the machine. "That was the last of my money."

"Maybe you'll think next time," I glared, as I made another turn and accelerated to enter the expressway.

"Jackson says it's not my fault. He says I'm like a cute puppy that is constantly getting into trouble," Reggie grinned, looking quite proud of himself.

Grady swatted the back of Reggie's head. "Puppies might be cute, but they need discipline," Grady scolded. "Bad, Puppy!"

I rolled my eyes and followed the signs for US-93 to I-40. It was going to be a long drive with a labradoodle in the car with us.

I drove for the first shift as Reggie and Grady slept. When Grady woke hours later, he made me pull into a rest stop and hand over the keys. I wanted to complain but knew I needed to sleep too, so I took the back seat where Grady had prepared a nest of blankets and pillows made out of coats and his shirts for me.

I was lights out in seconds.

I could hear her. She was crying, but the room was so dark, I couldn't see her. I should be able to see her. The small, cell window on the end wall should cast enough light to see around the room. Why couldn't I see her?

"Alandra? Where are you?" I whispered.

Her quiet cries echoed off the cold, damp walls.

"Alandra, come out where I can see you," I called into the blackness.

A cold, wet hand touched my leg, and I looked down. Alandra's hair was matted with blood, and her skull was split open. She stared up at me, but she wasn't seeing me. Her dead eyes forever looking through me.

I sat up screaming from the nightmare, trying to catch my breath, trying to throw the makeshift blankets and pillows away from me. I felt the SUV pulling to the side of the road and heard the cars honking around us, but I was still fighting off the images in my head. The smell of blood. The smell of fear. I gasped for air as the door in the back seat flew open beside me, and Grady pulled me into his arms as he climbed in.

Burrowing into his shoulder, I wished for him to make the nightmare disappear. Hoping the scent of him was stronger than the smell in that horrific room. Hoping his warm skin shook the chill off my body. Hoping he could pull me out from the hell that was torturing my mind.

"Shhh," Grady coaxed, as he rocked me back and forth. "I've got you. There you go, just keep breathing."

I could hear him. I didn't know how much time had passed with him holding me in the back seat, but I had finally calmed enough to hear him.

"How is she?" Reggie asked from the front seat.

"Just drive, Reggie. She's going to be okay," Grady answered.

I glanced up and looked at Grady through blurred eyes.

"I've got you," Grady whispered, leaning down to kiss my forehead.

Chapter Seventeen

I lay in Grady's arms for hours before I finally drifted back to sleep. When I woke later in the day, he was still holding me, rubbing my back and stroking my hair gently. I unclenched my fingers from his shirt and wrapped my arms around his shoulders, hugging him.

"Thank you," I whispered, kissing his neck.

"Always," Grady whispered back, hugging me in return.

Moving off his lap and onto the seat, he pulled the makeshift blankets up around me.

"Keep the blankets on until I dig out a sweatshirt for you. Your skin is like ice."

"Some fresh air would help. Can we take the next exit?"

"You sure?" Grady asked, leaning down to peer at me.

I nodded.

"Where are we?" I asked Reggie.

"The middle of Arkansas," Reggie answered. "It's about time you decided to wake up. I'm starving."

"I could use some warm food myself," I said, trying to stretch the muscles in my neck and back. "And, I could use a clean bathroom and a good walk."

"There's a town a mile up. They should at least have the basics."

Grady was still watching me closely but didn't say anything. I reached over and held his face and smiled. He turned into my hand and kissed my palm before sighing and turning forward to stretch his legs the best he could.

"I think a walk and some warm food sound good," Grady said. "But if Reggie doesn't get us to a restroom quickly, I'm going to take a piss out the window."

Reggie looked at me in the rearview mirror, and I shook my head no. He sighed and took the next exit.

Grady noticed the gesture and swatted Reggie in the back of the head.

"I wouldn't have made you wait," Reggie grinned.

"Yeah, right."

After a brief visit to the restrooms at a large truck stop, Reggie volunteered to walk to the restaurant next door to order food. It was a warm sunny day, and I was still too cold to bear the thought of sitting in an air-conditioned restaurant. Grady led me over to the picnic tables in the small patch of grass next door to the truck stop.

"You still have goose bumps." He rubbed his hands up and down my arms, trying to warm them.

"Distract me."

"Here?" Grady grinned.

"Not that kind of distraction, you perv," I said, swatting him in the gut.

"Fine," he chuckled, sitting down on the bench of the picnic table and pulling me onto his lap. "Let's see… Ah, I know. What was so funny about Bridget pretending to be Bones girlfriend?"

"That wasn't the funny part. Bones categorizes people based on what he knows about them. Bridget might be a club girl or a former club girl, but before that, she was a socialite."

"What?" Grady laughed.

"Yup," I grinned. "Bridget's family is loaded with a capital L."

"How'd she end up with the Devils Players?"

"I said her family was rich, not nice. It's not my place to say what all happened, but she's a hell of a lot better off where she's at now than where she came from."

"That sucks. I like Bridget. She's sweet and funny. Even if she does steal my wallet."

"She always gives it back," I laughed.

"Minus five dollars!"

"That's the penalty fee. If you catch her in the act, she owes you five dollars."

"Has anyone ever caught her?"

"I've made twenty-five dollars off her," I grinned, turning to look at him.

"That's my girl," Grady grinned, leaning in to kiss me. "You're warming up."

"I am," I nodded, kissing him again.

"Time out on the kissy-face," Reggie laughed, walking up with takeout bags. "Dinner time."

I slid off Grady's lap onto the bench seat and started pulling food out of the bags. Grady turned around to face the table but kept an arm around my waist. He wasn't ready to let me go just yet. And, truth be told, I didn't want him to let me go.

"I got a few meatloaf dinners, a few hot turkey dinners, and a few spaghetti dinners. You guys pick out what you want, and I'll eat whatever's left."

"Spaghetti," I answered.

"Slide me some meatloaf," Grady grinned.

"Hot turkey for me then," Reggie nodded.

I was starving. Dumping both the spaghetti dinners into one container, I settled in to eat.

Grady shook his head and started eating his meatloaf.

"You good now?" Reggie asked looking concerned.

"At the moment," I nodded. "It'll happen again, though."

"Was it the little girl? The one in the picture you showed Leo?"

I nodded and struggled to swallow the spaghetti I was chewing.

"Enough, Reggie," Grady warned.

Forcing the spaghetti down, I took a drink from the water bottle Grady handed me.

"Breathe, babe," Grady whispered, rubbing my back.

"I'm ok," I nodded, trying to convince myself. "Reggie, I can't talk about it yet."

"Jackson wouldn't tell me anything more than a little girl was hurt. I'm sorry, Kel."

Reggie placed his hand on top of mine, and I nodded again.

Taking a deep breath, I twirled my spaghetti with my fork as I let my mind wander.

"This hot turkey isn't as good as I thought it would be," Reggie pouted, eyeing my container.

"What a shame because this is really good. And, the garlic bread, yum," I grinned.

"This meatloaf is pretty badass too," Grady grinned, shoveling a large fork full into his mouth.

Reggie ate another bite of his turkey, scrunching his nose at the taste of it as he chewed and swallowed.

I slurped a long noodle into my mouth spraying spaghetti sauce everywhere. Grady laughed and wiped off my face.

"When do we turn off the highway to head further north?" Reggie asked, tossing his fork in with the hot turkey and sliding the container away. It must be really bad if Reggie left almost half of it uneaten.

"I have a place just outside of Atlanta we can stay at for a day or two. We'll rest there before we move up to Pittsburgh."

I slid my takeout container over between Reggie and I and handed him another plastic fork. I wasn't sharing the garlic bread, but I would share the spaghetti. My eyes were already bigger than my stomach.

"It'll be pretty late when we get there. Will we wake any neighbors?" Reggie asked before stuffing a pile of noodles into his mouth.

"It's a pretty remote location. No one will see us come or go."

"Can it be traced back to you?" Grady asked.

"No. I bought it under a friend's name. She doesn't even know it exists, but if I ever die, she'll be pleasantly surprised."

"Please tell me you've secretly bought property in my name too? Like the property across the road from the ranches?" Reggie asked.

"Sorry, Reg. No such luck," I grinned.

"Damn it," Reggie snapped his fingers.

"You act like you're poor," Grady laughed. "I have a pretty good idea how much you make working side jobs for Donovan and with your horse business."

"Sure," Reggie shrugged. "But Jackson still makes more money than I do. I'm trying to beat him."

"You're an idiot," I laughed, getting up to throw the empty cartons away.

"But I'm cute," Reggie grinned, following me with more trash.

I rolled my eyes as I leaned over to stretch my back.

"Ok, I'm too full to go for a walk now," I said. "I'll drive the rest of the stretch and get us to the safe house."

"Deal," Reggie agreed, rubbing his stomach with both hands. "I need a nap."

Reggie walked back to the SUV and climbed in the back seat. Grady tossed the last of the trash into the green barrel before wrapping his arms around me.

"Please tell me your safe house has a bedroom with a door and a lock," he whispered leaning over to kiss my neck.

"Three bedrooms, all with doors and locks," I answered before playfully pushing him away and walking toward the truck.

"Hallelujah," he laughed.

Chapter Eighteen

There must have been something terribly wrong with the hot turkey sandwich Reggie ate. We stopped at least thirty times for Reggie to either puke or run for a bathroom with his ass cheeks squeezed together.

At first, Grady and I laughed at Reggie's misery. But after a few hours, we were feeling sorry for him, and we all sighed with relief when I pulled up in front of the safe house.

As I was stepping out of the truck, I noticed one of the blinds flutter in the living room.

"Did you see that?" I asked.

"What?" Reggie asked, getting out of the back seat. "I need the bathroom again."

"Wait," I said, leaning back into the car and grabbing some napkins. "Take these and go behind the carport. Someone's in the house."

"You want me to shit behind the carport?!"

"Not really, but it's better than the alternatives."

I pushed him toward the carports, before checking my gun. Grady was already beside me with his own gun out. He was tense, as he scanned our surroundings.

"There's a motorcycle back here," Reggie yelled.

"License plate?" I called out.

"Michigan."

"Damn it," I said, stomping up to the door. "*Nightcrawler!* If you shoot me, I'm going to kick your ass!" I said as I threw open the door.

"Hey, Kelsey," Nightcrawler grinned down at me. "Come on in," he said, stepping away from the door and swing his arm out for us to enter.

He was wearing only a pair of boxers and was a good week past needing to shave. His long hair was ratted on one side, making me think we'd woke him.

"You better not be sleeping in my bed!" I snapped as I stomped past him inside.

"Explain why Nightcrawler is in your safe house," Grady sighed, putting away his gun.

"I have no idea," I said, glaring at Nightcrawler.

"Then explain how he knows about the house."

"After I escaped, I wasn't planning on coming home. Nightcrawler insisted I couldn't be alone, though, so we came here."

"So, you were in hiding with Nightcrawler? Just the two of you?"

"It was only for a day or two, I think," I nodded, as I set my shoulder bag on the dining room table, rummaging to the bottom of it to find some aspirin. "I stayed in bed a lot, so I'm not sure how long we were here."

"Umm, Kel?" Nightcrawler said.

"I don't want to hear from you yet," I interrupted Nightcrawler, finding the pills I was looking for finally.

I started to walk down the hallway, looking forward to a hot shower and a large fluffy bed.

"KELSEY!" Nightcrawler yelled.

I turned around as Grady pinned Nightcrawler by the throat against the wall.

Nightcrawler was a big guy. Usually dressed in leather and chains and had some badass tattoos. But he'd seen Grady fight, and he knew better than to try to defend himself. Grady had some wicked moves and could take on Bones and Donovan at the same time.

Grinning, I walked over and looked at Grady. His eyes were ice cold and locked on Nightcrawler.

"Did I forget to mention I was injured? And Nightcrawler literally stitched up my back?" I grinned.

Grady glanced at me but didn't release Nightcrawler.

"Or that I was in bed because I was sleep deprived and too weak to eat?"

He slowly lowered Nightcrawler until his feet touched the floor again.

"Or," I grinned, wrapping my arms around his waist, "that we left as soon as I heard you were arrested."

"You did forget to mention those things," Grady smirked, wrapping an arm around me.

"Oops," I grinned, pulling Grady with me down the hall.

"I should search the house," Grady said when we entered the bedroom.

"It's clear. Based on the amount of crap laying around, Nightcrawler's been here for at least a couple of weeks."

I unbuttoned his shirt as I kicked the bedroom door shut.

"Besides, you have a more important job."

"I do?" Grady grinned, as he worked the button open on my jeans.

"My shoulder is a little tender," I nodded. "I might need someone to help me take a shower."

Grady's grin turned wicked as he pulled my t-shirt over my head and walked me backward into the private bathroom.

When I woke the next morning, I changed into some jogging clothes and carried my tennis shoes out to the kitchen. The guys were sitting around the dining room table, drinking coffee. I slid onto one of the benches next to Reggie and stole a sip of his coffee. *Ick.* He put sugar in it.

"Good Morning, Sunshine," Reggie grinned, sliding his coffee back in front of him.

"*You* are not Hattie. I don't have to be nice to you in the mornings," I grumbled.

I finished tying my shoes and stood to stretch.

"You going for a run?" Nightcrawler asked.

"Yup."

"Want some company?"

"Nope."

Grady chuckled. He knew I only went running to help settle my thoughts and think out my next move.

I kissed Reggie on the cheek followed by Grady, before slipping out the front door and starting a slow jog down the driveway.

I had run a good mile before my heart started to beat harder and my body started to heat. I settled into a steady pace and kept going. My scattered thoughts started to align, and I focused on the present.

My first priority had to be the businesses. I had to cut off Jonathan's income source. His influence over other people was primarily based on the fact that he was wealthy. But to go after the businesses, I'd need more cash. Most of my funds were tied up in investments still. If I could find a buyer for the shipping company, I would have the money I needed.

Then there was his family. Jonathan had a strained relationship with his father and brothers and it wouldn't take much to cut those ties. His wife and children would be more difficult. I couldn't let them suffer the repercussions when his world started to break to pieces. I had to find an out for them, but their lives were too controlled by Jonathan to get a read on whether they would be willing to leave him.

His political career would fall with the media blowup of his companies crashing and his family abandoning him. Then, and only then, did I have a choice to make. Do I let him live? Or do I kill him?

Knowing I wasn't ready to make that decision, I turned and started back for the house.

Chapter Nineteen

"Where's breakfast?" I grinned, strolling into the house covered in sweat.

"Don't mention food," Reggie groaned.

"There're bagels and cream cheese in the kitchen," Nightcrawler grinned. "And, a fresh pot of coffee."

"Where's Grady?"

"Taking a shower," Reggie said. "And, no you can't join him. The rest of us need hot water, too."

"Well, you're no fun," I laughed, kicking off my tennis shoes before walking into the kitchen to get coffee and a bagel.

"So, who are you hiding from Nightcrawler?" I asked as I spread a generous layer of veggie cream cheese on my bagel.

"Pissed off a guy in Miami. Not sure what the fallout will be, so I was ordered to go find someplace to hide and lie low."

"Miami? What were you doing there?"

Nightcrawler looked down at the table as I settled on the bench across the table from him.

"Fess up," I glared.

Nightcrawler scrubbed his forehead with his palm before sighing and looking at me. "Some guy was running his mouth, and it got back to me. He was bragging about taking my niece and another woman to Pasco to be used as play toys."

Nightcrawler paused, trying to decide if he was going to tell me the rest.

"I killed him."

I nodded, sipping my coffee. "So, who's the guy you pissed off?"

"Mickey McNabe."

Reggie whistled in awe.

Mickey McNabe and I had history, a lot of it. After I had arrested him on some minor drug distribution charges, I mentored his only daughter for several years. When I fled Miami, Nola kidnapped the girl and took her to a man named Pasco. Pasco tortured her to death. He was the same man who had killed Nightcrawler's niece.

Overall, Mickey's a dangerous criminal, but he's also smart, logical and very resourceful.

"I'm not connecting the dots here," I said, shaking my head. "Who's the guy you killed?"

"I believe you knew him by the name of Badger."

When I left Miami, I had sent a message to Mickey in prison, letting him know Badger, his distant cousin, was a marked man due to his involvement with Nola. I didn't expect Mickey to let him live. Mickey wouldn't protect anyone associated with Nola, not after his only daughter's murder.

Grabbing my shoulder bag from the counter, I pulled out a burner phone and a contact book. I called Maggie.

"Agent O'Donnell," she answered.

"It's your favorite vigilante," I grinned.

"When I saw the unknown number, I figured it was you," she chuckled. "I was going to call you. I'm in the middle of a case and wanted your opinion."

"What's the case?"

"Kidnapping. A twelve-year-old girl went missing two days ago in a small town in Kansas. She's the third girl in five years from this area."

"Were the first two victims ever found?"

"No. Never seen again."

"Are the girls connected somehow? Same school? Church? Sport?"

"Not that we can find."

"I'm in the middle of my own case, but have Genie send me everything you have so far. I'll see if anything new pops out."

"I'd appreciate it," Maggie sighed. "You need backup for your case?"

"No. But I do have a reason for calling. What's the status on Mickey?"

"We found enough evidence to prove Mickey was set up for the murder. He was released last week for time served on the original charges, and the murder charges were thrown out."

"Wow. Mickey's out?"

Nightcrawler's eyes widened in surprise.

"For the moment," Maggie sighed. "I kind of like the guy, but I liked him better behind bars."

"Yeah, I get it," I chuckled. "Alright, send me the case file on the kidnapping, and I'll let you know if I find anything."

I disconnected the call and looked up the number to Mickey's gym. I asked for the manager and gave him my burner number. He'd get the message to Mickey.

"He's going to kill me, isn't he?" Nightcrawler asked.

"No," I laughed, shaking my head.

"You sure?"

"Not yet, but I will be soon. Don't sweat it. Mickey's dangerous, but he's smart. I'm not sure what's going on."

The burner phone rang, and I answered it.

"Call the hit off on my friend," I said.

"Just like old times, Harrison," Mickey laughed. "Which friend?"

"The one involved with Badger's untimely death. Badger had it coming."

"It wasn't retaliation against me?" Mickey asked.

"No, it was because Badger was a douche bag and bragging about taking Nightcrawler's niece to Pasco."

"Consider your friend free to do as he pleases. I was informed it had to do with something else. And, Badger had an expiration date anyway, so no loss."

"I was actually surprised to hear he was alive still."

"I was saving him for my release date," Mickey chuckled.

"Then Badger got off easy," I laughed. "Hey, you going legit now?"

"I'm moving that direction. My criminal record isn't exactly opening doors though."

"I'm looking to liquidate the shipping business. I need the cash for another project. You interested?"

"I can loan you the cash if you don't want to sell the company."

"The only reason I bought it was to force intel. So, if you're interested, or if you know someone who is, I'm looking to be bought out. But it has to happen in the next few days."

"Let me run the numbers. Have your attorney call me at this number, and we'll see if we can come to terms. But, I don't have enough to buy you completely out."

"I know a family in New Jersey that might consider partnering with you. Have you heard of Phillip Bianchi?"

"Infamous son of the mafia?" Mickey chuckled. "Yeah, I know who he is."

"Reach out. See if he's interested. He's also looking to move his family in a cleaner direction. It might be a good fit for both of you."

"Have your lawyer call me," Mickey chuckled, hanging up.

I grinned looking at the phone.

"Well? Am I a dead man?" Nightcrawler asked.

"No," I shook my head. "He was told you killed Badger as retaliation for something else. You're free to do as you please. I'd give him a day or two to spread the word, though."

Nightcrawler blew out a breath of relief. "I owe you," he nodded.

"Good. You can go to Pittsburgh with us then," I grinned.

"I'll go anywhere you want. I've been so fucking bored. Last night, I was hoping you guys were robbers so I could kick somebody's ass."

Grady's burner phone was sitting on the table and started to ring. I looked at the display and decided to answer it.

"Harrison."

"Hey," Wild Card said. "There's a warehouse down here with some shady characters coming and going. I need a couple more days to figure out what's going on."

"Not alone you're not. I just freed up Nightcrawler's schedule. I'll send him to meet up with you. If you need more guys, reach out to Donovan."

"Will do. Have Nightcrawler meet me at the marina at dawn tomorrow," he said before hanging up.

"Pack your bags, Nightcrawler. Wild Card needs backup in New Orleans."

"Hell, yes," Nightcrawler grinned, getting up from the table and barreling down the hall.

I was just about to head to the War Room when my phone rang again.

"Harrison," I answered.

"Bones is a moron," Bridget said.

"He can be," I laughed. "What's wrong?"

"He set me up in a hotel and told me to stay put. Said you'd officially lost your mind if you thought me coming to Pittsburgh was a good idea. I've been eating room service and sitting by the pool."

"Yeah, he's a moron," I sighed. "I'll be there tomorrow. Until then, do you have the charge card Katie gave you?"

"The shiny brand new card that has been begging to be used?"

"Break it in, babe. It's under a shell company's name and can't be traced back to me. Go find some fancy ass stores and buy both of us some top label clothes. Spend a fortune and make it public."

"But Lisa packed enough designer clothes for both of us."

"I'm expecting a fancy dinner party or ball in our future, so we'll both need gowns. But that's not why I want you to go shopping. You don't need Bones to gain access to the upper society. You need exposure. And, where do rich women find that?"

"At the most expensive boutiques in town," Bridget said. I could hear her smile over the phone. "I'm on it. By the time you get here tomorrow, there will be a serious dent in the charge card balance. Maybe I'll upgrade my room to the penthouse too."

"Have fun," I said, hanging up.

"I'm bored," Reggie said from beside me.

"Make another pot of coffee and then set up a conference line with Tech and Katie."

"Where's your laptop?"

"We don't need it," I said, walking down the hallway and moving the wall sconce. The door to the War Room opened. Laptops and monitors were already set up.

"This is definitely one of your houses," Reggie laughed. "Give me a few minutes to power everything up."

Grady had been gone too long, so I decided to check on him. When I pushed open the bedroom door, I saw him sitting with his back turned to me, watching a video on his laptop. The bed had been moved, and the files I had hidden under the bed were scattered about. Pictures of accident scenes. Police reports. Bank statements. And, the video that Grady was watching. All evidence I had hidden away, hoping no one would ever find it, but too scared to burn it.

"Stop," I said, my voice quivering, mimicking the voice of my younger self on the laptop screen. "Shut it off."

Grady turned and stared at me with tears in his eyes.

"Please. Just turn it off," I begged.

He turned back to the laptop and stopped the video. My hands shook as I gathered the files and stacked them into a pile.

"Kelsey?" Grady said, coming over to me and putting his hands on my hips.

I pulled away, backing up to the door, clutching the papers.

"No. Don't pretend," I said, shaking my head.

"Pretend?" Grady said, stepping toward me again.

I couldn't face him. I didn't dare look up to see the judgment, the shame, in his eyes. I turned and ran from the room.

Grabbing the kitchen trash can, I tossed the files inside and opened a kitchen drawer. I needed a lighter. I needed to burn it all. I never should have kept any of the evidence. I should have destroyed every scrap of information.

Grady came in and grabbed me again, but I spun away from him, pulling one of the drawers out and dumping its contents on the floor. I dropped to my knees, scattering the mess even further. There had to be a lighter. I had to find it. I pulled the next drawer out, dumping it on the floor. Silverware clattered loudly across the room.

I looked around, spotting Nightcrawler standing next to Reggie.

"Give me your lighter!" I yelled as I charged over to Nightcrawler.

I was pulling the lighter out of his inside cut pocket when Grady knocked it out of my hand. Before I could retrieve it, I was wrapped in his arms, and he was dragging me back to the bedroom.

"NO! I need to burn it!"

"Kelsey, you need to stop," Grady said, settling me on the plush carpet in the bedroom, pinning me between himself and the wall.

I turned away, but he forced my face toward him.

"Stop it! Look at me!" he ordered.

I couldn't. I couldn't look at him. I didn't want to see it. I closed my eyes and covered my face with my hands. Sobs racked my body as I curled into a ball and Grady held me.

"What the fuck, Grady?" Reggie's voice asked from somewhere nearby.

• • •

"Get the files out of the trash and hide them for me," he ordered. "Nightcrawler, get the flash drive out of my laptop."

Grady stroked my back and continued to rock me.

"You didn't have a choice, Kelsey," he whispered, holding me tight. "You had to save Charlie. You're not to blame."

"You don't understand! I did it! I planned it!" I yelled, trying to push him away.

He held me tight despite my efforts to push him away.

"You were a CHILD! You did the only thing you could think of to save her! You're not to blame!"

"I am. I chose to prostitute myself out to that man. I could have found another way. I've thought of a hundred different ways since then that didn't involve whoring myself out. And, that's what I am. I'm a whore, Grady. You saw the video."

"I saw a young teenager, risking her life to save someone she loves," Grady said, pulling me onto his lap. "I saw a young girl who was raped by a man old enough to be her grandfather and who was wearing a badge. You're not a whore, Kelsey. You're a fighter."

He continued to rock me, holding me so tight I could barely breathe.

"I love you," he whispered, stroking my hair back. "Do you hear me? I love you."

I wrapped my arms around him and buried my face in his neck.

Chapter Twenty

It took a long time for Grady to get me to calm down. When I finally quit crying, and the tremors eased, he left my side briefly to start a bath.

I was barely aware of my surroundings as he undressed us both and settled us in the warm water.

"Just relax," he whispered, pulling me to lean into him.

"You can't tell Charlie," I whispered. "She'd never forgive me."

"I don't think it's Charlie who needs to forgive you. I think it's time you forgive yourself."

"I don't know how," I admitted, pulling his arms around me.

"Start by telling me what happened," Grady said, tightening his hold on me.

"I overheard my dad talking to my uncle. He was asking if it was true. If they killed my grandparents. My uncle laughed and said it was my mother and my aunt's idea. He just had to tweak the car.

"My father just sat there. He didn't say anything for a long time. Then he asked how they got away with it. My uncle said my mother paid off the sheriff. My father got up and walked away. I thought he'd stop them. That he'd make it right. That he'd finally listen to me and help me save Charlie. But he didn't. He went back to pretending none of it was happening. He went back to telling me how good I was at making up tall tales."

Grady soaped up a washcloth and started washing my arms.

"Then what happened?"

"I knew I was running out of time. My Uncle was watching Charlie differently. Like a man watches a woman. I could see it. I think Charlie saw it too. I couldn't keep him from beating her. How was I going to keep him from raping her?"

"What did you do?" Grady whispered while running the washcloth across my shoulder.

"I'd been to the police so many times, always ignored, but I knew the station well. They barely noticed my presence when I would come in. So, I waited outside the building one day until the Sherriff left. Then I walked right past everyone and into his office. No one stopped me. I dug through his files until I found the unofficial police reports, the ones with the real statements, the real pictures, the real mechanical reports. He'd kept everything in case my parents turned on him. Next, I found his bank statements. I took those too, not knowing if they would help, but needing as much ammo as I could find."

"Where did you go?"

"I went to Nana's house. She lived in North Carolina but kept her house in town. I stayed up all night reading before I hid the documents in the cellar. I knew, as incriminating as the documents were, it wasn't enough. There was still no guarantee I could save Charlie. If I went after them, my uncle would want revenge." Rubbing my hands over my face, I released a shaky breath. I wasn't sure if I could finish the story. "I needed protection. I needed Charlie to be safe."

"You needed the sheriff's protection," Grady sighed. He dropped the washcloth into the water and began massaging one of my hands.

"I went to Ms. Bisson's house. I used to babysit for her and knew she had a nanny cam. I asked if I could borrow it. The whole town had heard me rant about my uncle hurting Charlie, but nobody knew what to believe. I think she saw the desperation in my eyes that day. She gave it to me and showed me how it worked. She didn't ask me why I needed it. She just let me take it. I went back to the Sherriff's house the next night. I had the nanny cam in the outside pocket of my backpack, and I set the bag on the kitchen counter. You saw the rest on the video."

"Yes," Grady said, kissing the back of my head. "I saw a desperate young girl easily convince an older man into having sex with her and crying out to stop when she realized it was a mistake. I'm so sorry you went through that."

"I made the decision," I said, curling my hands into fists, remembering that night.

"You made the decision to save Charlie. That was the decision you made. That's what you have to remember. And, you have to forgive yourself for the rest. You were brave," he whispered, kissing my cheek.

He unclenched my fists one finger at a time and began massaging my hands again.

"After that night, I had enough evidence on all of them. They couldn't turn on me or each other, or the house of cards would fall. I forced the sheriff to rent me one of his houses and for my parents to sign emancipation papers. And, they never acted against me to try to take Charlie away even though she was only twelve. I had them all in a vice, and I held them there for years."

"And, you never told Charlie?"

"No," I shook my head. "I don't want her to be ashamed of me. I don't want her to feel guilty. I don't want her to know what the price was for her future."

"She needs to know. It's part of her story too."

"I can't."

"Why did you keep the files?"

"For years, it was to keep us safe. Then I told myself it was to protect us if they ever interfered in our lives. But as I got older, I don't know why I kept them. I don't know why I couldn't destroy them."

"I think you do. I think you want to clear the record on how your grandparents died. And, I think you want your parents, your aunt and uncle, and the sheriff to pay for what they did."

"I do," I nodded. "But not at the expense of destroying Charlie. It would crush her to know the truth."

"She's strong. She's a fighter. You taught her that. She won't blame you."

I shook my head no. "Even if you're right and she isn't ashamed of me, she'd still blame herself. And, she'd be so angry. I'm afraid of what she'd do to them. This could destroy the person she's worked so hard to become."

"They need to pay for what they did. Whether they go to prison or a grave," Grady sighed.

"I can't agree to that," I sighed, shaking my head and standing up in the tub.

I grabbed a towel and dried off before slipping into the bedroom to get dressed.

As I pulled my hair back up into a clip, I tried to focus on other things. I needed to put the past back in a bottle and move forward. I had work to do.

Chapter Twenty-One

Reggie was talking to Tech and Katie over the teleconference line when I walked into the War Room.

"Nightcrawler leave?" I asked Reggie.

"A few minutes ago," Reggie nodded. He looked up at me and raised an eyebrow. "You okay, Sis?"

"I will be," I said before turning to the TV monitor. "Tech, did we get some files from Genie?"

"Sure did. I started sorting through them. We have three victims, all twelve years old. The first victim was kidnapped five years ago, the second was two years ago, and the third was last Tuesday. Genie ran dozens of scenarios trying to link the victims, but so far nothing overlaps."

"Twelve-year-old girls are big into social media. Pull everything you have for each girl for the two months prior to them being kidnapped. Let's see if any of their posts or tweets overlap."

"On it," Tech nodded and turned to start running another laptop.

"I got an alert on Bridget's charge card," Katie grinned. "Guess who bought a four-thousand-dollar purse."

"I told her to go crazy. Bones was shutting her out of the op, so she's blending in and trying to make new friends on her own."

"I'm so jealous," Reggie grinned.

"Focus, Reggie," I said, rolling my eyes. "Katie, what do we have on the girls' families and homes?"

"They had very different backgrounds. The first and third victims were from middle-class families. The second girl's mother lives on welfare checks. They all live in different towns too—a good ten to twenty miles away from each other."

"Can you map it for me?"

"I already did," Tech answered and reached over to strike a few keys. "I know how much you like visuals."

The other TV screen in the War Room lit up with a map of the northeastern corner of Kansas. Red dots marked the girls' homes. Blue dots marked their last known locations. None of the dots were anywhere near each other.

"Let's get Genie patched in."

"Here are the first victim's social media accounts," Reggie said, handing me a stack of papers from the printer.

"Genie's on with us," Katie announced.

"And, how's my favorite copper doing today?" Genie's giddy voice filled the room.

"Perfectly magical," I grumbled.

"Well then, put me to work. I hear you are taking a peek at the kidnapping case. Maggie's taking this one harder than usual. I think she really needs a save. We all do."

"Based on a quick glance of the files, I'm predicting this guy is middle income, organized, but not social. He's grabbing the girls in remote locations, but he had to have been watching them, known their routines."

"I agree," Maggie said. "Genie patched me into the call. But we don't know how long he stalked them before grabbing them or where they crossed paths with him."

I was reading the tweets of the first victim and looked back at the map. I felt Grady come into the room, setting a cup of coffee in front of me, but I was focused on the map.

"Get ready folks," Grady grinned.

I looked back at the social media printout.

"Tech, did the other two girls make recent trips to Topeka before they disappeared?"

"I just sent Reggie the second girl's accounts. You read hers while I do a search for the third girl."

"I'll race you," Genie challenged, and I could hear them both typing at high speed.

"Found it," they both said at once.

I had found what I was looking for in the second girl's tweets as well.

"Let me guess—downtown Topeka?"

"Yeah, a school trip to the museum," Tech answered.

"We checked Topeka. None of the girls were in the same building."

"No, but they were in the same area. Tech, map the museum, the first victim's doctor's office, and the second victim went to a symphony, so mark the hall."

The screen changed to the new locations, with new blue dots. They were several blocks away from each other. Too many blocks for them to walk.

"Genie, overlay the metro bus route," I said almost to myself as I turned my head to look at the map.

Yellow lines started to fill the map at warp speed.

"Maggie—,"

"I see it. Genie, get me an employee roster, bus cameras, and driver schedules for each of the days the girls were in Topeka. We need to figure out which buses they were on, and then we can look for any passengers or employees paying too much attention."

"Let me know what you find. But be careful. We both know the first two girls are dead. This guy won't hesitate to kill the third girl and run if he thinks you're close to catching him."

"You think she's still alive?" Maggie asked, sounding hopeful.

"Yeah, I do. Whether it's about sex, family, or companionship, I think he keeps his victims until he realizes they will never accept him. Then he kills them and finds a new girl."

"I'll let you know what we find," Maggie said, disconnecting.

Genie's live light also dropped off the monitor.

"You probably just saved that girl's life," Grady said.

"I just gave them a lead to follow. They still have a lot of work to do to track it down."

"Do you really think you can give up law enforcement?"

"I already have," I nodded and shuffled the papers into a pile. "Okay, where are we at with our own investigation?"

"I have a pile of shit for you to read through on the businesses," Tech said.

"And, I hired a lawyer," Katie said. "He's already in Pittsburgh in the same hotel as Bridget and going through copies of everything."

"Good. Send him a copy of my contracts and account books on Mayfair Shipping. I'm going to liquidate my investment to free up some cash. Have him review the numbers, and I'll send you Mickey's number. I need a reasonable deal to close in the next few days."

"Mickey's out of prison?" Grady asked.

I nodded. "He was released last week. The murder charges fell apart, and he had already served his time on the other charges."

"Good. I owe him a beer," Grady grinned, sipping his coffee.

I shook my head and looked back to Reggie.

"Reggie, call Texas and make sure all is well. Katie, call Bridget and talk BS. Socialites have ever-annoying ringing phones, and it will appear odd if she's not getting any calls. Tech, keep doing whatever you're doing. And, Grady, check in with Wild Card. Make sure he's not doing anything stupid without backup."

Grady snorted but followed Reggie out of the room. I settled in front of the computer and started reading through all the new data on Jonathon's businesses. Tech had sent thousands of pages. I started taking notes on the first one, determined to move on to the next phase of my plan.

Chapter Twenty-Two

"That's enough," Grady said, walking into the War Room and closing my laptop. "Tech, go to bed."

"Gladly," Tech yawned, on the TV screen.

"You didn't have to stay up because of me," I said, trying to reopen the laptop.

Grady placed his hand on top of it and pulled me from the chair.

"It's three a.m., time to call it a night," he said, pushing me out of the room.

"But I have more to get done."

"Good Night, Tech," Grady called out before turning me down the hallway.

I heard Tech yawn again, followed by a beep, so I was assuming he signed off. I sighed and followed the hallway down to the bedroom.

"I'm not tired," I complained.

"No, you're exhausted," Grady chuckled, reaching around me and unsnapping my jeans.

I pulled off my shirt and sat on the edge of the bed. I watched Grady pull my jeans off and realized he was right. I was exhausted.

He pulled me off the bed and peeled the covers back. Then with the help of a playful shove, I landed flat on my back on top of the silky sheets. I rolled onto my side as he walked around the bed and lay down beside me.

"Hi," I whispered.

"Hey, beautiful," he grinned, after gathering a pillow under him.

Grady was laying on his stomach, watching me, as I stroked a finger down his shoulder and back. I started to trace the tattoo of the panther on his shoulder blade and smiled.

"You're thinking of Eric," Grady whispered, stroking a finger across my cheek.

"Sorry," I said, leaning into his hand.

"Nothing to be sorry for. He was your friend. And, you loved him," Grady said.

He rolled to his back and pulled me to his chest.

"After you kicked me out of Texas, I went to Florida to visit Carly and Tobias and pay my respects," Grady said as he moved my hair away from my face. "I told them I'd bring you back to see them when you were better."

"They must hate me for getting Eric killed."

"Not at all," Grady said, shaking his head. "They're worried about you. Eric might not have been the love of your life, but he was just as important. They know you're grieving too."

I kissed Grady's chest and rested my cheek over his heart.

"How did you know I was thinking about Eric?"

"Oh, I've heard all about the whole spirit-animal hippy shit," Grady chuckled.

I looked up, grinning at Grady.

"The lion in love with the panther," Grady snorted. "You have the strangest friends."

"So why did you pick a panther for your tattoo?" I teased.

"Because it's a badass tattoo," Grady laughed, rolling us both over, so he hovered above me.

"You found out my secret today," I grinned up at him.

"And, why does that make you happy?"

"Because after you found out my darkest secret, you told me you loved me."

"Always."

"You can't promise that," I said, shaking my head. "Someday I might do something even worse."

"I don't care," he said, kissing my cheek. "I have things in my past I'm not proud of either. And, I'll make more mistakes, but they won't change who I am. And I am a man, deeply, madly, crazy in love with the most beautiful, funny, fierce, intelligent woman I've ever met."

He leaned in and kissed me gently.

"Always," he whispered.

"Always," I repeated his words, hoping they were true as I wrapped my arms and legs around him.

"Come on you lovebirds," Reggie yelled, banging on the door. "Time to get up. It's almost noon."

"I don't want to," I giggled, tugging the covers over my head and curling into Grady's chest.

"When this is over," Grady chuckled, pulling me up to kiss me, "it's you and me, right here, in this house, for a whole week."

"Hmm. Sounds wonderful. But you're forgetting I have a very neglected son who isn't going to let me out of his sight once this is over," I laughed, crawling out of bed.

"Fine," Grady said, getting out of bed and heading to the bathroom. "We'll wait until our honeymoon then."

"*Our what??*"

"You heard me," he laughed, closing the door.

"But I don't even know which State I want to live in!" I yelled through the door.

I heard him laugh as he turned on the water for the shower. A shower sounded lovely, but I didn't want to continue the 'honeymoon' conversation, so I dressed quickly and met up with Reggie in the kitchen.

"Anything new?" I asked Reggie as I poured a cup of coffee.

"Pops texted me a picture of him wrapped up in my celestial blue and cream afghan," Reggie sighed.

"I meant about the investigation," I smirked.

"I talked to Katie. She's still going through the business books and working with the lawyer on setting up the sale of Mayfair Shipping. Then I called Wild Card, and he said everything was fine. Nightcrawler called back a few minutes later and said it wasn't fine, and he was pulling some guys in to help. Said he'd call you later."

"That's what I was afraid of," I said rolling my eye.

"Doesn't surprise me," Grady chuckled, reaching past me to get a cup.

He smelled of soap and shampoo, and I couldn't help but to grin as I leaned into his bare chest. He was wearing jeans, but that was it.

"Well, I'll be damned," Reggie laughed.

"Shut up," I laughed and moved away from Grady before we ended up back in the bedroom.

"Never thought I'd see the day when Kelsey Harrison let the walls down," Reggie grinned, shaking his head.

"Like I had a choice with this one," I said, pointing my cup at Grady.

Grady leaned against the counter and grinned as he sipped his coffee.

I looked at the clock and groaned. It was indeed almost noon.

"Okay, we need to pack and get on the road. I planned on being in Pittsburgh before dinner, but now we'll be lucky to get there before bedtime."

"Not the way I drive," Grady grinned.

Grady drove, Reggie navigated, and I took over the back seat researching the businesses and taking calls from Katie who was acting as my liaison with the new lawyer. We stopped as few times as possible and true to his word, Grady made record time, pulling up just before eight o'clock.

When we entered the townhouse, all the lights were on, and I found Bridget in the kitchen. She looked completely different. Her hair and nails were so shiny the lighting in the kitchen reflected off them. Her beige suit was trimmed in silk, and she had matching Louboutin heels that made my heart flutter.

"The shoes!" I exclaimed.

"I know, right! I went a little nuts," Bridget giggled, turning one of her feet side-to-side so I could get the full effect. "I also picked you up a pair in navy to match a fabulous Armani pantsuit I found for you."

"I'm in love!" I grinned.

"Was I just replaced by a pair of shoes?" Grady chuckled, setting down a pile of suitcases and duffle bags.

"You weren't replaced," I shrugged.

"You were just moved further down the list," Reggie laughed, leaning down to get a closer look at the shoes. "Please tell me you bought me something!"

"Well, I bought something for Bones, but since he's an asshole, I'll give it to you. Does that count?" Bridget laughed.

"I'll take it. Gimmie-gimmie," Reggie said, holding out his hands.

Bridget retrieved a small box from the dining room table that was overflowing with boxes and bags of name brand clothes and shoes.

"Here," she said, handing Reggie the box.

Reggie gently set the box down and carefully opened it.

"Oooh. Those are sweet," I said, leaning around Reggie.

"They're cufflinks," Grady said from the other side of Reggie. "Who cares about cufflinks?"

"They're Korstantino cufflinks! These are the tiger eye design," Reggie squealed, jumping up and down hugging Bridget. "Jackson's going to be so damn jealous."

"Doubt it," Grady said, rolling his eyes.

"You're such a boy," Reggie said, shaking his head.

Grady threw his arms out to his side in a 'What does that mean?' gesture. I laughed and pushed him toward the door to retrieve the rest of the luggage.

"Bridget, what's the layout?" I asked.

"One small staff bedroom on the first floor and three bedrooms upstairs. I started hauling your clothes into one of the upstairs bedrooms, but then I ran out of room. I also filled the cupboards and the refrigerator with some basics but didn't want to get caught doing domestic activities like grocery shopping, so I ordered more groceries to be delivered tomorrow morning. Oh, and there's no secret War Room here, which was quite disappointing. But there is a den around the corner with a large internet-ready TV."

I walked around the kitchen and into the den. Rich, chocolate-colored leather couches were set on one side of the room, a heavy oak desk at the other, and an oak conference table with six chairs was stationed in the center of the room with a large flat screen TV at one end.

"Fancy," I grinned. "No more folding chairs."

"Not in this townhouse," Bridget grinned. "Grady's friend has good taste."

"I'll be sure to tell him you said so," Grady chuckled behind us. "All the luggage is inside. What's next?"

"Contact Bones and have him meet us. Tell him to make sure he's not followed."

Grady nodded, pulling his phone out.

"Reggie, can you make sense of all the clothes and luggage?"

Reggie nodded and walked away.

"Bridget?" I whispered after the boys had walked away.

"Yes?" she grinned.

"I need to see the shoes you bought me," I smirked.

"I'll go get them while you pull our dinner out of the oven," she said before running upstairs.

I pulled the lasagna and garlic bread out of the oven, careful to use my bad arm as little as possible. I found the plates and silverware and set everything on the dining room table while Reggie moved the last of the bags upstairs.

Bridget had already opened several bottles of wine, so I poured myself a glass as everyone came back and filled their plates. I slipped off to the side and tried on the Louboutin's Bridget had handed me. I smiled as I crossed the room, realizing they fit to perfection.

"You are so wearing those heels tonight," Grady chuckled from his seat at the dining room table.

"We're not going anywhere tonight," I said, turning my foot to the side so I could see the shoe from a different angle.

"Never said we were," Grady grinned.

"Oooh, you're bad," Bridget giggled.

I blushed a bit and took the shoes back off. Grady filled a plate, passing it to me. Still holding my wine glass in my right hand, I took the offered plate and a twinge of pain laced up my shoulder and into the base of my neck. Grady lunged for the plate, catching it as it slipped from my fingers.

"Damn it," I cringed, pulling my arm to my chest.

"It's my fault," Grady said, standing to massage it. "You've been doing so much better today, that I forgot."

"I should be able to carry a damn plate!"

"You will, but only if you listen to your body and take a break when it's telling you too," he grinned, kissing my neck.

"You're making fun of me," I snapped.

"A little," Grady whispered, leaning in to kiss my neck again.

"It's not funny."

"It kind of is," Bones chuckled from the entrance.

"I wasn't talking to you," I glared.

Bones grinned as he walked over to the table and pulled out a chair across from Reggie, filling a plate for himself. He startled when he noticed Bridget, posed with her legs crossed and sipping wine next to him.

"Mr. Hartwood, it's not polite to stare," Bridget informed him.

"Bridget?"

"Good for you. You figured out my name. Now, by all means, forget you ever knew me," Bridget said, before standing and walking into the kitchen to retrieve another bottle of wine.

"Wow. Was that you or Reggie?" Bones asked looking at me and then looking back at Bridget.

"Bones—," Grady tried to warn him.

"You clean up nicely, Bridge," Bones grinned, leaning back in his chair so he could better see her legs as she walked back to the table.

His grin was short lived when Bridget dumped an entire bottle of red wine over his head.

"Was that the 97 Bordeaux?" Rebecca, Bones' sister, asked stepping into the room and setting her purse in an armchair near the entrance. "I must say, it would have been better to pour a gallon of milk over his head. I would have drank the Bordeaux."

"I thought it a bit bitter," Bridget shrugged. "There's a nice cabernet if you'd like, though."

"Yes, please. Bones, go clean yourself up. You've made a mess of yourself, and you're getting wine on Dex's floors," Rebecca scolded.

"I've made a mess?" Bones glared, wine dripping off his hair and face.

"You told a woman she cleans up nicely—yes—you made a mess of things. Now go."

Bones stormed down the hall.

"Becca," Grady nodded, before tucking his forehead into my good shoulder and laughing.

"Sorry to intrude unannounced. I decided to come and gather some truths. The most important being, how long is my brother going to be in town driving me insane?"

"I actually hope he stays here permanently," Bridget said while pouring Rebecca a glass of cabernet.

"Absolutely not. He crashed another one of my dates. Either he leaves town, or I'm going to put a hit out on him. I know people. I can make it happen."

"Don't we all," Grady laughed. "And, luckily for Bones, all the people you know, he knows."

Rebecca sighed before taking a sip of her wine. "Hmm. Much smoother than the Bordeaux. Good decision."

"I'll call someone to clean the chair and floor tomorrow morning," Bridget said, looking at the mess she had made.

"I got it," Reggie said. "I'm a master when it comes to wine stains."

"How about my shirt? Can you get the stain out?" Bones said, stomping back into the room.

"I could get the stain out, but it'd still be an ugly shirt," Reggie grinned.

"This is an expensive shirt."

"That just means you have no fashion sense," Reggie grinned.

"I paid a hundred and fifty for this shirt."

"Please. That's nothing," Bridget laughed. "Kelsey's shoes were almost a grand."

"I know you from somewhere, don't I?" Rebecca grinned, looking at Bridget.

Bridget nodded. "Boarding school."

"Bridget Delano! Yes, now I remember. You were a year behind me, but we had some of the same classes because you were so damn smart."

"Just determined," Bridget smiled. "Determined to ensure I never had to go home again."

"Delano? Your last name is Dell," Bones said.

"I lied," Bridget shrugged. "I don't like people knowing my real name. Surely you understand, *Declan*."

I snorted, earning a glare from Bones.

"How is your family?" Rebecca asked Bridget, ignoring Bones.

"Still a bunch of assholes in expensive ugly shirts," Bridget grinned.

Bones shoved a chair to the side as he glared across the table at Bridget. Bridget glared back at him.

"Bones—Don't," I said.

Grady pushed Bones toward one of the recliners by the fireplace. He forced an irate Bones into one before stretching out in the other, to play guard dog over his friend.

"Let's talk business, shall we?" Rebecca smirked. "What do I have to do expedite Bones leaving town?"

"We actually could use your help," I said, nodding for her to have a seat. "First, I need Bridget to get close to someone. Jackie Vaughn."

"I can arrange that," Rebecca shrugged. "What else?"

"I'm getting ready to sell Mayfair Shipping so I can buy some other companies. I have no interest in running the new businesses, though. I just want to acquire them. Can you meet me tomorrow and give me your feedback on what I should do with them down the road?"

"So, you're buying them, but you don't want them?"

"Possibly, yes," I grinned.

"Intrigued. I'll clear my schedule for tomorrow afternoon."

"And, I was hoping you could throw a charity ball. I would expect you to hire someone to take care of the details, of course, but I need the invitations to come from you."

"When?"

"Two weeks."

"I'll set it up. Who do you need to attend?"

"Jonathan Vaughn."

Rebecca watched me intently as she took a sip of her wine. Slowly, she set the glass in front of her on the table. "I'll do it, on one condition."

"And, that is?"

"You make sure there's no blowback on Barrister Industries."

"He won't hold any power by the time I'm done with him."

"Splendid. I'll call my party planner tonight and get her started. I'm assuming you'll be paying to support the event?"

"Anonymously, yes. Pull the funds out of my investor account."

She nodded as she slid gracefully out of her chair. "Bridget, it was nice seeing you again. If you need to get close to Jackie, we'll need to go to breakfast tomorrow. Where should the car pick you up from?"

"I'm staying at the Hyatt, in the penthouse suite."

"Ten?"

"Perfect. Let me show you out," Bridget smiled, stepping away from the table and leading Rebecca to the door.

"I'm in some weird alternate universe," Bones grumbled from the chair by the fireplace.

"No, but you're definitely screwed, brother," Grady chuckled.

"Can I go shopping for ball gowns?" Reggie asked.

"Sorry, too late," Bridget said, returning to the room. "I picked up dresses today for Kelsey and I both. And, I've already made a lot of contacts. I have the phone numbers of six men who asked me out. Let me know if it will be helpful to go out with any of them. I also have three new BFF's that keep calling me constantly," she said, rolling her eyes.

She emptied five business cards and a bar napkin on the table. I flipped through their names.

"Paul Vaughn?"

Bridget nodded. "Jonathan's brother, but from what I can tell the family doesn't care for Jonathan. Paul wasn't much on talking about his brother's campaign when I brought it up."

"I don't think he's the right angle. We need to try to get access to the teenage daughter. I think getting closer to the wife might get you there."

"What am I looking for with the daughter?"

"You'll know when you see it," I said, looking up at Bridget.

"Shit," Bridget said, grabbing her wine glass and downing it.

"You sure you're up for this? You can back out."

"No," she said, shaking her head as she refilled her glass. "I'm in. Just tell me the bastard is going down, Kelsey."

"We're going to skewer and roast him over an open flame," I said, clinking our glasses.

Chapter Twenty-Three

Bones escorted an unappreciative Bridget back to the hotel around midnight. Reggie had long before went to bed. Grady was shutting my laptop once again, pulling me away from the business accounts.

When we got upstairs, I pulled my duffle bag out, only to find it empty. I opened the dresser and closet, finding everything was unpacked.

"What are you doing?" Grady sighed, coming up behind me and wrapping his arms around me.

"I was looking for a nightshirt."

"You don't need a nightshirt," Grady said, kissing down the side of my neck until he reached the neckline on my shirt, then pulling the shirt over my head to continue kissing down my back. "I have this image of you wearing those shoes, and only those shoes," he said as he unsnapped my jeans and dragged them over my hips.

"Seriously?" I laughed.

"Hell yes," Grady laughed, dropping the shoes to the floor in front of me.

"Why, Mr. Tanner, I would've never guessed you for a shoe-guy," I giggled as I kicked my jeans off before sliding my feet into the shoes.

I turned around. I was now wearing only a black bra, black panties, and the shoes, Grady searched my body with his eyes, as he walked backward to the bed and lay down, propping himself up with his elbows.

I took a step toward him, and he shook his head. "Only the shoes."

I slowly unhooked the bra and let it slide off my shoulders. Running my hands down my breasts, down my stomach, I snared my panties with one finger on each side, sliding each side down a few inches at a time until I leaned over, stepping out of them.

"Yeah, that's the look I had in my head," Grady grinned, pulling his boxers off and crooking a finger for me to join him. "I'm definitely a shoe-guy."

Six a.m. rolled around sooner than expected and I forced myself away from Grady and into the shower. I had just shampooed my hair when I heard the bathroom door open.

"No—," I laughed. "You're not invited. I have to be downstairs in ten minutes."

Grady pulled back the shower curtain and stepped in. "Then we better be quick."

"Damn it, Grady," I laughed, as he started licking my neck. "You better be very quick."

Since I had to lay low for at least a week, I decided to dress in comfortable cotton shorts and a cotton tank top. Hurrying so Grady wouldn't distract me again, I ran down the stairs barefoot, hopping off the last step and turning into the kitchen.

"Someone's awful perky this morning," Reggie grinned.

"Am I late?" I asked, ignoring his comment and filling up a cup of coffee.

"Tech and Katie are on the conference line, but Tech's still booting up computers. I'll fix you some fruit and oatmeal for breakfast and bring it to you."

"Thanks, Reg," I grinned, kissing him on the cheek and heading into the den.

"Oh, look," Katie said over the line, "Kelsey's got sex-glow this morning."

"Your roots are showing, Katie. Better get to a salon."

"Liar," Katie said, but she turned to one of the other monitors and tried to check her reflection.

Tech grinned and rolled his eyes.

"Where are we?" I asked as Reggie came in and set a bowl of oatmeal and a plate of fruit in front of me.

"The lawyer is meeting you at the townhouse at seven o'clock. Donovan hired one of his guys to chauffeur him back and forth and to taxi Bridget around when necessary too," Katie said.

"Good. Anything new from New Orleans?"

"I talked to Wild Card last night," Reggie said. "Large crates were being moved into the warehouse. He was going to sneak inside early this morning after things quieted down. He said he'd call afterward, but I haven't heard from him yet."

"Sounds risky," Grady grumbled, walking in and sitting next to me. He stole a giant strawberry from my plate.

"Sounds like Wild Card is impatient," I said. "But we can't set up for a long surveillance job either, so let's just hope he doesn't get himself in trouble."

"Nightcrawler and one of the other bikers were with him," Reggie said. "And, they had some scouts watching the building in case things went bad."

"We've made a deal with Mickey McNabe and the Bianchi family on Mayfair shipping," Katie said. "You'll cash out just below market value, which is more than you paid for it, but not much. The lawyer has the paperwork to sign."

"Good. I need the cash," I said, sipping my coffee and pulling my feet up into the chair.

I slid my plate of fruit away from Grady and slid him the bowl of oatmeal instead. He grinned and grabbed the bowl and spoon. I laughed and sucked on the giant cut of cantaloupe I held with my fingers.

"You're acting goofy this morning," Katie laughed. "I don't think I've ever seen you this relaxed."

"My son is safe. My friends are safe. The last bad guy goes down within the next two weeks. Life is good," I said, holding up my coffee.

"Cheers," Tech said holding up his hot cocoa.

"How's Bridget?" Katie asked.

"She's making progress," Grady nodded. "Rebecca is going to help her make some new connections today. Bridget's going around Bones. In fact, she poured a bottle of wine over his head last night."

"He said something stupid, didn't he," Tech grinned.

"Said she cleaned up nicely," Reggie grinned.

"Oh damn," Katie squealed. "Did anyone record it?"

"Unfortunately, no," I grinned. "Rebecca will be over this afternoon to look at any of the businesses I may be buying. I'm hoping she'll fold the management of some of them under Barrister's."

"Two would fit nicely," Katie agreed. "But we need a better game plan on the ones you don't want. The ones tied to bad books or illegal activity."

"We'll go through each when the lawyer gets here. What's his name again?"

"Herman Stykes. Despite the name, he's known to be a shark. Though, he's a little strange."

"How strange?"

"You'll see," Katie grinned.

"What about Carl's research on the messaging service?"

"Carl pulled twenty years of call logs, then extracted anything he could tie to Max, Nola, Pasco, and finally, Jonathan. Everything for Jonathan and Nola pointed to New Orleans. We also pulled anything mentioning the warehouse. Jonathan bought it shortly after the bar was shut down, so he hasn't owned it long."

"So, if he was able to keep the trafficking business open, it might be where he keeps his victims?" Grady asked.

"Maybe, but the bar was used to kidnap people from," Tech said. "The warehouse doesn't have any visitors and the neighboring businesses would make it too risky to move victims in and out."

"Maybe he drugs them," Grady shrugged. "Then puts them in the crates."

"It would still be too risky," I said shaking my head. "Jonathan owns the warehouse. He wouldn't take the chance of being caught in human trafficking and have it trace back to him. And, I don't think trafficking was really his thing. I never got the impression his involvement was anything more than entertainment for him."

Grady sighed and rubbed a hand down his face. "I hate this shit. I hate talking about this monster, wading through all these sick fucking layers of his personality. I'd rather just kill him."

"Here, here," Bones agreed, walking into the room. "Anything I can work on?"

"No," I said, shaking my head. "We're at a standstill until I start crushing his income."

"Bones can take me for a drive," Grady said, getting up. "I'd like to get better acquainted with the streets and neighborhood."

"You mean you need some guy time," I grinned.

"Unless you're willing to give me some girl time," Grady grinned down at me.

"Get out of here," I laughed, shoving him away. "Reggie will keep me company."

"I'd rather go shopping with Bridget," Reggie pouted.

"Maybe later, Reg. We'll see what her schedule looks like," I said, patting his arm.

Bones snorted as he followed Grady out of the room.

"Is that a good idea?" Katie asked.

"What?"

"Letting Grady and Bones go out unsupervised?"

"Like I could stop Grady? Besides, it makes sense. I'd do the same thing if I was him."

"So, you know he's going to go track down Jonathan?" Tech asked.

"Sure. He's coming up with a plan B," I shrugged. "He won't do anything unless we fail. And, we all know, I don't fail."

"But Grady thinks you might?"

"No," I laughed. "I think he's hoping I fail. He still wants to kill him but knows it would piss me off."

"What about Bones?" Reggie asked.

"I made Bones swear we'd do this my way. He'll have to stop Grady if it comes down to it."

"That's mean," Tech laughed. "You've got the two biggest bad-asses I know locked down."

I grinned as I sucked on the cantaloupe.

Chapter Twenty-Four

Herman Stykes was beyond strange. When he arrived, he adamantly refused Reggie's help to unload his files and slowly carried them in himself, one box at a time. Then he searched the townhouse for the best place to set up, deciding on the living room because it had what he deemed to be the best natural lighting. Then he requested the heavy oak dining room table be moved so he would have adequate work space.

With my bum shoulder, I wasn't allowed to help, so five foot Herman Stykes, with his pencil arms and gerbil size legs, lifted his side of the table up a half an inch, while Reggie held his end up a foot off the floor. I finally convinced them to use the rug to drag the table into the other room. Reggie made it work.

Once the table was moved, the lawyer started assembling piles of papers 'just so' and set up the whiteboard he brought with him at one end of the room. We watched him in silence for forty-five minutes while he ensured everything was in its proper place.

Reggie hooked up one of the laptops to the living room TV. Tech and Katie watched the snail-paced activity over the conference connection. Of course, they had the luxury of a mute button. They kept stepping away from the monitor so they could laugh. Reggie and I squirmed and continued to elbow each other.

"Can I get you something to drink Herman?" Reggie asked.

"Please, call me Mr. Stykes. And, yes, I'll have a raspberry tea please."

"I'm afraid we are fresh out of raspberry tea. Can I interest you in a coffee or orange juice?"

"No."

Mr. Stykes walked a circle around the room, checking everything one last time.

"Since there isn't anything appropriate to drink, let's get down to business. You wanted all the businesses analyzed for possible hostile acquisitions. Is that correct?"

"Mostly," I shrugged. "Katie, do we have all the attorney-client documents signed and in order?"

"Yes. We're covered."

"Good. Mr. Stykes, my goal is to financially destroy Jonathan Vaughn."

"Well, then," he said, looking back at the piles of papers. "I'll need to make some changes. Please give me a few minutes."

We stood and watched Mr. Stykes move piles of paper around the table for twenty minutes. I was ready for a shot of tequila by the time he was ready.

"Yes, this will work," he nodded to himself.

Turning to me he said, "Are you ready to begin or do you need to take a break first?"

"I think we better get started," Katie insisted, covering her laugh.

"Very well then. These four businesses are what we call crap. They have high expenses, low profits and are barely staying in the black. This business is solid, but Mr. Vaughn is only a small stakeholder."

Mr. Stykes moved from the far end of the table to the center and straightened the center stack of folders. Hovering his hand over the next file, he began again.

"This is the company he's trying to sell. It makes a decent profit, but nothing off the charts. This one," he said, pointing to the thicker file, "is his main company, JV Dagger Innovations."

He looked at the folders closest to me. Without moving any closer, he pointed to them. "Those look shady as hell. I don't want to know what he's doing with them."

"This company," I said walking over and tapping my finger on the folder in the center of the table.

"No!!! Please don't touch! You'll get your germs all over my papers. Touch your own papers," Mr. Stykes said, leaning over the piles of papers, trying to protect his documents.

I stepped back and put my hands in the air in surrender. I looked over at Reggie, but he had turned away laughing. Tech and Katie had us on mute and had stepped out of the monitor's range again.

"I do apologize Mr. Stykes. I'll behave now," I said, trying to hide my grin.

I waited for Mr. Stykes to walk his circle around the room again, ensuring his documents were still in their proper place.

"JV Dagger is Jonathan's baby," I said after he had completed his circle. "He's trying to sell the other company to add cash to JV Dagger and at the same time, refuel his campaign fund. How desperate is he to find a buyer?"

"He's offering just under market, but with a cash offer, we could cut him lower."

"And, do I have enough money from the sale of Mayfair Shipping?"

"Yes. You could also pick up the crap companies if you wanted, but if your interest is to financially ruin him, eventually he'll have to file bankruptcy on them."

"I do want the four crap companies as you call them. Two of them, I think would pull a profit if we cleaned house."

"Very well then. I can start negotiating a cash deal with all five companies if you wish. I'll use the package deal to drive down the price."

"As soon as the sale goes through, I want the businesses with shady books turned over to the IRS by whatever covert means you determine is best. I'll alert the FBI of the one that appears to be a front for illegal activity."

"The one in New Orleans?" he asked.

"Yes. We're checking into that one a bit closer."

"I don't want to know—," Mr. Stykes said, holding up his hands to stop me.

"Okay."

"Do you want to go after JV Dagger Innovations? If your goal is to ruin him, we'll have to do something about that company."

"After the sale of the other businesses, how soon do you think it will take Jonathan to reinvest the money into his company and political campaign?"

"He's behind on some payments, so he'll make a wire transfer as soon as possible. I'd say two days after we close, give or take a day."

"And, once he funds the account, can he pull the money back out?"

"It's incorporated so it would take a few days, but most of his capital will be wrapped up in the company. If he pulled the money back out, it would hurt the company."

"Then let's help him dump his money into it as quickly as we can. Then we'll sink his mother ship."

"Oh, I see. Yes. Yes. That would ruin him for sure," Mr. Stykes nodded, pushing up his thick dark glasses. "What about the company he owns a minority share in?"

"Jonathan's reputation will soon be taking a dive in the national media. They'll find a way to push him out and what little money he makes on them, won't save him."

"Yes, Yes. This will be fun," Mr. Stykes nodded straight-faced as he started to re-arrange his papers again.

Reggie stepped out of the room and returned a minute later, handing me a shot.

I looked at the clock. It was only 8:30 a.m. I downed the shot anyway.

"One more thing," I said. "My name can't be traced to any of the purchases. If he finds out it's me, he'll pull out of the deal."

"That's not a problem. I've already created layers of shell companies. He'd have to postpone for months to dig through the names to find you. Hope you don't mind, but I took the liberty of naming the top shell company as Sunshine and Partners."

"I think that's a very fitting name, Mr. Stykes," I grinned over at Katie and Tech.

"I need a beer," Reggie said, walking out of the room.

"Perhaps, Sir," Mr. Stykes called to Reggie. "Do you have available some filtered spring water and lemon?"

"We do. I'll grab that for you," Reggie said, as he continued out.

"I'm going to get started on negotiations. If I can have the room for the next two and a half hours, undisturbed, I think that would work the best. Otherwise, I'll need to transfer the files back to the hotel, and the lighting right now in this room is most ideal."

"I'll leave you to your work. If you need anything, feel free to let us know."

Reggie walked in with a bottle of water, a plate with a lemon, and a cutting knife. He set them on the corner of the table and walked out. Mr. Stykes started panicking about the placement of the plate and bottle, and I rushed to exit the room.

Reggie and I regrouped in the den and reconnected with Tech and Katie.

"You really didn't think I needed a warning?" I asked Katie.

"It was just too much fun letting him surprise you. He really is great at what he does."

"Send me the contracts on the sale of Mayfair Shipping, so I'm ready to sign when he's done. I probably won't need either of you until mid-afternoon so you can do whatever until then."

"Sounds good," Tech grinned at Katie.

"Don't get any ideas. I'm going to the store to check on construction," Katie laughed as Tech shut the laptop, disconnecting the call.

"Ah, the season of love," Reggie grinned. "So, what's my next assignment?"

"Well, you decide. Do you want to read the contracts for me or figure out something for lunch?"

"I'll go slave away in the kitchen," he pouted.

I opened up the file Katie had sent to me and sighed. It was four hundred and twenty-seven pages. I really wish Reggie would have picked the contracts.

Chapter Twenty-Five

Lunch came and went, without any sign of Bones or Grady. Mr. Stykes re-emerged at precisely 11:25 a.m. and declared he had a very agreeable verbal deal for the purchase of the businesses. He would be returning to his hotel to type it up and deliver it to Jonathan's attorney by one o'clock. I wasn't sure how you could type up a contract that quick being I was only half way through the Mayfair contract, but Mr. Stykes didn't seem concerned.

I listened to Reggie sigh loudly for the third time before I dug out a pile of cash and told him to be back by 6:00. He was out the door before I could blink.

I relocated to one of the recliners in the front sitting area. Tucked under a throw blanket, I took notes and continue reading while I drank an oversized cup of coffee.

"Wake up!" Rebecca shouted from above me.

I jumped out of the chair, sending everything crashing to the floor.

"Shit, sorry," she laughed, picking up the laptop, notepad, and pen I had dropped.

"Damn," I laughed. "I can't believe I was sleeping so deeply. It must have been the contract. It's so damn boring, it put me in a temporary coma."

"What contract?"

"The sale of Mayfair Shipping. Mr. Stykes needs me to sign it later today, but I can't seem to read the damn thing."

"Herman Stykes?"

"The one and I hope, the only."

"Print the contract, and I'll go through it."

"It's 427 pages."

"Yes, but I'm familiar with Mr. Stykes' work and a lot of the information is standardized in all his contracts. I'll spot anything out of place."

"It's your eyeballs," I shrugged, taking the laptop and setting it on the breakfast bar. "How do I send this to the printer?"

She laughed and slid the laptop in front of her.

"Where's the dining room table?" she asked.

"Mr. Stykes needed it moved to the living room because the natural lighting was better."

"Yes. That sounds like the one and only Mr. Stykes," Rebecca laughed. "His quirks are worth it, though. I've never seen such airtight contracts. And, he can be a sneaky bastard too."

"The printer is in the den. I have the other files I want to go through with you in there too."

"Sounds good. Got any beer? It's been one of those kinds of days."

I opened the refrigerator and grinned. "Bridget stocked the fridge."

"What's that mean?"

"We have three kinds of beer, or we can make a pitcher of margaritas."

"Margaritas it is then," Rebecca laughed, opening the end cupboard and getting out a blender. She then turned and pulled two glasses out of the middle cupboard on the second shelf.

"So, who's this Dex guy? The one who owns this place." I grinned.

Rebecca froze and looked up at me. She turned back and looked at where she pulled the blender and glasses, knowing where they were stored.

"You can't tell Bones. He'd flip out," Rebecca grinned.

"Wasn't planning on telling anyone. But I've been reading that damn contract for hours, so I need something more exciting to talk about for at least five minutes," I grinned, leaning onto the counter top to wait for her to spill the story.

Rebecca wriggled her nose and grinned as she looked back at me. "He was in their unit. After he had served, he went into private security overseas. We hooked up when he was home on a two-week vacation last year, but he ended it when I refused to tell Bones."

"Why do you care what Bones thinks?"

"Because he sets fire to every relationship I've ever been in," Rebecca sighed. "I didn't want to see their friendship ruined too."

"And, you don't think their friendship is already strained because you asked Dex to keep a secret from Bones?"

"If I was thinking clearly, I never would have started a relationship with him at all. He's only home maybe twice a year which is a major negative. But, damn, he's smoking hot," she grinned. "He makes me laugh. And, he likes the fact that I'm this crazy insane business woman running a company. He actually told me he's proud of me. No one's said that before."

"I need a visual," I said, gesturing for her phone.

She pulled up a picture of the two of them together. She was laughing trying to take the picture as he was kissing her neck.

"He is hot."

I scrolled through the next few photos. In all of them, Rebecca was laughing while Dex was holding her. They looked great together.

"You screwed up. You need to fix this," I said, setting down the phone.

"It's too late."

"Bullshit," I said, adding some more tequila to the blender before she capped it. "Tell Bones you met this terrific guy who makes you laugh and who isn't intimidated by your job and you let him go because you were afraid of Bones ruining it."

"And, what if Bones goes all ape shit crazy when he finds out it was Dex?" she asked, before pushing the button on the blender.

I waited for the blender to stop before I answered.

"Two things can happen. One, Bones is happy for you and you live happily ever after. Or, two, Bones goes ape-shit, calls Dex and yells at him. You still win because Dex knows you finally came clean."

"What if he's already found someone else?"

"Then he hides overseas," I shrugged. "And you continue dating losers until you're an old maid."

"Nice. Thanks a lot," she laughed, filling the glasses.

We moved our drinks into the den, and I picked up the giant stack of papers from the printer and tossed them to Rebecca. She grabbed a highlighter and started highlighting small sections as she flipped the papers over. When she had a good twenty pages marked up, I started looking at her highlights. She was marking only the particulars of the sale; the rest was all legal non-sense. It took less than twenty minutes for her to break it all down for me.

"Looks good to me, though if you can hold the company for longer, I'm sure you could sell it at a higher price."

"No," I shook my head. "I need to sell now in order to buy these." I pulled five of the folders from the pile on the table out and moved them in front of her so she could read them.

I sat back and drank my margarita. She was only on the third company when I finished my drink, so I stole her untouched glass. By the time she was halfway through the last business, I had refilled both our drinks.

"Well," she said, leaning back in her chair. "Four of these are barely in the black, and the other is doing only moderately better."

"Agreed," I said setting down my glass and moving the papers around in a very Herman Stykes kind of way.

I pulled specific inventory sheets from two folders and placed them on top of a third folder. Then I paired folder four and five together.

"Now, what do you think?" I asked.

"Mergers?" she grinned, looking at them again. "What's the goal?"

"Jonathon's going to be dumping a pile of green into JV Dagger Innovations. I want to target the companies to become his biggest competitor, stealing his best vendors and clients. By consolidating some aspects of the companies, I could leverage them better against him."

"So, merge the three manufacturing and development companies to compete for the best supply deals and new product lines. Then merge the other two companies to hit the servicing-side of his revenues," she nodded. "It could work, but it would take a lot of time."

"To completely crush him, yes, it would take several months. But to start causing damage to an already tipsy company? I think if we put our heads together we can create absolute chaos. As soon as the funds are wired and secure, we can put enough heat on the company that if he tries to pull the money out, everyone else would abandon ship."

"And after you tank JV Dagger?"

"Then I'm left with two companies positioned to make strong profits," I shrugged. "Barrister's would be a nice fit for their oversight."

"After the re-organization, it would be a very nice fit," Rebecca grinned, clinking our glasses together.

• • •

Chapter Twenty-Six

Bridget arrived mid-afternoon and made us a second pitcher of margaritas while Rebecca and I mapped out the plan for the restructuring of the manufacturing businesses. By the time we started with the servicing business plan, the doorbell rang, and I went to answer it.

After checking the peephole, I swung the door open, stepping back as Mr. Stykes strolled past me into the living room.

"I have the contracts. We can close on everything tomorrow. Are you prepared to sign?" He began laying out contracts with signature tabs.

"I'm ready when you are."

After making me collect my own pen, Mr. Stykes had me sign the corporate documentation for the ownership of the company Sunshine and Partners. Then he asked who would be representing the company as the official signer during the closings.

"I'll do it," Bridget grinned, stepping into the room. "No one knows that Bridget Delano is associated with you."

"It could be risky. What if Jackie Vaughn questions your involvement in the sale?"

"I just spent most of the day shopping and eating with Jackie. The last thing on her radar is anything to do with her husband. And, her husband doesn't seem to have anything to do with her either, unless it's for a photo opportunity."

"In my opinion, Mr. Vaughn is too distracted," Mr. Stykes said. "I doubt he will even look at the signature."

"No one would blink an eye if a Delano were to make such large purchases," Rebecca said, stepping into the room. "It doesn't matter that Bridget hasn't been associated with her family in years. Anyone seeing the name would assume it was all part of the great dynasty."

Bridget snorted.

"Fine. But make sure the closings are split. I don't want her in a room with Jonathan Vaughn. I don't want him to even see her at the end of the hall."

"There are conference rooms at my hotel," Bridget nodded. "I can stay in the penthouse, and Mr. Stykes can handle the rest in the conference room."

"Yes, but get the Gladesview conference room," Mr. Stykes nodded. "It has the best lighting."

I signed the authority documents, giving Bridget all the power to execute the contracts. Rebecca read all the sales contracts and rattled off the parts and pieces I needed to know. I nodded at Bridget to sign.

My phone rang as we were wrapping up.

"About time you called in," I answered, turning to walk to the den.

"It's been a busy day," Wild Card sighed.

"You have information, or just checking in?"

"I have more pieces to the puzzle but haven't put anything together. I emailed some pictures to you as well."

"Give me a minute," I said, before putting the phone on speaker.

Rebecca, Bridget, a curious looking Mr. Stykes followed me into the room. I accessed my email and brought up the pictures on the large wall monitor.

"What am I looking at?" I asked.

"Counterfeit handbags," Bridget laughed. She stepped closer to the pictures to look at the various purses and totes. "Wow. These are good."

"Why am I looking at counterfeit handbags?" I asked.

"Good question," Wild Card answered. "That's what we found in the crates at the warehouse. We snuck in early this morning, but we didn't sneak out before another delivery showed up. We had to hide in a closet until they left again. When they did leave, I followed one of the men, and Nightcrawler followed the freight truck. The truck led nowhere important. The guy I followed went to an abandoned mansion out in the bayou. Creepy as hell out there."

"Perhaps on Willow Estates Road?" Mr. Stykes asked.

"Who is that?" Wild Card asked.

"My lawyer," I answered. "Speak freely."

"Yeah, the mansion was on Willow Estates Road. How'd you know?"

"Jonathon Vaughn moved into the house to live with his uncle at the age of eleven. No one knows why. When his uncle died, he inherited the house and all the other assets."

"That's where the bodies are buried," I said.

"Like where we can find dirt on Jonathon?" Wild Card asked.

"By the look on Kelsey's face," Grady said, stepping into the room. "I think she meant in the literal sense."

Grady moved me over to a chair, pushing me down into it. The room was tipping on an angle.

"Stay with us," Grady whispered, handing me a bottled water.

I nodded and sipped some water. For a second, I didn't think I'd be able to swallow it, but as he rubbed circles on my back, it finally slid down.

"What now?" Bones asked. "Do we call the FBI in?"

He must have walked in with Grady and heard the phone conversation.

"No," I said. "They can't do anything based on me having a gut feeling."

"They'd believe you," Grady said.

"But that won't get them a warrant."

"So, what do we do?" Wild Card asked.

"We wait. But we need to watch the house. I don't want Jonathan to be able to hurt anyone else before we take him down."

"I'll set up a watch with Nightcrawler and the other bikers. I also called Ryan. He's available to help."

"What about Leo?"

"He has him out at his fishing cabin. He's off the grid until we figure out what to do with him."

"No. Ryan stands guard over Leo until this is all over. I can't take a chance on him double-crossing us."

"I'll relay the message," Wild Card said. "I'll buy a tent or something and camp out close to the house to keep an eye on things. That way we won't need as many guys."

"You realize there are gators and snakes out there, right?" I laughed.

"I'll figure out something."

"Some of the old estates have servant's quarters in close proximity to the main house," Mr. Stykes said. "I'd inspect the property for empty cottages or outbuilding with lofts."

"I'll do that," Wild Card said.

"Be careful," I warned.

"I got this," Wild Card said, hanging up.

"Are we missing all the fun?" Tech asked, walking into the room.

My body shot out of the chair as I turned to see Katie, Tech, Anne, and Alex, all standing in the den, grinning at me.

"What the hell are all of you doing here?" I asked.

"We're family," Alex shrugged. "Where the hell else would we be?"

I threw myself at them, pulling them in for a big group hug. I had happy tears streaming down my face as we all talked at once. Mr. Stykes found an immediate excuse to leave. Everyone else moved into the kitchen and settled around the breakfast bar. Katie and Rebecca mixed up more pitchers of margaritas as Alex filled me in on the family.

"Lisa was throwing a fit that she wasn't able to come," Alex grinned his bright white smile. "I think Donovan is glad Abigail's too young to be away from her mother. And, girl, she is the cutest thing. I can't wait for her to get bigger so I can start dressing her in style."

"No pastels, please," I laughed. "Sara's pastels are enough."

"No pastels for Abby," Alex said, shaking her head. "I'm already looking for black boots in her size."

"A baby in bitch boots—Badass," Katie laughed.

Anne rolled her eyes.

"How'd you manage to leave without Whiskey handcuffing you?" I asked Anne.

"I didn't give him a choice. I told him if he loved me, he'd stay and watch over Sara."

"Oh, and I'm sure it went just that smoothly," Katie laughed, passing out the drinks.

"There may have been a little bit of an argument," Anne grinned.

"Well, I'm glad you guys are here," I said to Anne, Alex, Tech, and Katie. "Tomorrow I'm purchasing five companies. I need them restructured into two companies. This kind of transition usually takes several months, but I need it to happen in a few short days."

"Game on," Katie grinned. "Put us to work."

Bones and Grady moved the dining room table back into the dining room. Rebecca retrieved the business files. Tech brought out the laptops, and Katie moved the pitchers of margaritas to the table. Once we were re-organized, everyone jumped in with both feet.

Alex and I worked the final plans for the manufacturing businesses while Rebecca and Katie worked on the restructuring plans for the service businesses. Grady and Bones helped Tech run backgrounds on all the employees from all five companies. Anne sorted through the results, writing up bios on everyone. Bridget, unable to sit still, started cooking dinner.

Reggie returned just as Bridget declared dinner to be ready. We slid our papers and laptops to the center of the table and ate around or in-between the piles.

"I have a confession to make," Rebecca said, looking up at Bones.

"I'm not your priest," Bones chuckled.

"No, just my jailor," she mumbled.

Bones set his fork down. "Now what have I done to piss you off?"

"It's not what you did. It's what I figured you'd do," she sighed. "I had an affair with someone last year. I fell in love, but I kept it a secret. I didn't want you to know about it."

"Is he married?" Bones smirked.

"No. It was Dex," Rebecca blurted out before downing the rest of her drink.

Bones stood, glaring across the table at Rebecca.

Grady's head shot up and focused in on Rebecca. A slow grin finally surfaced, and I relaxed, knowing Rebecca would have another ally.

"I can see that," Grady nodded. "You two would make a good couple."

"I saw the pictures," I said. "They look adorable together."

"Is he good looking?" Katie asked.

"Panty-melting hot," Rebecca laughed, despite Bones looking ready to throw himself across the table. "And, the best sex of my life."

Grady and Tech grabbed for Bones, dragging him toward the kitchen. He huffed and puffed for a few minutes before storming out of the townhouse.

"Win-win? Right?" Rebecca asked me, looking nervously at the front door.

"Relax. Dex is too far away for Bones to go after," I laughed. "Bones will have to resort to yelling at Dex over the phone."

"That was the plan?" Grady grinned, coming back to the table.

"Yup," I nodded. "Dex needs to find out Rebecca's not hiding anymore."

"It *was* a good plan," Grady chuckled, kissing the top of my head. "Only one major problem."

"What?" Rebecca asked.

"Dex is flying in tonight. Bones is going to pick him up at the airport."

"Oh shit!" Rebecca said, bolting out of her chair. "What do I do? He'll kill him!"

"Damn," I sighed. "Bones is going to get arrested at the airport if we don't stop him."

"Why would Bones get arrested?" a man asked, closing the front door behind him.

"Hey, Dex," Grady grinned, jogging over to help Dex with his bags. "We were just talking about you. Bones is on his way to kill you."

"What?" Dex laughed. "Why would—,"

"I told him," Rebecca interrupted.

"You did?" Dex said, dropping the rest of his bags before walking over to stand in front of Rebecca. "Why? Why now?"

"Because I was tired of hiding that you were the best thing that ever happened in my life," she admitted.

"About fucking time," Dex said, before pulling her into him and kissing her.

"And, I think that's our cue," I laughed, grabbing a laptop and a stack of papers.

Everyone grabbed as much as they could carry and we quickly relocated into the den.

"We need to figure out who is sleeping where, before it gets much later," Bridget said.

"I can sleep on one of the couches," Anne said.

"Tech and I can sleep in the small bedroom downstairs," Katie said.

"Where will I sleep?" Alex asked.

"You can stay in my penthouse suite," Bridget grinned. "It's getting lonely there by myself."

"Sweet," Alex grinned. "I've never been in a penthouse suite before."

"That will work," I nodded.

We settled back into our research and didn't see Dex or Rebecca again. Bones called Grady around midnight and said Dex never showed up at the airport. Grady said he'd help find him in the morning and hung up. We all chuckled and called it a night.

Despite grumblings from Grady, I slipped a nightshirt on before sliding into bed beside him. He wrapped an arm around me as I laid my head on his shoulder and slowly traced the deep scar across his abs.

"How?" I asked.

"Afghanistan," he whispered, before kissing the top of my head. "Shrapnel. Car bomb was detonated as we were patrolling a small town."

"I'm sorry."

"Nothing to be sorry about. It happened. It's part of my past, not my future. There were a lot of guys that weren't given the option of having a future."

"How are the flashbacks?" I asked, propping my head up to look at him.

"Gone, I think. Of course, I can't promise that if another bomb goes off, I won't have a relapse again," Grady grinned.

"I'm not worried," I giggled. "I know how to distract you until you come out of it."

I leaned in and kissed him. It was a gentle romantic kiss until he rolled me onto my back and took over. Much like he'd taken over our first kiss when I was trying to distract him during a flashback.

"Hmm," Grady moaned. "I like your methods much better than the shrinks."

"I have a special talent," I grinned, as I reached under the covers and stroked him.

"About that nightshirt," Grady chuckled, pulling it over my head.

"What nightshirt?" I moaned, as he put his lips against my body.

Chapter Twenty-Seven

The next day was a madhouse of making phone calls, signing contracts, finalizing our battle strategies, and doing a late-night walk through of all five businesses. Donovan arranged for Carol, our favorite bean counter from the store, to drive down to meet up with us. Katie hired three administration temps and an unemployed human resources director to join the takeover staff. Alex found movers to handle the offices and the manufacturing businesses. Grady, Dex, and Bones organized security for the next few days.

Bones wasn't speaking to Dex or Rebecca, but he wasn't trying to kill Dex either. We decided it was good enough for now.

By the time we went to bed, we were ready to meet with the employees in the morning for all five companies at the manufacturing plant, which offered the most standing room space. Until then, all the buildings were locked down, with security preventing anyone from entering.

At eight a.m. sharp, we walked into the manufacturing plant as one team.

"Good morning everyone," I announced loudly, though you could have heard a mouse take a turd in the quiet room. "Thank you for meeting us at one centralized site this morning. I will try to make this brief."

Tech set up a table off to the side for the human resource director, Annette. Carol and one of the temps set up a table a few feet away. The remaining two temps stayed with Katie and Anne.

"I'm not going to bore you all with a long-winded speech. Everyone wants to know the same thing—do you still have a job? The majority of you do, but there will be people leaving today. Let's just get this over with, shall we? Ernest Carper, Julie Eckert, and Marissa Forest, please come up to the front of the room."

Three nervous individuals dressed in suits walked forward.

"Your employment is being terminated on the grounds of embezzlement. If you wish to fight this termination, I will turn over the records to the police and make it a criminal matter. Please see Carol at the second table."

The two women turned white as a ghost. The man's face turned beet red, and his eyes turned cold.

"Don't even think about it, Ernie," an older man dressed in a factory uniform said, stepping forward. "You heard the lady. Walk out or go to jail, but if you make one move against her, I'll beat you to a pulp."

I grinned as Ernie huffed off.

"We're not all bad, ma'am," the man nodded, before stepping back over with his coworkers.

"Your name?" I asked the man.

"Bart Carpenter, ma'am," the man nodded.

"Thank you for your assistance, Bart," I nodded.

I looked back down at my list.

"The following people are not being let go because of anything they have done, but because the new organization will no longer support such a large managerial staff. Each of you will be given a severance package and a recommendation letter. I wish you all the best."

The companies were top heavy, too many bosses and not enough workers. There was no other solution. Katie stood beside me, helping to pass out the severance envelopes as I read the list of twenty-two names. They relinquished their security badges and keys, and Carol explained the arrangements for them to come back the next day to pick up their personal belongings.

When I announced the last name on the list, Diego Hernandez, many of the factory workers started complaining. I looked up at the young man in question as he nodded respectfully, and held a hand out to quiet the workers. When they calmed, he walked over to collect his packet. I stopped Katie from handing him the envelope mid-air.

Walking over to Bart, I asked, "What don't I know about that young man?"

"He's the only one from the management team that ever listened or cared about the company. He didn't have much authority, but he did what he could. When Jenny was terminated for missing too many work shifts, he stood up for her and made them rehire her. Her son has cancer. She's doing the best she can."

"I'm going to be turning these companies upside-down and shaking the dust off them. Do you think he can handle it?"

"He's got some good ideas, and he's got a lot of energy," Bart nodded. Several of the other employees around him nodded as well.

"Alright," I shrugged. "Katie, change of plans. Mr. Hernandez will be joining our team."

"You got it, boss," she grinned, tossing the severance envelope into one of the HR boxes.

"Just like that?" Diego asked.

"I seldom act on a whim when it comes to business. I suggest you just roll with it," I grinned.

"Yes, ma'am," he grinned back.

"I have a question for a Mr. George Banker," I called out.

"That's me," an old man shuffled forward.

Several of his coworkers looked sadly at the ground.

"Mr. Banker, my question is, if you had your choice of retiring financially comfortable or to continue working, which would you choose?"

"Is this a trick question?"

"No, not at all," I grinned. "I'm truly asking."

"Well, as much as I would miss everyone, if I could afford it, I'd retire." He had answered the question honestly, but he held a nervous breath as he waited to see if it was a mistake.

"Very well then," I said, pulling an envelope out of my satchel. "According to my calculations, you've worked in this building as a janitor for over fifty years under different company names. Many of those companies failed to provide retirement options. As a reward for your longtime service, you will find a substantial retirement package inside this envelope. And you are welcome to visit whenever it pleases you. Happy Retirement."

"This is for me?" Mr. Banker asked, looking inside the envelope.

"Is it enough money, George?" a man's voice called out.

"More than enough," the old man nodded with tears in his eyes.

Anne walked over and guided him to a chair. She sat next to him with a gentle hand on his shoulder.

"I have fifteen more layoffs, unfortunately. I am willing to consider retaining anyone on this list who would consider working an alternate job description. It will be up to you. Carol is the woman sitting over at the table. She has a list of the positions we have available and will help in any way possible. If you are not interested in an alternate position, Katie has a severance package for you."

"This is bullshit," a man called out.

"Yeah," another man yelled. "Go to hell bitch."

"I would put a cap on those tempers, gentleman. You are not in a sports bar. You are in a place of business."

"Suck my cock," the first man said, storming toward me.

"That took longer than I expected," Katie grinned, handing me the envelopes and stepping in front of me.

Attempting to push Katie out of his path, the man abruptly found himself face-first on the floor with his arm pinned behind his back. The second guy came barreling straight at Katie when Bones stepped in front of him. The guy came skidding to a stop staring up at Bones.

"Get them out of here," I ordered.

Grady, Bones, and Dex hauled both men out. They wouldn't be getting severance packages.

Katie grabbed her clipboard, walking over to the factory workers to find out what the two men's names were. I started calling out the next list of layoffs. Half of them walked out with their severance packages. The others hurried over to Carol to find out what other jobs would be available.

I carefully watched the expressions on the faces remaining. This would be the prime opportunity to cut any other bad eggs out.

"Not bad," the young manager, Diego, called out. "You knocked out a lot of overweight salaries and some of the trouble makers."

He grinned widely at me with his hands in his pockets and rocked back and forth on his feet.

"Shut the fuck up, Taco," a burly man toward the back yelled. "Nobody wants to hear your spic ass talk."

"Yeah, man," the guy next to him laughed. "Fucking Hispanic prick."

The young man's smile broadened as he winked at me.

"Dex? Grady? Would you please escort those two gentlemen to their vehicles? They are no longer welcome here."

Dex and Grady met the two men halfway across the room and escorted them out. When the doors closed a round of chuckles broke the silence.

"Nicely done, Diego," I grinned. "Ok, let's get down to business. The rest of you are still employed, but we have a lot of changes to make in a very short period of time. We will be rolling three manufacturing plants into this space. The other two manufacturing buildings will be put up for sale. We will also be using the large office building next door to expanding our sales, marketing, and product design teams. We will be focusing a lot of our energy on new products to make sure we can maintain a strong income after the current product lines fizzle out. Additionally, we have another building where we will be focusing on professional services such as advertising, accounting, and even capital acquisitions. That is where the majority of the fancy suit people here today will be going," I grinned. "It's going to be very fast-paced, challenging, and if you're successful, financially rewarding."

Everyone looked around and grinned.

"Everyone who works in one of the factories will follow Alex," Katie called out.

Alex stepped out and raised his hand, and more than a third of the room followed him over to the far side where he had set up design layouts of the new production lines. Bones discretely followed the crowd.

"Everyone else, check the list Anne is posting to see if you will be working in the administrative building next door or at the other office building," Katie called out. "Kelsey will take the lead in the admin building, and Anne and I will be in charge at the other office building. Everyone will regroup in the entrance lobbies."

Grady and I escorted our group to the adjacent building to get started. First order of business was to pack up the belongings for those no longer employed. We worked quickly, boxing and labeling everything and relocating the belongings to the front reception area where security guards would monitor the belongings being picked up.

"That was the easy part," I sighed. I looked up the stairs at the three floors to be sorted and shifted.

"Piece of cake," Diego grinned next to me.

"I'm getting too old for this shit," I laughed.

"Let's start on the first floor then," he chuckled, leading us off to the right into the first glass room filled with desks and filing cabinets. "This is going to be the sales and purchasing teams, right?"

"You got it. What was it before?"

Diego looked puzzled for a moment and looked around.

"Karrie—," he called out.

A young woman turned around.

"What did you guys do in here?"

"Nothing," she shrugged. "We were supposed to do purchasing, but there wasn't enough to keep us busy. We ate a lot of cake and bagels."

"Well, at least you're honest," I laughed. "Let's start with sorting the filing cabinets."

The first box I lifted when Grady wasn't looking about dropped me to my knees. Luckily, Diego was there to grab the box.

"Listen up," Diego called out. "Do not lift or move anything beyond your own capabilities. We don't want anyone getting injured today. And, that goes for our new boss too. She seems to have a bad shoulder, so stop her if you see her doing something stupid."

"I like him," Grady yelled out from across the room.

"Nobody asked you," I yelled back.

I went back to sorting files while rubbing my shoulder occasionally.

"Karrie? Is there a good place to store the files we need to keep but don't need readily available?"

"Well, there's a big storage room over there, but it's full."

"What's in it?" I asked as I followed her over.

She didn't answer. She just opened the door and let me look for myself. The room was about twenty by twenty and stacked with racks and shelves of old phones, typewriters, computers, and printers. Most of it was at least twenty years old.

"Can you start making some calls and see if there is anyone in the area who would take this stuff off our hands?"

Karrie giggled. "I'll find someone."

"Damn," Diego sighed, looking into the room.

"Start dragging it out. We need the space. If Karrie can't find someone to take it, I'll have a dumpster dropped off."

"I need some extra labor," Diego called out, before stacking three typewriters and carrying them out.

I was about to step further into the room when I heard someone behind me.

"Don't even think about it," a woman grinned, stepping in front of me and taking an old monitor.

"You best get out of here," another woman grinned. "We're not going to let you move anything."

I heard Grady chuckle before he pulled me out of the room and lightly shoved me back toward the desks.

It was after nine by the time we returned to the townhouse. We had sent the employees home at four, but we had stayed to finish walking through our assigned buildings.

"Man, I'm beat," Dex said, leading us inside.

"Too tired for food?" Rebecca asked while removing takeout from the large bags on the counter.

"Never too tired for food or sex. Do I get both?" Dex grinned.

"Knock it off," Bones growled.

Rebecca focused on the food glancing nervously at Bones as he stomped toward the table. Dex chuckled as he walked over and wrapped his arms around Rebecca. Her shoulders relaxed as she leaned into him.

"Alex? How'd the factory go today?"

"We got most of the equipment in the factory moved to one end. They are going to test run the new layout tomorrow while we set up the equipment that is being moved over from the other buildings. We should be up and running by the end of the week. We are going to be behind on a few orders though."

"Who has the order sheets? I'll have someone call the clients in the morning."

"I brought home copies of all the pending orders for the month. I'm only worried about the ones for this week, though."

He slid a file across the table to me, and I tucked it in my satchel. I was too tired to look at it.

"Katie, Anne, Dex? How'd the professional services building go?"

"It's a great building," Katie grinned. "Plenty of room to expand. In fact, there's a big corner office with lots of natural light that would be perfect for an acquisitions attorney we know."

"You can pitch the idea," I laughed. "I have no idea if Mr. Stykes would be interested."

"I already made an appointment with him for tomorrow," Katie grinned. "How did your building go?"

"Good. But man, there's a lot of crap to move," I laughed. "I swear they haven't thrown anything away in forty years."

"And, they won't allow her to move anything," Grady chuckled, sitting next to me and opening a beer.

"Did you tattle on her," Alex asked.

"Didn't have to," Grady grinned. "Diego read her like a book and ordered everyone to make sure she didn't lift anything all day."

"I'm really glad Bart saved him," Alex said.

"The guy who stood up to Ernie?" I asked.

"Yeah. Bart's a line foreman. Well respected," Alex nodded.

"I'm glad he saved Diego too. I promoted him to manager of the new design and product development team. What do you think of Bart being promoted to run the factory?"

"I had my sales pitch all planned out to sell you on that very idea," Alex chuckled, sliding into the chair across from me.

"Sold. Make it happen. He's loyal and honest. And, if the other employees respect him, then they will stay."

Looking around, everyone appeared tired but in a good mood. Well, except for Reggie. He looked a bit depressed.

"Reggie, how did the other factory buildings go?"

"Boring. I just walked around empty buildings all day."

"That's a good thing, Reg," I grinned. "Alex will get them emptied by tomorrow, and then you're free again."

"Jackie Vaughn is busy tomorrow, so is there anything I can do to help?" Bridget asked as she started setting plates of food on the table.

"I want the third floor re-arranged and set up differently in the admin building. It's going to be for the design teams. It's super un-inspirational right now. Want to take a crack at turning it around for me? It involves shopping for things like whiteboards, corkboards, and edgy workstations and getting rid of the outdated cubicles and fluorescent lighting."

"Sounds fun. I'll get online tonight," Bridget giggled, skipping back to the kitchen area.

I rolled my eyes.

I longingly stared at the plate of grilled chicken and pasta Rebecca set in front of me.

"You can't lift your left arm anymore can you," Grady chuckled, leaning over to cut my food.

"The only thing I moved today was paper," I whined, rubbing my shoulder.

"You moved folders all day, for twelve hours," Grady grinned. "Diego's wife has an old arm brace he's bringing in tomorrow, and like it or not, you're wearing it."

"Am not," I argued.

"You are too," Grady said, as he set my silverware back down. "Or we are locking you out of the building."

"I own the building."

"Legally, though, I have the authority to ban you from the building," Bridget giggled, sitting beside me.

"I hold grudges," I warned.

"No, you don't," Bridget laughed, slurping some pasta.

Even though I didn't want to, her antics made me laugh. She was behaving like the old Bridget—the high energy, over the top girl I knew so well, instead of the polished socialite.

I watched Bones grinning at her from the end of the table. He had been missing this version of Bridget too.

Chapter Twenty-Eight

The next morning, I asked Diego to assign out tasks while I went to meet with the manager of the sales team. I found her in her new office, leaned back in her chair watching something on her cell phone. When she noticed me standing in her doorway, she set the phone off to the side and sat up straighter.

I slid a copy of the order sheets that were going to be delayed for delivery and asked her to reach out to the clients and let them know. She assured me she'd take care of it. I left the office, stepping around the corner into the small break area.

"Karrie," the manager called out, not leaving her office.

"Yes, Mrs. Cappen?" Karrie said, rushing across the room to the office.

"The new owner wants someone to call these customers and let them know their orders will be late. I have no idea why. It's not like anything ever gets shipped on time around here."

"I can call them," Karrie agreed, stepping further into the office to take the list. "When shall I say they can expect the shipments?"

"She said it would be no more than five days late, but really, who can believe that?"

"Was it Kelsey who told you it would be five days?" Karrie asked.

"Yes, that woman. Do we know her last name? What kind of owner uses their first name? So, unprofessional."

Karrie walked past, heading toward her desk. After calling Tech to tell him to pull Mrs. Cappen's security access, I picked up an empty box, carrying it into Mrs. Cappen's office. She was already zoned in on her cell phone again.

"Pack your belongings. You won't be staying on with us," I said, dropping the empty box on the floor before leaving the office.

I alerted one of the guards to monitor Mrs. Cappen as she packed her belongings before I went to the second floor to inform Annette, the new HR director. She grabbed a few files and jogged toward the stairs.

"Did I scare her?"

"No," Carol chuckled. "But it's common practice to involve the HR director when terminating employment so they can get all the paperwork settled."

"I didn't know that," I grinned. "I've never had an HR director."

"Katie and I always tried to get to the employees and take care of things once you left the room."

"Figures," I said rolling my eyes. "How is it going up here?"

The first floor was the sales and purchasing team on one side of the building and conference rooms on the other side. The second floor was split between HR, some miscellaneous administration positions, and the accounting department. The third floor was new product design and development.

"Accounting is struggling, but HR is running smooth. And, we have some admins feeling a bit out-of-sorts without a good understanding of what they will be doing."

"I can't make them feel better about that until I see where they are needed and what they are needed for. A few of them may be pulled to the other floors, but some will stay here to help whoever needs it."

"I get it. Annette and I just keep trying to reassure them there will be plenty of work to go around as soon as we are up and running."

"Thanks. I'm glad you could make the drive to help."

"With the store under construction, Katie has been struggling to keep a lot of us busy. I'm glad I could be put to work," Carol grinned. "Besides, it's always fun to watch you wield your power."

"Whatever," I rolled my eyes. "What can I do to help up here?"

"Nothing until you are wearing the arm sling Diego brought in for you. Everyone is under orders to stop you otherwise."

"Fine," I grumbled, pulling the ugly thing out of my shoulder bag. "This is so stupid."

"Accounting files for the other two manufacturing companies—," she pointed toward the stacks of folders. "We are keeping out anything for the last two years. Everything else needs to be labeled and marked to be put in the storage room. Anything useless like the three boxes of typewriter manuals gets tossed."

As it turned out, with the full administrative staff and accounting staff working with me, they only need me to make decisions of what to store, put in the filing cabinet, or throw out. The stack quickly disappeared. When the accountants started arguing whether the new file layout should be by date or alphabet, I led the administration staff away.

"Okay ladies and gents," I grinned. "I hear everyone is a bit anxious about what your day-to-day work will be. I can't answer that yet, but I know at least two of you will be needed upstairs to work with the product design group. Anybody interested in moving upstairs?"

Three hands shot up.

"Fine," I grinned. "All three of you can go. Find the woman who looks like a pixie and let her know you need workstations."

They laughed, racing off toward the stairs. I grinned at their antics. This place might be in total chaos right now, but the people were good people.

"The rest of you, pick a desk and set it up to your preference. Then I want you to brainstorm together on ordering new supplies and updating internal documents with the new company logo and name."

"Do we have a p-n-g of the new logo?" one of the women asked.

"A what?"

"A picture file," Diego laughed. "Do you even have a new logo?"

"No," I grinned. "Can't we just scribble out something?"

"No," Diego grinned. "Chrissy, call Marty and tell him to work with Scott and design a new company logo."

A woman raced to a desk by the window and made a call. All the other admins raced to their wish-list desk and claimed their piece of real estate. One of the older women looked about, settling at one of the unclaimed desks, seeming uninspired.

"If you haven't filled the receptionist position, she's the one," Diego whispered.

"Then go tell her for me," I whispered loudly back.

When I got to the third floor, I had to turn in circles twice to be sure I was in the same room as the night before. Electricians were installing the new lighting. Versatile workstations were being assembled. Two large administration desks were set up near the entrance door. Another administration desk was near the two large offices that now served as conference rooms.

"Do you like it? Do you like it?" Bridget bounced up and down in front of me.

"I do," I grinned.

"I want to paint the walls too, but Diego said I had to wait because he wants the design teams working at full speed by this afternoon."

"See if you can get painters in this weekend, while the offices are closed."

She squealed, hugged me, and took off toward one of the administrators.

"You realize she wants to paint the room yellow and blue, don't you?" Diego laughed behind me.

"Bridget's ideas usually sound cuckoo, but she knows what she's doing," I grinned.

"I hope so," he chuckled. "We have our first brainstorming session at one o'clock. Do you want to join us?"

"Nope. I'll need to meet with you before that meeting, though. After that, just let me know when you have something ready to pitch."

"Let's meet now then," he nodded.

I followed him into one of the conference rooms and closed the door.

"Have you noticed that I haven't assigned anyone to manage the entire building nor it's tie-in with the manufacturing building yet?" I asked.

"Believe me, everyone noticed. I've been telling them that most likely you or one of your other employees will stick around for a while and run things."

"We don't live here," I said, shaking my head. "And, we don't want to."

"So, what's the plan? Or can't you share that yet?"

"Short term, I want you to take the role. This floor will still be your priority, but the rest of the time you will be coordinating with the other managers. Bart will run the manufacturing warehouse. I'll be assigning someone new to the Sales Manager position today."

"Mrs. Cappen?" he asked.

"She took a permanent leave this morning," I shook my head. "I'm thinking Karrie, but I'll have to see if she can step up to the plate."

"So, you want me to coordinate short term?"

"If you do well, it could turn into long term," I shrugged. "But, I have a company in mind that will take over ownership review, and ultimately, it will be up to them to decide if you stay in charge. They are fair, and I respect the CEO completely. She's tough but flexible. She rewards good talent too."

"Sounds good," Diego grinned.

"Now the tricky part," I said, pulling a file out of my shoulder-bag and sliding it across the table.

"Ugh. JV Dagger Innovations? I thought we were done with that SOB."

"My goal is to compete against them. I want you to focus on any new products that position us to steal their market share or any supply vendors we can lock into a non-compete deal. We will be openly and directly targeting the company, anything we can do to hurt their bottom line."

"You know Jonathan Vaughn is nuts, right? I mean he's running for governor, so everyone looks up to him as a superstar, but I've sat across the table from him. He's freaking scary."

"I know. Believe me, I know," I nodded.

Grady walked in and sat down.

"We're in a meeting," I grinned.

"Like I care," he grinned back.

Diego chuckled and went back to flipping through the file.

"What if he comes after me? Comes after my family?"

"I won't be making your position public until this is all over. And, until then, we will have full security at all the buildings. Everyone's already following your orders. It won't matter if we wait a few weeks to make the official announcement."

"You promise the employees will be safe?"

"Yes," Grady nodded. "We have more men coming. They'll handle any blowback."

"I need you to come up with ideas that will hurt JV Dagger financially. I already have a starter list," I said, pulling a pad of paper out. "See what you can come up with to add to it. We need to be positioned to strike by Friday."

"You also need to keep this quiet," Grady said. "The more people who know, the bigger the risk is that Jonathan will be warned that Kelsey is coming after him."

"I won't tell anyone. They won't ask, anyway. All these moves would be smart business moves," Diego nodded. "You're really taking him down?"

"Someone needs to," I shrugged.

"That's what the buyouts and mergers were about?" Diego grinned. "I was trying to figure it out, but nothing made sense. I've never heard of Sunshine and Partners. And, really, it sounds like something someone made up as a joke."

"It sort of was," I grinned. "Feel free to pitch a new company name too."

"We'll have a new logo and company name by lunchtime. I'll forward it to the admin team so they can start doing an overhaul of all our documents."

I nodded and stepped out of the conference room, followed by Diego and Grady.

Two guys were waiting impatiently to showed Diego a pile of printed artworks. He dug through them and narrowed it down to two.

"Neither of these is the logo we want, but keep following this idea. We need something edgy."

"All that effort for a logo?" I asked.

"I thought you were leaving?" Diego grinned.

"I'm gone," I laughed, moving back to the stairs.

I was almost to the first floor when a frantic Karrie called up the stairs to me.

"Kelsey, one of the customers is irate about their delayed order. He says he needs the stock in two days or he'll pull his business accounts. I don't know who to talk to because you fired Mrs. Cappen."

"What would Mrs. Cappen have done?"

"Nothing," Karrie shrugged. "She would have blamed me and said I didn't tell her."

"So, what do you think we should do?"

"I think someone should talk to Bart. Maybe there's enough stock ready to fill part of this order. And, if not, we should consider overtime pay to fill the order."

"Well, let's go talk to Bart then," I nodded, leading her out of the building.

Chapter Twenty-Nine

By one o'clock I decided we should leave to give the staff some space without strangers watching over their shoulder. Grady, Alex, Bones and I drove over to the professional building that Katie and Anne were getting organized.

The first thing I noticed, was the lack of security at the front of the building. We walked in, unannounced, and into the main offices. Two security guards were flirting with some of the office girls. Bones growled and headed their way.

"Let's go," Grady chuckled, pulling me down another walkway.

"Weren't those Donovan's guys?" I asked as I was shuffled inside an elevator.

"They used to be," Grady grinned.

We stepped off the elevator on the fifth floor of the seven-floor building. Last time I talked with Katie, she was somewhere in the area of the fifth floor. The large open area of cubicles was a disorganized mess, with boxes stacked everywhere. Furniture was being moved in and out of offices. I walked down an outside row, following along the office doors until I got to the end and turned left. I followed the length of the walkway but still didn't spot Katie before turning left again. Three doors down, sitting on a stack of boxes, elbows braced on knees while she leaned over massaging her temples, was Katie.

"That bad?" I laughed.

"This is the worst floor yet, and I have two more to go," she whined.

"So why is all the furniture being moved around?" Grady asked.

"Because these advertising people are insane!"

"Try again?" I asked.

"Because they argued and complained so much I finally walked away and they took that as they could do whatever the hell they wanted."

"Where's Dex?"

"He went to break up a fight on the accounting floor."

"Which floor?" Grady grinned.

"Fourth," I laughed.

Grady turned back to the elevators, and I dragged Katie off from her box to the center of the storm where the receptionist looked absolutely freaked.

"Is there an intercom for this floor?"

The receptionist nodded and pushed a few mysterious buttons on the phone before handing me the handset.

"Attention ladies and gentlemen, this is the owner speaking. Set down whatever you are carrying and come to the center reception desk if you want to keep your jobs."

I hung up, and by the time everyone gathered around, Dex and Grady stepped off the elevator.

"Boys, do a walk-thru for me. Anyone still hiding in an office or moving furniture is fired. I don't care who they are," I said.

They both headed off in different directions.

• • •

I waited, grinning. I was predicting there would be at least two. I was wrong. Grady and Dex escorted five employees into the elevators.

"Stop at HR on the first floor," Katie called out over my shoulder.

Grady and Dex grinned as the elevator doors closed.

"Now then," I said. "Do we have an understanding of how this employee vs. employer thing works?"

Some of the professional movers who were standing off to the side chuckled.

"Gentleman," I grinned at them. "Can you move all the furniture back into the offices?"

"Even if that means moving it into the office we just took it out of?" one of the guys laughed.

"That's exactly what I mean."

Several of the executives glared over at me.

"Oh, no, you don't," I said, pointing at three of them. "Katie, escort these three down to HR. They no longer work here."

"Fine by me," Katie said, directing them over to the elevator.

"You," I said pointing to one of the secretaries. "How was the staff organized before we purchased the building?"

"Everything to the left was sales, and everything to the right was advertising. Marketing staff had the center offices."

"Thank you. As everyone knows, the sales staff has been moved to another floor. I want each advertising person to pair up with a marketing person. If you can't pick a partner, I'll assign one to you."

One of the marketers and one of the advertisers ran to each other and linked arms in good humor. It was obvious they were friends. Everyone else seemed to stand back, seeming unsure.

I turned back to the receptionist. She was biting her thumbnail. Looking at the other assistants standing around, I spotted Rebecca sitting in the corner, hair braided crookedly down her back, wearing a dowdy outdated suit, and spinster fake glasses. I grinned but didn't tattle on her.

"Administration staff, please go into the conference room and write down all the names of the associates here. Then you will decide the pairings based on what you know of their personality, likes and skill levels."

Rebecca looked down at the desk grinning but grabbed a pad of paper and a pen and followed the rest of the admin staff into the conference room.

"You can't be serious?" one of the associates said. "You are putting our careers in the hands of our secretaries?"

I shrugged.

"It makes sense," another associate chuckled. "Those of us who treated them with respect will get good partners. Those who didn't, well, you might not survive the change."

"You two," I said pointing to my only paired team. "You will be taking the two offices before the corner office at the end of this hall. Gather only your belongings and your client files and get them moved."

"My stuff is still in one of those offices," one of the men complained.

"Do you think they are going to steal it?" I laughed, hands thrown up in the air.

"Who gets the corner offices?" another man asked.

"No one," I answered. "The way I see it, with the people we just fired, we will have plenty of offices without using them. We can turn them into meeting rooms and create a sign-out sheet at the front desk for when they are needed."

"That's fair," another employee nodded.

A few more nodded in agreement.

The administration staff came out of the conference room in record time.

"Since I'm the temp," Rebecca said, while pushing up her glasses, "I was asked to give the assignments out."

I nodded. "Go ahead."

Rebecca read off the pairings, and I sent each pair in different directions down the halls. Soon it was just the admin staff and the receptionist left. The receptionist slid back behind the safety of her desk.

"Okay. I'm going to count to three, and then the rest of you will run to pick the team you want to work with. The temp gets stuck with whoever is left since we are short on administrators."

"We get to pick?" one of the women grinned.

"One, two, three, go—," I called out, laughing as they raced down the halls in different directions.

* * *

I wasn't surprised to find the pair without an administrator was the team arguing loudly near the receptionist desk.

"Try to make it through the day," I patted Rebecca's shoulder.

She snorted but didn't say anything as she went to smooth down the escalating argument.

Grady, Dex, and Katie stepped off the elevator and looked around.

"Where is everyone?" Katie asked.

"Getting settled in their new assigned offices and getting to know their new working partners," I grinned.

"And, the corner offices?"

"No one gets them," I shook my head. "I need you to have the furniture replaced for meeting rooms and set up a sign-out sheet for them to be reserved."

"I can set up calendars for signing them out electronically," the receptionist said.

"Thank you," Katie smiled, before walking down the hall to make sure everyone was behaving.

"Enough!" Rebecca yelled over the top of her feuding pair. "Like it or not, you two are stuck together. Either act like professionals and prove you have this company's best interest in mind or quit before you get fired."

Both associates quickly glanced over at me before nodding to Rebecca and working together to move their boxes into their new offices.

"What's Rebecca doing dressed like that?" Grady whispered to Dex.

"She's pretending to be a temp named Becky," Dex grinned. "I kind of like the nerdy glasses."

The receptionist's head popped up, and she looked at us.

"If you keep her secret, she can help pick the bad apples out of the barrel," I said, leaning in so only she could hear.

She grinned and did the zip the lips motion. "I knew she wasn't a temp," she giggled. "She directed us in that conference room like a pro."

"Yeah, she's a little over qualified," I laughed. "She's the CEO of Barrister Industries."

"No shit?" she laughed, before realizing she had sworn and covered her mouth with both hands.

"No shit," Dex nodded, chuckling.

Chapter Thirty

We made it all the way to the top floor, getting everyone reassigned into workspaces. When we finally called it a night, many of the employees were still working, organizing files, or calling clients. Mr. Stykes was keeping three furniture movers busy moving tables and chairs, so they were 'just so'. I was still surprised he agreed to take the lead counsel position in the acquisitions department. He said he couldn't turn down the natural lighting the job provided.

"I think things went smoother after the advertising and marketing floor," I smirked, following Katie into the townhouse.

"They were horrible," she groaned. "I don't want to go back to that floor, ever again."

"I'll take them tomorrow. You can work with Stykes on setting up the staff he will need."

"Deal," she nodded.

"I'll be moving over to the other building tomorrow too," Tech said, moving past us and opening up the refrigerator. "I need to get everyone access to the servers but want different servers per floor. We'll be the only ones who can access all the files."

Tech pulled a beer, uncapping it, and made a half ass attempt at tossing the cap toward the sink.

"Rough day," I grinned.

"Just long. I had to replace a lot of equipment at the manufacturing administration building. Took longer than I planned. Everyone was very helpful, though."

"The atmosphere at the other building isn't as friendly, but the equipment looks newer."

Tech sighed.

"I'll make the rounds with you tomorrow," Bones grinned. "They're all scared of me."

Bridget giggled and passed Bones a beer.

"Oh, Diego wanted me to give you a file," Bridget said, bouncing across the room to her bag.

I walked over and took the file. Inside were sign-off sheets for the new name, logo, and several contract proposals.

"He did all this in one day?" Rebecca asked, looking over my shoulder.

"No, he did all this since about eleven o'clock this morning," I grinned.

"It seems unfair for Barrister's to step in. We'll be taking a cut of the profits without having to do anything," Rebecca chuckled.

"I think it will balance out with all the effort the professional building is going to require," I laughed. "Why didn't we fire those two idiots who argued all day?"

"Because according to the secretaries, they are mean, but very talented. Give me a chance to turn them around."

"It's your ears that have to listen to them bitching," I grinned, shaking my head.

"I have a plan. I want to pitch to them to come up with the marketing and advertising plan to rebrand the servicing building. I can steer them to look at JV Dagger Innovations and stealing their clients."

"Can you trust them?"

"If they think they'll pull in more clients, they'll dig in and be cutthroat about it."

"Good. We only have one more day before we need to start hurting the company publicly." I looked around the room. Everyone had settled in with drinks but listened and waited to see if I needed anything else. "How are the rest of the buildings going?"

"The three buildings you are selling are now empty and shut down," Reggie said. "I decreased security and reassigned people to the other sites."

"Tomorrow, can you do a walk-through of the occupied buildings and see if you notice anything we missed? Nobody knows you. So, they won't know to be on their best behavior."

"I get to be the secret office spy?" Reggie grinned.

"It's kind of fun," Rebecca said. "I text Katie or Kelsey, and they show up a few minutes later and fire the awful people."

"Do I get to have a fake name?"

"No," Tech said, tossing his empty bottle into the recycle bin. "I'm not setting up another security badge just so you can play James Bond."

"That's the name I wanted to use," Reggie pouted.

"Next?" I laughed.

"The accounting floor is up and running in the servicing building. I plan on spending my time tomorrow in HR to get them organized," Anne said.

"The manufacturing plant is up and running," Alex said. "I'm helping Diego lock down vendor contracts. We are setting up face-to-face meetings for Friday morning. With the consolidation of the manufacturing, most of the vendors won't hesitate to lock down a deal."

"Sounds like everyone has a plan in place. Work together if you need assistance. Bridget has the signing authority for the companies, so if you know it's something I'm agreeable to, just hand her a pen."

My phone rang. I stepped into the living room to answer it. "Kelsey."

"This is Mr. Stykes. Do you remember me?"

"Of course, Mr. Stykes," I answered, rolling my eyes. "What can I do for you?"

"I just wanted to inform you that during the real estate closings, I had a casual conversation with Mr. Vaughn about a company jet that was up for sale. I just heard the sale closed and Mr. Vaughn sunk a significant amount of his cash into the purchase of the jet. The funds were wired out this morning."

"Frivolous spending," I laughed. "I love it."

"That was all. Good day," Mr. Stykes said, disconnecting the call.

"Good news everyone," I announced, walking back into the main room. "Jonathan sank several million into purchasing a private jet this morning."

"You're kidding," Rebecca grinned.

"Nope. Mr. Stykes planted the idea at the closings."

"I told you he was a sneaky bastard."

While everyone was unwinding from the long stressful day, I slipped upstairs to steal some alone time. After a brief call to Nicholas, who was eager to get off the phone because he had a friend over, I changed into a comfortable outfit and stood looking out the second-floor window. A light rain obscured most of the view and the buildings and street below blurred as the sky darkened from the storm passing over.

"Hey," Grady whispered, entering the bedroom and wrapping his arms around me.

"Hey," I answered, leaning my back into him.

He held me as we stood silently looking outside. As time slipped past, the tension in my neck and shoulders increased. I focused my mind, puzzling over the events of the last few days.

"What's wrong?" he asked.

"I'm not sure," I shrugged, scanning the street below us. "Maybe it's just that everything seems to be going too smoothly."

"I don't think the chaos of the last two days has been smooth," Grady chuckled. "You and your family are just too good at working together to accomplish insane deadlines."

"Perhaps."

"You do realize you and your friends just consolidate five businesses into two in a matter of days, don't you? That should have taken months."

"It's not that," I shook my head. "I feel like something bad is coming."

"Like what?"

"I don't know. I'm retracing everything in my head. Angry ex-employee? Jonathan having a mole at one of the companies? Something. Something feels off."

"Then I'll alert security to be extra cautious," Grady said, kissing my cheek before he moved away to go back downstairs.

The sky outside rumbled as the storm passed over. I stepped away to follow Grady, and the glass in front of me shattered.

"Sniper!" I yelled as I dove for the glass-covered floor.

I hoped everyone downstairs heard my warning and took cover. Grady came rushing in the door, using his body to cover mine, as he dragged me into the hallway.

"Kelsey?" Bones yelled from somewhere in the house. "Where's the shooter?"

"I don't know. Somewhere east of the townhouse," I yelled.

Safely out of the room and back downstairs, I sat on the dining room floor with my family. Katie sat beside me bandaging my left arm. The bullet had barely grazed the skin. If I hadn't turned away when I did, I would have been dead.

Grady, Dex, Reggie, and Bones were searching for the shooter. I dug my phone out of my back pocket and called Ryan.

"Is Leo still under your supervision?" I asked him.

"I've got eyes on him right now. Why?"

"Sniper just took a shot at me."

"Wasn't him but I'll see if we can figure out who it was."

"I'll call a friend of mine as well. Thanks."

I hung up and called Benny the Barber, the legendary hitman of Miami.

"It's Kelsey. Someone just tracked me down again and took a shot at me. What are you hearing?"

"The reward for killing you went up yesterday with an open contract. First assassin who finds you and takes you out gets the pot of gold. I wouldn't be surprised if a few of your doppelgangers are accidentally killed."

"Is there a way to shut it down?"

"Not unless you're dead."

"Lovely. I've gotta go," I said, hanging up. "Shit!"

"What is it?" Tech asked.

"The price went up on killing me, and it was posted as open season, meaning the first one who hits the mark gets paid. Every hitman in the business is looking for me."

"That's good news," Dex said, walking hunched over into the dining room.

"How is that good news?"

"It means whoever found you won't tell anyone else where you are. He wouldn't risk someone else getting to you before he makes the shot."

"So, Jonathan might not know I'm here yet?"

"Exactly. We just need to track down one guy and then you're in the clear again."

"We lost him," Bones said, coming in the front door followed by Grady.

"We found shell casings on the rooftop across the street, but he's long gone. Tech can you get us access to any nearby security feeds?"

"In a minute," Tech nodded.

He had two laptops on the floor in front of him, and he was typing frantically.

"Ok, I found the posting on the dark net. If we catch this guy, I can post in his place that you're dead. It will buy us some time. Hopefully, by then, Jonathan finds himself in a financial bind and won't be able to restart the contract."

"So, find the shooter, fake a death, bankrupt an evil politician?" Rebecca laughed a little hysterically.

"Piece of cake," Alex grinned.

Chapter Thirty-One

"Absolutely not," Bones yelled the next morning.

"That's the stupidest idea I've ever heard," Dex yelled, supporting Bones.

"Hear her out," Grady sighed.

"You can't be serious?" Bones said.

"She's earned the respect to at least be heard before we shut her down," Grady answered.

"Time is our biggest challenge right now," I began again when everyone had quieted. "This guy knows I'm here. He's probably been watching me for at least a day or two. He needs to get to me before anyone else discovers my location. We know from the video feed and the shell he left behind that he's not the best of the best where hitmen are concerned. He'll see everyone else leave and he'll get antsy. He'll make a move."

"When you are here alone, without any backup?" Bones said.

Bridget walked over and put her arm around Bones' waist. He sighed, and moved her in front of him, folding his arms around her.

"I'm trained. He won't see me as a threat."

"You can't do this without backup," Dex said.

"Won't work," Tech said. "If he's been watching her, he's seen the rest of us as well. Even if we did manage to somehow sneak back in unseen, he could have a simple heat sensor that would show how many people are inside the townhouse."

"You'll wear a jacket?" Grady asked.

"Yes," I nodded. "I don't have a death wish."

"You're considering this?" Dex yelled.

"What if you were the target? Would it make sense for you to be the bait?" Grady asked Dex.

"Yes. If it was me, it would make sense. We've been doing this stupid crazy shit for years."

"So, has Kelsey," Bones sighed, sitting on a nearby bar stool and pulling Bridget with him. "She's trained for this."

"Because she was a cop?" Dex asked.

"No," Katie said. "Because she's been fighting to save her family and keep herself alive for years. She's been in worse situations. We have to trust her."

"Everyone, pack up," Anne ordered. "We leave in five minutes. No more arguing."

Grady walked over and folded me in a hug. "I don't like this," he whispered.

"I know," I chuckled. "I don't like it either, but this guy is trigger happy to get to me first. This is the quickest and safest plan to neutralize him."

"We'll be only a few blocks away. You let us know as soon as he enters the townhouse."

"I will. Promise."

"I love you."

"Always?" I grinned up at him.

"Always," he whispered before kissing the top of my head, loading a Glock, and following Dex and Bones out of the townhouse.

"Testing coms," Tech said over the earpiece.

"Reading you clearly," I answered.

"You've got Grady and Bones on coms a few blocks away. I'm in the server room at the servicing building."

"Sounds good. Grady?"

"I'm right here," he answered.

"Thanks," I said, taking a deep breath.

"Keep your eyes and ears on the townhouse. Be alert."

"I'm going to read some files in the den. I'll be ready."

"We can be there in less than three minutes when you send the signal."

"Copy," I said, nodding to myself as I settled in the den to work.

Three hours later, nothing. Not a peep. I was getting uncomfortable wearing the flak jacket, and my stomach was rumbling. I slid my Glock into my holster and went to the kitchen to make a sandwich. As I closed the refrigerator door, juggling the turkey, bread, and mayo, I realized I was standing face-to-face with a man I didn't recognize.

Throwing the sandwich makings at him, I swung the refrigerator door back open before barreling the other direction. "Now," I yelled, as I ran, pulling my gun out of my holster. "Now! Now!"

With no time to turn and shoot, I threw a stand to the floor as I ran past it and ran into the living room. I could hear him thrashing through the debris directly behind me. He grabbed hold of my left shoulder, and bright stars blocked my vision as the pain raced up my neck and down my arm.

I pivoted and swung the butt of the gun into his temple as hard as I could.

Still gripping my shoulder, I felt him pulling me downward as he dropped to the floor. I pushed away from him and stepped back, holding my gun on him. Blood trickled from his temple as his eyes slid closed.

"Got him," I called out as tires screeched to a stop in front of the townhouse.

"We're here, don't shoot," Grady yelled as they came charging in. "Bones, search the house."

Grady grabbed flex cuffs and secured the man on the floor before checking for a pulse.

"Why didn't you shoot him?" he asked.

"Couldn't," I answered, shaking my head. "He was too close. He surprised me."

"How close did he get?" Grady yelled, glaring at me.

"He was a foot away by the time I noticed him. He appeared out of nowhere, like a ghost."

I could hear Tech laugh over the coms before he spoke. "One of the guys who accepted the contract has a handle name of Spirit-Walker. I bet it's him."

"He *was* very quiet," I nodded.

Tech chuckled, but Grady continued to glare.

"House appears to be clear," Bones announced, returning to help Grady lift the unconscious man off the floor.

"How'd he get inside?" I asked.

"Back patio door was ajar. He must have jimmied the lock," Bones shrugged.

"And, you didn't hear him?" Grady yelled.

"I'm telling you, he was like a ghost," I shrugged.

"Spirit-Walker," Tech corrected me.

"Shut up, Tech," Grady growled.

Bones smirked as he helped drag the bad guy out of the room and down the hall. I wasn't sure where they were going to put him. More importantly, I didn't care.

"Get me some photos so I can post your demise," Tech said.

"Give me a few minutes," I answered before disconnecting the coms.

Walking back into the kitchen, I set my Glock on the counter and started removing as many of the Velcro straps as I could on the flak jacket. Grady strode toward me to remove the rest and lift it up over my head.

"Never again," he whispered, as he lifted me into his arms and kissed me.

When the kiss ended, I found myself straddling his lap as he sat on a barstool. I wasn't even aware I'd been moving.

"I don't know," I grinned. "I think I need to do that more often if this is the reward."

Grady slapped my ass, before lifting me up and setting me on the next barstool.

"So, I take it you were making a sandwich when your guest arrived?" he chuckled, getting up to pick up the bread, mayo, and turkey still scattered on the kitchen floor.

"I got hungry," I sighed.

Grady chuckled.

"Grady, make us lunch while I help Kelsey get these pictures taken," Bones ordered, coming in with a tote bag of supplies. "Rebecca has a theater friend that sent over everything we need."

Twenty minutes later, I was lying on the hardwood floor in a pool of blood with a fake gash across my neck, eyes frozen in an open position. Bones took a picture from a distance and then a close-up, with the flash off this time, so my eyes didn't involuntarily blink.

"And, that's the money shot," Bones grinned, looking at the picture.

"Do I really look dead?"

"Yes," he grimaced. "I don't think Grady should see these. Go get cleaned up, and I'll send the pics to Tech."

Upstairs I started with peeling the fake gash off my neck and dumping it in the trash. My jeans joined the disposable pile next. I was trying to get my shirt off without lifting my left arm when Grady slid into the bathroom and helped me.

"How bad is your shoulder?"

"Hurts."

He got out some Tylenol as I started up a shower. I downed the pills and stepped in. A minute later, Grady stepped in behind me.

"Tell me again," he said, turning me around to face him. "How's the shoulder?"

"I'll live," I grinned.

Grady lifted me and pinned my body with his against the cool tiles as he started stroking my body with his tongue. Best-Medicine-Ever.

We didn't leave the shower until all the hot water was gone. Back in the bedroom, we laughed as we helped each other warm back up. It was another hour before we dressed and went downstairs, only to find a note from Bones that he had given up waiting for us and went back to the professional building. Grady took that as a green light to maneuver me into the den and onto the conference table.

"No more," I giggled, twenty minutes later. "I'm starving, and we're going to get caught."

"I'll feed you, but I couldn't give a shit if we get caught," Grady grinned, giving me a hard peck on the lips before he stepped away to re-fasten his jeans.

I laughed and jumped off the table. Luckily, I still had my shirt on, but I was having trouble with only one arm getting my pants on again. And, I didn't trust Grady to help, so I moved to the other side of the room.

"I'll behave," he chuckled, walking over to help me. "You need to get an ice pack on your shoulder. After lunch, I'll give you a massage."

"Ice pack, yes. Massage, no. I need to get some work done. Tomorrow is day one of our financial strike against JV Dagger Innovations."

"Fine," Grady grinned, walking toward the door. "Then the massage can be later tonight. But we're going to bed early."

I shook my head as I started up several laptops.

Deciding to work in the dining room, Grady helped me catch up on my research for the rest of the afternoon. Reggie was the first one home and said he'd start dinner. Within an hour, everyone else started filing in.

"How did today go?" I asked.

"Great," Katie nodded. "Reggie weeded out a sexist pig who had cornered a secretary, and Tech found a woman feeding her porn addiction at work. Both were let go. And we have all our ducks lined up for tomorrow. New ads are ready to go live bright and early, thanks to Rebecca."

"How much longer are you going to be undercover?" I asked Rebecca.

"Tomorrow morning I will inform the board that I have been looking into taking over the new companies. Should be a slam dunk. After that, I plan on re-introducing myself to your staff as the CEO of Barrister's."

"I thought you wanted Barrister's left out of this until it was all over?"

"I changed my mind," Rebecca shrugged. "If Barrister's is publicly backing the companies, it will speed up the financial impact to JV Dagger Innovations. Bones and grandfather are backing the play, and we agreed to increase security. It's a smart company move, and if Jonathan wants to take it personally," she shrugged, "then we'll be ready."

"I don't like it," Dex complained.

"I'll need a personal bodyguard," Rebecca flirted, dragging a manicured finger down his cheek.

Dex smirked, pulling her closer to him.

"How's the hitman?" Bones asked, rolling his eyes at his sister.

"I haven't checked on him," Grady grinned. "I've been busy."

"I'm sure you have," Bones muttered, walking down the hall.

"Where are we keeping the hitman, anyway?" I asked.

"Chained up in the mechanical room," Grady shrugged.

"What are you going to do with him?" Anne asked.

"I called Maggie. Her and Kierson are coming tomorrow to picked him up," I sighed. "Hopefully they can keep it quiet."

"Is she still working the kidnapping case?" Tech asked.

"No," I shook my head. "They caught the bad guy and saved the girl."

"Was he connected to the bus routes?" Tech asked.

"He rode the metro every day. They think he's involved in other disappearances, but they're still processing the evidence and reviewing years of footage." I shook my head, trying not to think of the kids that were not as lucky.

"Even if they find other victims, you still helped save that little girl. She's home with her family," Anne smiled, squeezing my hand before moving over to the kitchen to help Reggie.

"Damn straight," Grady grinned beside me.

"Well, if there's no sniper on the loose, I'm going back to my apartment," Rebecca said, gathering her belongings.

"I'm staying with you tonight, just to make sure it's safe," Dex grinned, walking out with her.

"I need to head back to the penthouse. I'm meeting Jackie in the morning," Bridget said.

"I'm ready when you are," Alex nodded, standing up.

"I'll go too," Bones said, walking back down the hall.

"Is anyone staying for dinner?" Reggie asked.

"You'll still have a half dozen people to feed," Katie said. "And, I'm starving, so hurry up."

"I need to check on Carl," Tech said.

"What is Carl working on?" I asked.

"I gave him a list of all the employees on floors two through seven. He's setting up their new security logins."

I nodded but didn't say anything else as Tech disappeared around the corner.

"Tomorrow's his birthday," Katie whispered. "What the hell are we going to do?"

"Tech's birthday?" I asked.

She nodded, looking nervous.

"I can make a cake," Anne whispered.

"I'll plan something for dinner," Reggie said.

"Text Bridget, and have her pick up balloons and decorations," I said.

"What about presents? I don't know what to buy a biker slash computer geek!" Katie complained.

"Call Sara and Bones," I grinned. "They'll think of gift ideas for us. As for a gift from you, maybe a trip somewhere fun."

"Like a Disney cruise," Grady chuckled.

"He'd love that!" Katie squealed.

"I can't believe it," Tech called, walking back into the room. "Carl got everyone programmed *and* the new firewalls set up."

"Bonus!" I grinned. "What's left to do?"

"Nothing," he shook his head. "That would have taken me another week to finish. The regular IT staff can take it from here."

"So then, you can keep a digital eye on Jonathan for me tomorrow?"

"Sure," Tech grinned. "I might even do it from here, sitting around in my boxer shorts."

"Or you could get dressed and join me," Katie said. "That way, if we run into any problems with the new ad campaigns for the social media accounts, you'll be close by to fix it."

"Fine," Tech sighed. "But Saturday—I'm in my boxers all day."

"Deal. We'll get a hotel room, so you don't creep everyone else out."

"No one will care," Tech said, rolling his eyes. "Hell, the den smells like sex."

My face turned bright red, and I turned to flee, but Grady stopped me by tucking me into his side as he chuckled.

"Dude, that's my sister," I heard Reggie complain.

"She made me polish the table afterward," Grady laughed.

Chapter Thirty-Two

It was agreed I'd lay low at the house and keep an eye on the prisoner until Maggie or Kierson arrived to pick him up. I didn't think it was a good idea to lead them to the mechanical room where he was chained up, so I moved the hitman to the dining room and secured him to a pillar. Grady wouldn't like it, but Grady was with Bones scouting out the banquet hall for next week's charity ball.

The hitman was creepy. His eyes kept following me as I moved about the townhouse. I was considering dragging him back into the mechanical room when the doorbell rang.

Saved by the bell, I went to the door to answer it.

Maggie and Kierson both slid inside and Kierson, without a word, went straight to the prisoner. He replaced the zip ties with metal cuffs and pulled him off the floor.

"You should have called the local cops," Kierson grumbled.

"Couldn't," I shrugged. "I'm supposed to be dead, remember?"

"Yeah," Maggie laughed. "Genie got an alert yesterday that you were dead and she wouldn't stop bawling long enough for me to explain that it was fake. She saw the photo and just flipped out."

"Yikes. She mad?"

"No. She's going to enlarge the picture and have it framed in her office."

"Why?" I laughed.

"She says it will make her coworkers think she's tougher," Kierson said, rolling his eyes. "I'll get this guy transported to the local office and then swing back to pick up Maggie."

After Kierson left, Maggie helped herself to a cup of coffee and joined me at the breakfast bar.

"You've been distant lately," she said.

"I've been trying to decide how I want everything to play out."

"As in the legal way or the six-feet-under kind of way?"

"Maybe," I shrugged.

"You've only killed out of self-defense. Even in the house where Nola held you captive, the only death that was questionable was the housekeeper, and the other victims all gave statements that the woman was evil. What makes this situation different?"

"I'm not sure I can pull it off," I admitted. "I can damage him. Financially ruin him. Destroy his career and family. But what if — what if in the end—he's still free to hurt someone else? Free to go after someone I care about? I couldn't live with that."

"So, he's one of the men who hurt you? When Nola had you?"

I nodded but didn't say anything.

"We have a lot of DNA samples from New Orleans that were never matched. Maybe his DNA will be one of them."

"And, if the DNA doesn't match then I've played my hand. The FBI knows who my target is."

"Do you have anything else on him? Anything else that could put him away?"

"Just a hunch," I sighed.

I took another sip of my coffee before turning to face Maggie.

"He has a family house in another state. I'm guessing that's where he buried his victims' bodies."

"We can get a warrant and do a search," she grinned. "I don't have to put in the report where the tip came from."

"Won't work," I said, shaking my head. "You'll never get a warrant without solid probable cause. He's too politically connected."

"Who is he?" she whispered, though no one else was around.

"Until I decide my end game, I can't tell you."

She nodded and let it go.

By the time Kierson returned to pick up Maggie, we had brainstormed on several of Maggie's cold cases. She was going to run with some of the ideas and see if they led anywhere. The entire team had a vacation coming up, three long weeks off, so they didn't want to take on a new case, and instead were reviewing some of their unsolved cases.

The thought of taking a three-week vacation made me smile. Was it even possible to think of all of us being safe enough to do such a thing? For me to travel with my son, my friends, and family, with Grady? To walk in the open fresh air and not have to worry about someone recognizing me or shooting at one of us?

I sighed as I escorted them to the door and said my goodbyes. As I closed the door behind them, I felt very alone.

"Go away. I need to work," I snapped at Grady when he tried to distract me from my computer work.

"What's wrong," he snapped back, slamming the laptop closed.

"What the hell did you do that for?" I yelled.

"Because you're acting like a bitch and I want to know why."

Reggie and Katie bailed from the den, leaving us alone.

"Nothing's wrong. I just have work to do, and you keep distracting me."

"Bullshit. You've been over those files a hundred times."

"And, I'll keep going over them until I know I'm ready," I yelled back.

"That's it," Grady growled, standing up and throwing me over his shoulder in the process.

"What the hell do you think you're doing? Put me down!" I yelled, beating my good arm against his back.

"I'll put you down when I'm ready!" Grady yelled as he stormed out of the room and down the hall.

I continued to fight him as he opened a door and walked down a set of stairs. I didn't even know the townhouse had a basement. I paused in my attack, to lean up and look around.

At the bottom of the steps, Grady dropped me rump first on a stack of mats along the wall. He stormed over to a shelf and tossed boxing gloves at me.

"You want to box!? With me only having one arm?" I yelled, tossing the gloves back.

He put on one glove, on his right hand, and moved his left arm behind his back, grinning at me.

Grady was left-handed.

"Fine, I'll play," I glared, putting the right-handed glove on and moving my left arm behind my back.

I was sweating down to my toes a half an hour later, but neither of us had the upper hand. Turns out, with Grady not using his dominant arm, we were well matched. I wasn't the only one breathing hard.

"You ready to talk yet," he chuckled.

"Not yet," I glared and tried for another leg sweep.

My leg found purchase, twisting behind his, but as he lost his balance, he took me down with him. We both hit the mat hard, the air whooshing out of our lungs. When we were able to breathe again, we broke out laughing.

Grady rolled on top of me.

"Talk to me," he ordered.

I looked up at him as the tears slipped past my guard.

"Please," Grady whispered, placing a hand on my cheek.

"I'm scared."

"Why?" he asked, stroking my cheeks clean with his thumb.

"I don't know if I'm strong enough to stop him. What if I fail? What if he kills me or someone I care about before I stop him? What if I have to fight, and I can't because of this stupid arm? What if—,"

"Stop. Shhh," Grady whispered, before kissing me briefly. "I'm right here. I'm not going anywhere."

"Promise?" I asked, my lower lip trembling.

"Ahh, babe. Always," he promised, leaning in to kiss me again.

Grady and I lay on the mats and talked for another half an hour before I was emotionally back in one piece again.

"Shit! Tech's birthday!"

"It's fine. Rebecca kept Tech late at the office, and everyone else was finishing the decorations and dinner. He should be here any moment, though, so we should go upstairs."

Grady helped me up from the floor but didn't let me go. He stared down at me and stroked the side of my face.

"Always," I whispered to him.

He nodded and pulled me to follow him up the stairs.

Chapter Thirty-Three

Tech was grinning from ear-to-ear as he blew out his birthday candles.

"Thanks, everybody," he said. "I've never had a birthday party before."

"Never?" Rebecca asked.

"Nope," Tech grinned. "This is the first."

"Well, hot cocoa with whip cream for the birthday boy," Anne grinned, setting a mug in front of him as Reggie started serving the cake.

"And, you have to open the present from me first," Katie grinned, passing Tech a card.

Tech opened the card and read it, kissing Katie afterward, before opening the second envelope inside the card.

"A Disney Cruise? Sweet! Can we take Sara and Nick?"

"I was thinking just the two of us."

"But you won't ride the water slides with me," Tech grinned.

"I didn't think of that," Katie said, rolling her eyes. "We'll see if they can come when the date gets closer. I booked it for next month, hoping everything settles down by then."

"Open mine next," I grinned, passing a present down the table.

"It's from BOTH of us," Grady grinned, throwing an arm around me.

Tech tore into the box until enough of the paper was off for him to see what it was.

"Holy shit! It's a 3D Virtual Gaming system! Sweet!"

Tech jumped up and ran out of the room with the box, heading for the den.

"Well, there goes the birthday boy," Katie laughed. "Who wants cake?"

"Is he coming back?" Bridget pouted.

"We probably won't see him again for a few days," Bones chuckled.

"But I got him new sneakers."

"I got him more games for the 3D thing, but I think I'll hold off and give them to him when we get back home," Anne laughed.

"Might be a good idea," Katie grinned.

"How did today go?" I asked.

"Busy, but good," Katie nodded. "We hit the social media sites hard with the rebranding ads. Alex locked down some major vendor contracts. Diego scored on a new production line design that should knock the wind out of Jonathan's sails. And, the last time I checked, we had booked four of JV Dagger's clients for professional services, both for accounting services and promotional services."

"Definitely a busy day."

"Most of the staff is working tomorrow too," Bridget pouted. "I had to move the painters to come in on Sunday."

"Is there a crisis I don't know about?"

"No. They're just energized and ready to prove what they are capable of," Rebecca grinned. "They seem to be excited about Barrister's stepping in for oversight control too."

"The realtor called. She already found a buyer for one of the older buildings. Katie and I read the contracts and even had Mr. Stykes give it a glance before we told Bridget to sign off."

"We getting a decent price?" I asked.

"You're making money on the deal, that's for sure," Katie grinned.

"Carol wants to know if she can stay on for a couple of weeks," Anne said. "She's bouncing between the manufacturing admin building and the professional services building working with the HR and accounting departments."

"It's up to her, but she can head home whenever she wants to."

"She knows," Alex nodded. "She's been bored lately, though."

"I met Jackie's kids today," Bridget said, looking over her shoulder to make sure Tech hadn't returning. "I think you're right about the daughter, but there's no way I can get her to trust me in less than a week. She has completely shut down. And, Jackie is blind to it."

"Jackie's probably so busy hiding the abuse she's going through, she can't see through the fog," I sighed. "Just stay connected with Jackie then. Hopefully, by the time the charity ball comes around, she'll trust you enough to believe us when we tell her our suspicions."

"About the ball," Rebecca said, pushing around a piece of cake on her plate. "I had one of the guests call and ask if they could bring another couple who will be in town visiting. I couldn't say no, without sending up red flags."

"Who?" I asked, my voice turning cold.

Rebecca looked up at me and then turned to look at Bridget.

"Noooo," Bridget said, shaking her head. "Hell no."

"I'm sorry," Rebecca said. "I didn't know what to do."

"It's ok, Bridget," I said, hurrying over to her.

Her body was shaking. Bones looked confused but wrapped a comforting arm around her.

"We'll get you out of town tomorrow morning," I said, holding her hand. "I'd never ask you to be in the same room with them."

"I just… can't," she said looking up at me with tears streaming down her face.

"I know," I said, pulling her in for a hug. "It's Okay. Really. I don't blame you."

"Who are we talking about?" Bones asked, tightening his arm around Bridget's waist.

"Her parents," Rebecca whispered. "They're horrible people. Especially her father."

Bridget started to crumble. Bones swooped her up, carrying her into the living room.

"What happened?" Tech asked, stepping back into the dining room.

"Bridget's parents are coming to town," I answered.

Tech's fists clenched, and he glared at the floor.

"If I can convince her to stay, can we destroy them too?" Tech asked me.

"That would require Bridget to agree," I sighed. "I'm sorry, Tech, but I don't think she can handle facing them. It could do more harm than good."

He strode into the living room.

"Do I even want to know what kind of fucked up shit that was about?" Dex growled.

"No, you don't," Rebecca said, leaning into him.

Chapter Thirty-Four

I did a quick tour of all the businesses Saturday morning. Looking around, you would have thought it was a Monday. A full staff of employees raced to meetings, copiers, filing cabinets and to catch the next ringing phone. The factory was running all three product lines, trying to build stock for the same-day shipping orders Diego wanted to promote by the end of the month.

As busy as everyone was, no one needed my assistance, so I asked Grady if we could take a drive.

"Did you talk to Nicholas this morning?" Grady asked as he exited the highway.

We had driven out of the city. All the tall buildings and crowded roads were a good half an hour behind us.

"Yeah. He told me to hurry up and catch the bad guys."

"I talked to him last night," Grady nodded. "He wanted to know how many chores I thought it would take to earn a 3D gaming system like Tech's."

"I'll have to build a game room if I move back to Michigan," I grinned.

"When."

"What?" I asked, turning away from the scenery we passed to look at Grady.

"Not if, but when you move back to Michigan," Grady said, pulling my hand onto his lap. "You need to be with your family."

"What about Texas? What about Charlie moving back to Miami?"

"You'll visit Texas. And, they'll visit you. As for Charlie, who knows where that girl will land. But she's an adult now. She has to figure life out for herself."

"And, you?" I asked, afraid of the answer. "Are you ready to go home?"

"I go, where you go," he said, pulling my hand up and kissing my palm. "Always, remember?"

"That's not fair to you," I sighed.

"There's not much for me in Montana anymore. A few friends and relatives," he shrugged. "I sold my house a couple years back. I wasn't there enough to maintain it."

I closed my eyes, leaning my head on the window, feeling the short quick bursts of sunlight that appeared between the trees. "It's too much to think about right now. And, truthfully, the thought of going back to selling clothes makes me want to run for the hills."

"No one said you had to sell clothes," Grady chuckled.

"Then what? Be a stay at home mom?" I snorted.

"No," Grady laughed. "The kids would revolt."

I laughed because I knew he was right.

"Hey look—," I grinned, pointing to a building up ahead. "A little diner. Can we stop for a burger?"

"Sounds good," he grinned, pulling into the parking lot.

As we ate lunch, I thought about Grady and my son, and the life I wanted to have. My son's safety was my first priority, but I knew I couldn't keep hiding in Texas. Grady was right. I wanted to go home. I wanted to go back to Michigan.

And, deciding what to do with Jonathan could threaten that future. If I chose to kill him, I could be arrested and lose the chance of raising my son. I wasn't willing to do that.

I dropped the French fry I was holding and pulled out my cell phone, calling Maggie.

"We need to talk," I said when she answered.

"I can be there in an hour."

"Best hurry before I change my mind again. And bring Kierson with you," I said before hanging up.

"Feds?" Grady grinned, stealing some of my fries.

"Reading my mind again, Mr. Tanner?"

"Wasn't hard," he smirked.

I threw a fry at him, but he caught it and ate it. He ordered two to-go milkshakes and paid for our lunch. It was time to go back and finish this.

When we returned to the townhouse, I warned everyone that Maggie and Kierson would be arriving soon, and I'd be officially looping them in on the plan. Everyone nodded, as Grady slid into a chair and started working with Bones, Dex, and Tech on studying the security set up of the banquet hall.

"You going to finish that?" Tech asked, eying my milkshake.

"Have at it," I said, sliding the cup to him. "I'm going to be in the den."

I wasn't surprised when Bridget followed me in. She slid her backside up on top of the table.

"How are you doing?" I asked.

"I'm a mess," she sighed, staring at the wall in front of her.

"I figured you'd be in Michigan by now."

She nodded, not looking at me. "Can I ask you something?"

"Sure," I said, taking a seat in one of the chairs.

"Are you scared?"

"My situation and your situation are different Bridget."

"But are you scared?" she asked, turning to look at me.

I nodded. "Yesterday afternoon I cried like a baby."

"I want to face them. Face him. But what if I can't go through with it?"

"Why do you want to face him? So, you can finish the assignment and stay close to Jackie?"

"No," she shook her head. "I need to confront my father. I need it to be over."

"It'll be hard."

"But you'll be there, right? And, Bones? I'll be safe?"

"Of course, you'd be safe. But your father won't go down easy. What if he starts yelling at you? Calling you horrible names? Are you prepared for that?"

"I can't keep running," she admitted, with tears streaming down her face.

"I'll make you a deal. Call Haley. If she agrees this is a good idea, then we'll humiliate your father at the charity ball."

* * *

"I already talked to Haley. She said — Game on," Bridget grinned, as the tears continued.

"I'll set it up," I nodded, standing and placing a hand on her shoulder in support. "But if you change your mind, that's okay too."

Bridget slid off the table and turned to leave. Neither of us had noticed Bones leaning against the doorway.

"Maggie and Kierson are here," he said to me, but his eyes never left Bridget's face.

He grasped Bridget's hand and led her out of the room.

I pulled the phone sitting in the center of the table toward me and dialed Genie as Maggie entered.

"Is this my favorite coworker or my favorite copper?" Genie giggled answering the phone.

"It appears you have both of us on the line," Maggie called out to the speaker phone, as she sat.

"Hey Genie, I have a favor to ask. It's not necessary to get in trouble using the FBI's database, but Tech's too close to this one so I can't ask him."

"Your wish is my command. Give me the goods," she giggled.

"I need everything you can find on Bridget Delano's family, specifically her father, but I want whatever intel is out there."

"Bridget... Delano..., Oh, my goodness, our Bridget?" she squealed.

"It's all good, Genie," I assured her. "Bridget asked me to help her expose her family. She knows I'll be digging for dirt."

"Poor girl. I don't know what's going on, but I'll send you everything I find."

"Thanks," I said, before hanging up.

"Delano?" Maggie asked.

"She's been going by Dell, but Delano is her real name."

"As in the 'Delano' family?" Kierson asked, entering the room.

"The same one," I sighed. "Bridget didn't have a fairytale upbringing, despite the money her family has."

"Is this why you called?" Maggie asked.

"No, I'll handle this. I called because I can't kill the guy I'm going after," I chuckled.

"Thank you, Jesus," Maggie sighed, leaning her head back into her chair. "I've been waiting months to hear you say that."

"I bet," I grinned. "It's been pretty touch-and-go. But now that I've officially decided, I need to loop both of you in on some of the things I know, and some of the things I suspect."

Grady sauntered in and set a cup of tea in front of me.

"Why tea?" I asked.

"Because you need to sleep tonight," he grinned, pulling out a chair beside me.

"Yeah! This isn't going to be another one of your all-nighters," Tech laughed, walking into the room loudly slurping the last of the milkshake. "Katie said I still have another birthday present coming."

Tech wiggled his eyebrows up and down and Katie, who had followed him in, whopped him in the gut.

Katie and Tech sat on the other side of the table and Tech brought a picture of Jonathan Vaughn up on the screen.

"No," Maggie said, looking back at me in total shock.

"Yes," I sighed.

"Shit," Kierson said, sitting in one of the chairs and rubbing his forehead. "You've got to be fucking kidding me. He's running for governor!"

"There goes our vacation," Maggie sighed, thumping her head on the table.

"We plan on taking him down this week, so you'll be in the clear after next weekend," I grinned.

Kierson rolled his eyes. Maggie got up and walked out of the room. When she returned a few minutes later, she carried in several glasses and a full bottle of whiskey.

"Here's to Kelsey saying she's taking down the bad guy in a week," Maggie grinned, tossing back the drink.

"She may plan on dealing with him this week, but generally after Kelsey walks away, we're left with a pile of reports to file and evidence to process," Kierson grumbled, tossing his own drink down.

He slid the glass to the center of the table and looked at me.

"Was he one of the men who hurt you?" he asked.

Grady reached out and placed a hand on my forearm.

"Yes, but that wasn't the worst of it."

Tech stood and walked over to close the door and dim the lights.

"I'm going to stop Kelsey and give you the basics," Tech said. "She's getting stronger every day, but she still has trouble talking about some of the things that happened," Tech spoke mechanically as he displayed additional photos on the wall monitor "Yes, Jonathan Vaughn was one of the men who tortured Kelsey. He realized though he wasn't hurting her emotionally, so he switched tactics. He started bringing women," Tech change the display screen up to three women, "and eventually a young girl, into the room to torture. He made Kelsey watch as he killed them."

Maggie leaned forward in her chair, before turning abruptly and running out of the room.

"Keep going, Tech," I nodded, stepping out of the den and closing the door behind me.

I caught up with Maggie down the hall in the half bathroom. I closed the door and turned the exhaust fan on before I helped hold her hair as she vomited.

"Shit, I'm sorry," she gasped between heaves.

"Nothing to be sorry for," I said. "Just help me take the bastard down, Maggie. He can't walk away from this. He can't have his freedom."

She spit into the toilet, before pushing away and leaning against the wall.

I wet a washcloth and filled a cup of water, handing both of them down to her.

"Just give me a minute," she nodded.

I slid out of the bathroom, giving her a few minutes of privacy.

"She need anything?" Reggie asked in the hallway.

"A toothbrush and maybe some dry toast."

He walked away and I returned to the den.

"Kierson is caught up with everything I know of what happened during your captivity. We were just about to explain your master plan."

"I hope it's a good one, Kelsey," Kierson said, rubbing his jaw. "This guy is going to be tough to take down."

"By the end of the week, there shouldn't be much left of him," I grinned.

Grady snorted.

"We already started Phase One: The financial ruin of Jonathan Vaughn," Katie grinned.

"And, how much prison time does that involve," Kierson asked, reaching for his glass and the whiskey bottle.

"None," I shrugged.

Maggie stepped back into the room and resumed her seat. She was munching on some dry toast.

"I anonymously purchased some businesses Jonathan was selling. We turned around and consolidated them, aiming them like a missile right back at his mother ship, JV Dagger Innovations."

"He took the money from the sale and used it to refuel his campaign and JV Dagger Innovations," Katie said taking over.

"He also blew a big chunk of money on a private jet," Grady grinned. "Plus, he paid off the hitman who supposedly killed Kelsey."

"But JV Dagger is our target," Katie said. "With all of his financial eggs in one basket, we started stealing his clients, his vendors, and his manufacturing line. We already stole seven large accounts. The company will be looking down the barrel of bankruptcy by the end of the week."

"Holy shit," Maggie laughed.

"Oh, they ain't done yet," Grady drawled, chuckling as he reached out to hold my hand.

"His family will fold when he goes down," I continued. "The immediate family cell is broken by years of abuse, and the extended family doesn't like him, so they'll abandon him the first chance they get. That leaves his political career. We need to destroy his career using consecutive blows so he's constantly trying to scramble to spin a story. First, the media will be tipped-off that his company is in trouble."

"Already in play," Katie grinned.

"Then the second blow will be when the FBI raids his warehouse in New Orleans and finds counterfeit handbags," I grinned looking at Kierson.

"Do you have enough for a warrant?" he asked.

"Sure, but the FBI can't detain him yet. It would help if the investigation is public though."

"Why not arrest him?" Maggie asked. "I would think a picture of him in handcuffs would help your plan."

"I need him to be available for a little longer," I said. "The third blow will be when I tell the world he raped and tortured me, along with killing three women and a young girl. That performance will be in front of his most influential backers, and will be recorded by the media."

"And, when is this public announcement," Kierson asked.

"This Friday at a charity ball. It's going to be a grand event. You'll need a tux of course," I grinned.

"You're not kidding, are you?" Kierson asked.

"His reputation will have taken such a hit by Friday he'll be scrambling for PR moments," Maggie laughed. "He'll show up to the charity ball early to do damage control."

"Nice profiling," I grinned, winking at Maggie.

"What happens after you tell the world he's a monster?" Maggie asked.

"The FBI arrests him of course. I wouldn't be telling you any of this if I'd decided to go with option B."

"Option B might be easier," Kierson grumbled.

"Don't tempt me, Jimmy," Grady said.

"Right, sorry. I forgot some of you would consider that a real option," Kierson said, rolling his eyes. "Option A, then. I'll need the details on this warehouse with counterfeit handbags so I can alert the fraud unit. As far as arresting him after the party, your witness statement would be enough to take him into custody and get a warrant for his DNA. But, we can't be sure his DNA will match one of the samples we collected in New Orleans."

"They," I said, pointing up to the picture of the three women and a young girl, "didn't die easy deaths. That much DNA would have been hard to clean up. Matching their DNA to the scene supports my version of events."

Grady squeezed the hand he still held. I intertwined our finger, keeping my connection with him.

"Without physical evidence directly linking him to the murders, a good lawyer can get him released," Maggie said.

"But, he'll be almost broke," Katie grinned, leaning back in her chair. "And, he'll be publicly humiliated. A good lawyer isn't going to want to tarnish their name by defending him."

"There's also the fact that if we can tie the other victims to the crime scene, corroborating my story, then you have probable cause for a warrant."

"A warrant for what?" Kierson asked.

"He inherited his uncle's estate in Louisiana. Jonathan has a thug in New Orleans who does a walk-through of the estate and grounds every week. I think it's where Jonathan buried his victims."

"And, if we come up empty? If your hunch is wrong?" Kierson asked.

"Then plan B," Grady said, looking coldly at Kierson.

"Or we go to trial with what we have," Maggie added quickly. "We exhaust all efforts just like any other case."

"No matter how this situation ends," I said, interrupting a potential argument, "the FBI needs to start their investigation without detaining Jonathan. He has to be at the charity ball if you want him stripped of his influence and power. The FBI won't be able to get anything to stick until we break him first."

"Agreed," Kierson nodded. "I need to make a phone call."

Chapter Thirty-Five

"I'm proud of you," Grady whispered, pulling me on top of his bare chest and kissing my forehead.

I pulled the sheet up to keep the chill from the air conditioner off my skin.

"I haven't done anything yet."

"You're fighting back. The legal way even," he chuckled. "Though I think Kierson secretly wishes you'd have chosen option B."

"I couldn't risk going to prison. It wouldn't be fair to Nick, Charlie, Hattie, everyone, including you," I said, kissing his chin. "Jonathan Vaughn has stolen enough from me. I won't let him have my freedom too."

"As I said, I'm so damn proud of you," Grady said, rolling on top of me.

Then he proceeded to show me just how proud.

"Time to get up, sleepyheads," Katie said, pounding on the door.

"It's Sunday," I yelled.

"The local TV network is interviewing Jonathan," she yelled.

"Shit," Grady said, as we both jumped out of bed and raced to get dressed.

He was quicker than I was. I only had my socks and sweatpants on by the time he turned around and dropped a sweatshirt over my head. He swung me up, carrying me down the stairs and into the living room. When he set me down, I saw everyone else was dressed similarly. I managed to work my right arm through the sleeve before Grady pulled me down to sit beside him on the floor and helped me work my other arm through as we waited for Tech to replay the interview.

"Anything good?" I asked.

"I only caught the last part of it. I was making hot cocoa," Tech grinned.

"What time is it, anyway?" Anne asked, sitting next to me on the floor, trying to straighten her bedhead.

"Almost seven," Katie giggled, sitting on the other side of Anne. "And, you might as well quit trying to fix that mess. There's no hope."

"Pause!" Anne yelled louder than necessary.

Everyone froze and turned to Anne.

"We at least deserve coffee if we are up this early on a Sunday."

Anne scrambled to the kitchen. Grady and I raced after her. Grady got the grounds out, Anne filled the water carafe, and I pulled out clean coffee mugs from the dishwasher. When the pot started brewing, the three of us stared whiled it slowly fill. We heard the front door open, and in walked Dex and Rebecca.

"Did you watch it?" Rebecca asked as Dex handed out the large cups of specialty-blend coffees they had brought.

Anne and I added some ice cubes to ours so we could drink them immediately.

"No," Grady chuckled. "Tech recorded the interview, but we needed coffee first."

"You saved us," I laughed, leading the group into the living room.

"Dex, you need a new coffee pot. Yours is too slow," Anne scolded him.

"I don't drink coffee," he shrugged.

"I'll pick up a new one this afternoon," Rebecca agreed as she camped out on the floor with us.

"Did you watch the interview?" I asked her.

"Yeah, but I'll wait to see what you think," she grinned.

We were just about to start when the doorbell rang. We all sighed as Dex went to answer it. He returned with Maggie and Genie following him into the room.

"What are we doing?" Genie giggled, sitting on the floor next to Rebecca.

"About to watch Jonathan's interview," Rebecca grinned. "Do I know you?"

"Genie, just Genie," she said, holding her hand out to shake Rebecca's. "I'm another one of Kelsey's sidekicks."

"She's also an analyst for the FBI," I laughed. "What are you doing in town?"

"The other analysts were being mean to me again, so I decided to come here," she grinned.

"Is everyone ready yet?" Tech complained.

"Dazzle us with your technical skills and hit play," Genie said to Tech.

"Smartass," Tech chuckled, hitting play before sitting behind Katie to watch the interview.

The interview had been live. And, though it was early in the morning, Jonathan had dragged his wife and both his daughters with him. After walking out on the stage, the older girl quickly stepped between her father and younger sister, acting as a barrier.

"Please tell me—," Maggie started to say.

"We'll get the girl away from him as soon as possible, Maggie," I whispered.

The reporter started with congratulations on the current rankings in the political campaign before switching gears to Jonathan's businesses.

"The financial market is buzzing about some companies you sold earlier this week to an unknown buyer. What was the reasoning behind the sale?" the reporter asked.

"I had been considering selling two of them when I was approached about selling five. With the upcoming election, my focus will be pulled into political matters, so I chose to sell. Of course, JV Dagger Innovations remains under my leadership and is continuing to thrive."

"Thrive? Have you not heard?" the reporter asked.

"Excuse me?" Jonathan said, maintaining his pleasant facial expression, but his shoulders tensed and his eyes darkened.

"The businesses you sold were consolidated, in what seems to be an overnight transition. Now the two remaining companies are targeting JV Dagger Innovations. I've been able to confirm that not only has JV Dagger lost a dozen of their top clients, but we also confirmed late yesterday that Barrister Industries will be stepping in to oversee the new companies."

"Obviously, I'm aware of the changes to my formerly owned companies," Jonathan said, though his body language contradicted the statement. "Let me assure you that even if Barrister's does step in, the companies will in no way be able to harm JV Dagger Innovations. We will continue to lead the industry in this area for professional outsourcing."

"And, the vending contracts that were negotiated to push JV Dagger out of competitive deals?" the reporter asked.

"Again, JV Dagger is a strong company. Everyone runs to the shiny new toy, but they always return to the solid, stable environment where their interests are protected."

"Let me ask this," the reporter paused, "Who owns the new companies?"

"As in most cases, large corporations with multiple investors pool their funds to acquire businesses. It really doesn't matter who the owners are," Jonathan chuckled, reaching his arm across the back of the couch and trying to look relaxed.

"We have investigators working on tracking back the ownership and have so far been unable to identify any individual person. The only name we've discovered so far is Bridget Delano."

"Well then, there you have it. The Delano family is indeed wealthy enough to purchase multiple businesses on a whim."

"But why are they specifically targeting your company then?"

"I'm sure it's just a coincidence. I've known the Delano family socially for years," Jonathan shrugged.

"Let's watch one of their new advertisements," the reporter said, nodding to someone off-camera.

Jonathan and his family watched the ad on the flat screen at the side of the stage. He had obviously not seen it before. It directly targeted his company, and by the time the 45-second video had ended, Jonathan was no longer able to contain his anger. The older daughter shifted closer to her sister and mother.

"Well, it looks like I do have a competitor," Jonathan chuckled without humor. "The new owners have obviously not done their homework, or they would have known how foolish it was to attempt to uproot a company of JV Dagger's size and reputation."

"But the question is, who are *they*? The Delano's?" the reporter asked.

"Ask me in another week," Jonathan smiled. "Because that's how long it will take me to demolish whoever is behind this."

"And what of the rumors that you own two other companies being reviewed by the IRS for tax fraud? Is there any truth to those allegations?"

"Don't be ridiculous," Jonathan said.

Having said all he intended to say, Jonathan stood and motioned with his hand to guide his family off stage.

"Shit," Genie giggled. "You did that?"

"Katie, call Bridget," I said, climbing up from the floor. "I don't want her left unprotected since she was named in the interview."

"I already texted her," Anne said. "Bones is pissed, but she's still meeting Jackie for breakfast in the hotel's restaurant. Alex is joining her for the meeting though."

"I don't like it," I said.

"Dex and I will go and do our bodyguard thing," Grady said, kissing my cheek before shoving Dex out of the room.

"I'll go with you," Reggie called out. "After breakfast, I can help Bridget and Alex finish the shopping for tuxes and the rest of the gowns we'll need for the charity ball."

"Can you have Bridget pick me up a dress too?" Rebecca asked. "I'm not wearing last year's design if they're walking in looking like movie stars."

"You're already on the list," Reggie grinned, holding out a piece of paper.

After refilling my coffee, Genie and Maggie followed me into the den. I pulled up the photos Wild Card sent me last night. I had called to tell him that the feds were taking over the warehouse building. He walked the perimeter of the old plantation house again, taking pictures from every angle, before packing up and relocating back to Texas. Nightcrawler had opted to stay in New Orleans to be available if needed.

"Genie, is there a way to get more information on this house? Old records or designs?"

"It depends on who owned it before Jonathan's uncle," Genie said, pulling out her laptop. "I'll give it a whirl, though. It's old enough I should be able to find something useful."

"I need a project," Maggie said, pulling out a chair and thumping her fingers on the table. "Put me to work."

"Can you go through the file we have on Bridget's family and give me a profile on her parents and her grandfather?" I asked, sliding three files of data and notes down the table to her.

"Sure," she agreed, scrunching her forehead. "But why? What does this have to do with Jonathan?"

"Bridget came out of hiding to help me. Her family plans on cornering her at the charity ball and Bridget wants to discredit her father and ruin him. I just hope she's strong enough to handle it."

"She has you," Genie said. "As long as she has you and the rest of the family, she'll be Okay."

"Damn straight," Tech said as he entered.

"Where's Katie?" I asked.

"Cooking," Tech snorted. "She started yelling at me when I tried to help, so I came in here."

"Is Anne out there?" I asked.

"Anne ran upstairs to shower," Tech said, shaking his head.

"So, Katie's unsupervised?"

"Rebecca's watching, but she seems just as clueless in a kitchen."

"Should we be scared?" Maggie asked.

Before I could answer, the fire alarm went off. We raced to the kitchen, just as Katie was pouring water into a pan of bacon that was on fire.

"No!" we all yelled, but it was too late, as the fire roared and spattered in every direction.

Tech pulled Katie out of the kitchen as Maggie yanked Rebecca away. I danced around the flames, grabbing the extinguisher from under the sink. Stepping back, I pulled the pin and doused the entire area down with white foam.

Fire out, I turned off the stove and unplugged the electric fry pan.

I grabbed two bags of bagels from the fridge and a tub of vegetable cream cheese, carrying them into the den. Everyone, including Rebecca and Katie, followed me.

"Oh, no, you don't," I chuckled at Katie and Rebecca.

They pouted but went back to the kitchen to clean up their mess. The rest of us fixed a bagel.

I was about an hour into studying aerial photos of the Louisiana plantation house when I sighed loudly.

Genie giggled beside me. "What's wrong?"

"I have no idea what I'm looking at. I don't know anything about Louisiana architecture or plantations."

"What do you need to know?" Maggie asked, pushing her own laptop away and looking at mine.

"What are these buildings?" I asked, pointing to some small structures near the back of the clearing.

Maggie took my laptop and moved the pictures to the wall monitor.

"Looks like crypts," she said, stepping up to the TV to get a better look.

Genie took control of the laptop and zoomed in.

"Definitely crypts," Maggie said, now that the image was bigger.

"Crypts? As in those little buildings, you put bodies in? Why not bury the body like everyone else?" I asked.

"Can't," Tech answered. "The water table is too high in most areas. You're likely to be seeing Aunt Ester's body come back up during the rainy season."

"Ewe."

"Exactly," Maggie chuckled. "That's why crypts are used. It's also why many of the old plantations are built to enter from the second story."

"So, they don't have basements?"

"Sometimes if the entrance level is high enough, they'll have partial cellars or passageways," Genie shrugged. "But basements like what you have in Michigan are pretty uncommon in the South."

"The mansion has a raised entrance, so either there is nothing under it, or it might have a partial cellar, right?" I asked.

"That would be my guess," Maggie nodded after Genie switched the photo to the plantation house.

"Then what? What would be the expectation inside the house?"

"I'm speculating here, but I'd expect to see a grand stairway to the second floor near the front of the house and smaller stairways for servants in the back of the house. The bedrooms would be upstairs, except for some possible small bedrooms for servants in the back of the first floor. The kitchen would be in the back too. The front of the house would typically be seating areas like parlors, dining rooms, etc."

"What about all the chimneys?"

"Fireplaces. They would have been the main source of heat at one point. Most of the chimneys appear old, probably not even functional," Maggie shrugged. "This one looks like it was added in the last decade or so. It probably goes to a living room fireplace or maybe a woodstove."

"So, hardwood floors? Old windows and doors? Outdated electrical?"

"Again, I'm guessing, but I would say yes," Maggie nodded.

"Then why the new door on the side of the house, but not any other updates?"

Genie flipped through several photos until she found one showing the side door toward the back of the house.

"Maybe it was damaged?" Tech said.

"No, Kelsey's right, it doesn't make sense. The front porch is falling apart, some of the windows are broken, but you add a steel door with deadbolts onto a back entrance?" Maggie said.

"Where would that door go?"

"I'm guessing a kitchen area," Maggie shrugged. "But I'm doing a lot of guessing today."

"I can't find layouts online anywhere," Genie said. "There hasn't even been a parish inspection in the last sixty years."

"And, what the hell is a parish? I don't get that either," I said, throwing my hands up.

"Stressing, Babe?" Grady chuckled, walking in and wrapping an arm around me. "Louisiana uses the term parish like the rest of the country uses the term county."

I sighed. Genie giggled.

My cell phone rang, offering me a much-needed distraction.

"Hi Hattie," I grinned, answering the phone as I walked out to the dining room.

Rebecca and Katie were putting the final spit and polish on the kitchen. The cleanliness didn't diminish the black scorch marks running up the wall and onto the ceiling. Dex was standing there with his hands on his hips, glaring at the floor.

"Sunshine, I need your help," Hattie said.

"What's wrong?" I asked, fully focusing on the call now.

"It's Henry and Pops. What on earth am I going to do? Henry keeps finding reasons to stay longer. I feel like a yo-yo being pulled back and forth. I can't take much more of this."

I could picture Hattie hiding in the kitchen, wringing the life out of kitchen towel as she paced back and forth.

"I can't believe Henry's still there," I laughed.

"It's not funny! This morning they almost started fist fighting over who would sit next to me at the breakfast table. If it wasn't for Jackson and Sara taking both the chairs next to me, someone would have earned a black eye."

"Well, I think it's sweet," I grinned.

"I called you for help, so start helping young lady, or I'll turn my frustration toward you," she scolded.

"Okay. Okay. But you're not going to like what I have to say."

"Say it anyway."

"You need to choose."

"I can't," Hattie sighed. "Both of them could make me happy."

"There's a difference between making your life pleasant and being madly in love, Hattie. Which one rocks your boat," I giggled.

"Rocks my what? Oh, never mind, I know what you're eluding to. And, that's not what's important."

"Then what's important? What's the most important thing for you to be eternally happy in this world?"

"I need to be with you and the rest of the family. I can't have a life without all of you in it."

"You'll always have us. But you can't base this decision on geography either. Figure out which one of them you're in love with and then set them both straight."

There was a long pause on the other line.

"When this is over, will you choose to live in Michigan or Texas?" Hattie asked.

"Nice try," I laughed. "I'll answer the question after you've dealt with your man problems."

"Fine," Hattie snapped. "I have to go. Henry's picking me up for a picnic."

Hattie disconnected abruptly.

"Hattie ok?" Katie asked, her forehead strained with lines of concern.

"She'll be fine," I nodded. "She still has Henry and Pops competing for her attention, and it's wearing on her nerves."

"Two men fighting over her," Rebecca grinned. "How sweet."

"Not to Hattie," I laughed.

By dinner time, we were all exhausted, and Katie ordered pizzas. Reggie, Alex, Bones, and Bridget returned carrying armloads of garment bags. After doling them out, Bridget ordered everyone to try their tuxes or gowns on so they could ensure the fit was correct. Grady's pants were a bit too long, and Alex pinned them to have them tailored.

Knowing I was done working for the night, I emptied the well-stocked liquor cabinet onto the counter and mixed up a cocktail.

"I'd love a cigarette," I giggled.

"I'm surprised you quit," Reggie said.

"Between Pops, Hattie and Nick, I didn't have a choice. They ganged up on me."

"I'm glad," Grady said, reaching past me to pour some Captains into a glass. "I only smoke when you smoke, so as long as you abstain, it will mean I'll behave."

"Sure, drop all the pressure on me," I laughed.

"He used to blame me," Dex grinned.

"And, after Dex quit, he blamed me," Bones grinned, pulling a beer from the refrigerator.

"So, you basically only smoke when someone else is smoking?"

"Never think about it otherwise," Grady shrugged.

"That's so unfair," I laughed.

"Well take your mind off it," Maggie ordered, bumping me with her hip to get to the booze. "What's the game plan for the next few days?"

"Keep hitting JV Dagger hard from the business front. The IRS audit will start Tuesday. If we can leak the illegal handbags on Wednesday, Jonathan will be thoroughly frazzled by Friday. And, we need to make sure security is tight at the reception hall."

"We have security under control," Dex nodded.

"Anne, Rebecca and I will take care of finishing off JV Dagger," Katie said.

"I'll get ahold of the party planner tomorrow and make sure everything is up to snuff for the charity ball," Bridget said, handing a bottle of wine to Grady to uncork.

"Then we'll just keep chiseling away," I shrugged.

"You need to get out of town for a few days," Tech said. "Everything falls apart if Jonathan finds you in the city."

"I'll just hide here until it's over," I cringed.

"You? Staying inside for four and a half days?" Bones laughed.

Grady wrapped an arm around me, pulling me into him. He was quietly chuckling behind me.

"I can handle it," I grumbled.

"No, you can't," Katie laughed. "No long drives, no bike rides, no boat rides, no horseback riding, staying confined inside until Friday? Please. If you did survive it, then you'd end up making us so miserable we'd wish you had left. You're already cranky."

"Then I'll sneak into the offices."

"Too dangerous," Maggie said, shaking her head.

"No one seriously expects me to leave, do you?"

"If it was one of us, you'd have already put us on a plane," Bones shrugged. "You actually put everyone in danger by being here."

"Then everyone should leave. This is my plan. I can't leave."

"Don't be stupid," Anne said, tossing a manila envelope onto the counter in front of me. "You'll be on teleconference calls with us during the day, jogging trails in the evening, and sleeping in comfort at night. You'll still be in charge, you'll just be out of town."

"What the hell is this?" I asked, opening the envelope.

"You're cabin rental," Anne shrugged. "It's in no-man's-land about two hours from here. I've already packed a bag for you and Grady."

"Don't—," Katie said, stopping me from saying anything. "This is the smart move, and you know it. It doesn't mean we don't need you. It just means the odds of Jonathan figuring out what we are up to decrease with you hidden away."

"So, this was planned behind my back?" I asked.

"More like discussed and agreed we'd have to be united in presenting it to you," Reggie grinned.

"Don't argue," Bridget grinned. "Slip off to your secluded cabin, equipped with Wi-Fi of course, and finish the plan for Friday. We'll be waiting for you when you get back into town."

"You all suck," I sighed.

"You think they suck because you know they're right," Grady chuckled.

"Think of it as resting up before the big fight," Alex grinned, still wearing his tux and swirling his wine glass.

"Yes, because heaven forbid, you'd allow yourself to just enjoy a romantic get-away," Anne said, rolling her eyes. "But whatever, finish your drink and get the hell out of here."

"You just want to steal my bed, so you don't have to sleep on the couch," I fake glared at Anne.

"I already put clean sheets on the bed," Anne smirked.

Chapter Thirty-Six

Stepping into the cabin, a chill ran down my spine. It wasn't the cold air, but the emptiness. Grady was scouting the exterior of the property while I checked the inside. I knew he'd be back any moment, but I still felt alone. Like when I was held captive by Nola. My only interaction with anyone was when she chose to torture me.

I stood there, staring at the nothingness surrounding me. I didn't see the old fireplace, built out of cut stone. I didn't see the queen size bed in the corner with a thick, handmade quilt. I barely noticed the woodstove with the old fashion top burners or the manual pump kitchen faucet. I just felt the cold, damp air seeping into my bones.

"Hey," Grady whispered, pulling me into the warmth of his body. "You're shivering."

I turned and wrapped my good arm around his shoulder, clinging to him.

Grady pulled me tighter into his body. "I'm right here."

Burying my face in his shoulder, I tried to hide the tears. Grady lifted me and carried me over to the bed, where he sat with me on his lap, and pulled the blankets up around me.

I woke to the sound of songbirds tweeting soft melodies. I opened my eyes to find myself curled into Grady, fully dressed, with a hand-sewn quilt tucked tightly around me and his arms cinching me to him. I reached up and stroked the side of his face, in awe of how peaceful he looked.

"Good morning," he whispered, without opening his eyes.

"I didn't mean to wake you," I whispered back, grinning as I watched the corners of his mouth curl into a smirk.

"You get to wake me anytime you want," he said, turning into my body and nuzzling my neck. "It's one of the rules."

"Oh yeah? And, what are the other rules?"

"Hmmm. I think it's best if you learn them one by one," he said kissing along my collar bone.

"Do any of these rules cover who makes coffee in the cold cabin that only has an archaic woodstove?"

He chuckled again, dropping his forehead to my chest. "I'm thinking it will be my job," he laughed.

"Since I have no idea how to start the thing, I think you're right," I said, shoving him toward the edge of the bed.

"One cup of coffee, coming up," he grinned, kissing me on the cheek. "In about 15 to 20 minutes of course."

"Seriously?"

He just laughed and went to the woodstove. I wrapped the quilt around me and got out of bed.

"So, is there a bathroom around here?"

"At the back of the kitchen. It has an old pull-string toilet flusher, but it's just for looks. The cabin has real plumbing."

"Hot water too?"

He tossed another log in the woodstove. "Yup. And, a clawfoot tub big enough for two. Why don't you go fill the tub while I get the stove started? I'll come join you as soon as the coffee is on."

Draping the blanket over a rocking chair, I wandered past the kitchen to find the bathroom.

Grady was right about the hot water, and soon I was almost swimming in the deep tub.

"Coffee, for My Lady," Grady said as he entered and handed me a cup.

I took a sip before setting the cup on the long shelf that ran alongside the tub. Grady stripped and stepped into the water, his back to the other tub end, facing me. He lifted my feet to prop across his thighs and started massaging deep circles into my arches.

"Why are you sitting all the way down there?"

"We need to talk," he sighed.

"I get the feeling I'm not going to enjoy this conversation."

"I need to know what happened last night, Kel. I can't help you if I don't understand. Was it a flashback?"

"No," I shook my head. "I knew where I was."

I ducked under the water to wet my hair. When I came back up, I grabbed the shampoo.

"Kelsey," Grady said, pulling me by my legs, so I slid across the tub toward him.

He took the shampoo away from me and set it on the shelf.

"What happened? You need to either tell me or a shrink. You decide, Babe."

"I'm fine. Really," I said looking up at him. "I just felt—I don't know—overwhelmed, maybe? It was the cold and the small dark room. It just reminded me of being alone in the basement dungeon. I wouldn't see anyone for days except for the housekeeper who occasionally brought me water. And, she wasn't allowed to speak to me."

"I thought there were other prisoners?"

"They were in another area," I said, shaking my head as a chill ran down my back.

"Ok," he said, leaning forward and kissing my forehead.

"That's it? I wig out and ruin our first night in a romantic cabin, and you're just 'okay' with it?" I grinned.

"Now I know," he shrugged, pulling me forward another foot, so I was sitting on his lap. "Until we know you're better acclimated, you won't be left alone in dark, isolated buildings."

"That's ridiculous," I laughed. "I need to just get over it."

"That's not how this works, Babe. It takes time."

"How much time?"

"Does it matter? Are you getting sick of me already?" he grinned.

"No, but I don't want a babysitter either," I pouted, kissing his chin.

"You seem to do fine when you're outside or when lots of noisy people are around, so you'll only have a babysitter the rest of the time."

"I'm not agreeing to that."

"I wasn't asking for your permission," he chuckled before kissing me.

"Hmm. I like this tub."

"I have something for you," Grady whispered as he leaned over the edge of the tub.

He held something in his hand, and in one smooth move, slid it onto my left ring finger.

"It's my ring," I said, looking down puzzled at my own ring.

I had purchased the ring at a going out of business sale last year. It was an emerald cut diamond flanked by two pear-shaped diamonds. But now, it had sapphires embedded around the center stone.

"I sent Lisa the money to buy the ring. Now, I'm re-gifting it back to you," he grinned.

"And, the sapphires?"

"They remind me of how bright your eyes get when you're angry or happy," he whispered. "Each time I saw your eyes sparkle, I think a fell a little more in love with you."

"My eyes don't sparkle," I laughed. I pulled back, turning so I could lean into him, as I stared down at the ring.

"Your eyes sparkled with anger the first day we met. You held a gun on me and demanded to know who I was," he chuckled, as he soaped up a washcloth.

"It wasn't the best time for visitors," I said.

"You were fierce. I knew instantly if I moved the wrong direction, you'd shoot me."

"It wasn't personal."

"No, it wasn't. You were fierce because I was a threat to your friends. I respected that."

"Tell me another."

"Later that day you came charging out of the back bedroom with only a wet towel wrapped around you yelling for Charlie. But it wasn't the anger I remember, it was your eyes shining with unshed tears after you decided to let her go undercover to watch for Nola," he ran the washcloth down my arm to my hand. "You were scared for her."

"She did well."

"Yes, she did. But it was your love for her, both to protect her and let her make her own decisions, I remember."

I leaned my head into his shoulder, relaxing my body to listen to him.

"I've seen your eyes sparkle when you laugh with your family. They shine when you cry. They burn bright when you're angry."

Grady pulled me up and turned me. I was once again straddling his lap. This time, though, I could see the passion in his eyes. His hands stroked down my body, feeling possessive, powerful, intimate.

"But my favorite is when they appear to melt when I make love to you," he whispered as he kissed down my neck and stroked my breasts. "When your eyes glisten with passion, and you looked up at me, calling my name as you come."

I held Grady's face in my hands and looked at him. I let him see it all as I lifted for him to enter me.

Chapter Thirty-Seven

"Quit it," I laughed, pushing Grady away an hour later as I tried to get out of bed. "I need to get dressed and get some work done."

"Fine. I'll see what we have around here for breakfast."

Grady tugged on some sweatpants and started walking around the corner to the kitchen area.

"Grady?"

When he glanced back at me, his grin vanished. "What's wrong?" he asked, walking back to kneel in front of me.

"The curtains? Can we open them?"

I knew in my head it was a charming log cabin, but with the dark brown log-made walls, the dark floors, and the curtains closed, it just felt—dark.

Grady didn't press me for more details, merely walked around the cabin and took all the curtain rods completely down. Bright sunlight flooded the small space. I felt my chest relax and my breathing was suddenly easier.

"Better?" he asked, piling the stack of curtains and rods in the corner.

"Much," I nodded.

"Holler if you need me," he said before walking into the kitchen.

I looked down at the ring that meant so much more to me now that it was wrapped in sapphires. I grinned, as I pulled the ring off and slid it onto my right hand. Grady wouldn't notice the difference, but Katie and Anne would get the wrong impression if it was on my left hand.

Stealing one of Grady's oversized shirts to wear, I booted up all three laptops on the coffee table in front of the couch. I could hear Grady shuffling supplies around in the kitchen. I opened a Skype line with Tech and started working.

I worked most of the day on either business strategies or researching the plantation house, but at sunset, Grady told everyone I was off the clock and closed the laptops.

"I didn't even get to say goodnight."

"It was implied," he said, pulling me off the floor where I was sitting. "Come on. We can go for a run before dinner."

As much as I disliked running, it helped to unwind, so I laced up a pair of shoes and joined Grady on the front porch to stretch.

"We following the road?" I asked.

"The woods are sparse enough to jog through," he shook his head. "There's a trail that follows up the ridge."

"Lovely," I rolled my eyes. "Incline running."

Grady took the lead, and I stayed on pace a few feet behind him. The last of the day's sunbeams blasted rays of orange and pink. We were only about a mile in when Grady slowed to a stop and reached back to pull me into him. Displayed below us, was a view of the sun setting behind a thick set of woodlands. The light shimmered and bounced around the trees, glistening off the top of the slow-moving stream that ran into the woods. I smiled, leaning into him.

"We need to get back," Grady whispered, holding me.

"Not just yet," I sighed, enjoying the moment.

"Did you bring a flashlight?"

"No. Did you?"

"No need," he grinned, turning me around and pushing me toward the trail. "I plan on being back before it gets dark. Can you keep up?" he asked, over his shoulder as he ran at a much quicker pace down the trail.

"Shit," I laughed, as I hurried to catch up.

The next few days were more of the same. Evenings and early mornings, Grady and I would spend time cooking, soaking in the tub, running the trails or spending too much time in bed. We talked for hours about his family, my family, my time as a cop, his time in the military, and the cases he was assigned to with Donovan's security company.

And during business hours we worked on research assignments and talked with everyone over Skype, whether they were in Michigan, Texas or Pittsburgh.

By Friday morning, I wasn't sure I was ready to leave.

"We can come back," Grady said, reading my mind.

"This isn't home," I said shaking my head. I moved my arms up around his shoulders, sighing when I realized that once again, Grady had moved the ring from my right hand to my left.

It had become a game between us. He'd wait until I was asleep or extremely distracted by other body parts to move it. My friends and family never questioned me about the ring, but looked every day to see which hand it was on.

"Someday you'll forget, and it will just be there," Grady chuckled.

"It's not that simple. Besides, we haven't even discussed it."

"There's nothing to discuss. When I know you're ready, I'm marrying you," Grady shrugged.

"Just like that?"

"You belong to me, you just don't know it yet," he grinned, kissing me briefly before walking over to load our bags.

"I belong to you," I snorted. "You make me sound like a horse."

"I like horses," Grady chuckled, getting behind the wheel of the SUV. "Now hurry up. We're supposed to be back before lunch."

"Good," I laughed. "I'm ready for a real meal that doesn't involve using the woodstove."

"Did you ever look in the pantry?" Grady chuckled, pulling the SUV down the drive.

"No, why?"

"There was a coffee pot and microwave stored inside," he laughed.

"Shut up! You didn't tell me?" I said, hitting him in the stomach.

"It was more fun watching you fight with the woodstove while you were having caffeine withdrawal."

"Paybacks, Grady. They are a coming."

"I look forward to it," Grady said, grabbing my hand and kissing my knuckles.

Lunch was takeout from a local Italian restaurant. I moaned through every morsel of my bruschetta chicken pasta, as everyone around me laughed.

"Didn't you feed her?" Katie asked Grady.

"She's not a big fan of peanut butter and jelly sandwiches."

"I also don't like burnt grilled cheese sandwiches."

"I did pretty well with the soup, though."

"You only had to open the can and wait for it to boil. The hot dogs I made were much better."

"So, neither of you had any real food?" Rebecca asked.

"We made do," Grady grinned, tossing a chunk of his breadstick at me.

I caught the chunk of bread and dipped it into the sauce on my plate.

"It wasn't horrible. But it was a far cry from Hattie's cooking."

"Speaking of Hattie," Katie grinned. "Did you hear Henry went back to Michigan?"

"No, she didn't mention that," I grinned. "And, Pops?"

Katie shrugged. "I have no idea what's going on. Hattie's being secretive."

"I asked Sara to spy," Anne giggled. "She was bored anyway."

"That's so wrong," Bones chuckled, shaking his head.

"It won't work," I said. "Hattie will figure out what Sara is up to in ten seconds flat."

"Of course. But Pops won't," Anne giggled.

I laughed and looked around the table. At the end of the table sat Genie and Maggie. Genie leaned in to say something to Maggie, and I noticed a bruise on her jaw.

"Genie? How'd you get that bruise?"

"That's a good one, isn't it?" she grinned. "I have a better one on my wrist."

She pulled up her sleeve to show me a handprint of a bruise wrapped around her wrist.

"What the hell?" I yelled, standing up.

"Chill, Kelsey," Maggie said, standing up and holding her hands out. "We've been in the basement gym learning some new self-defense moves."

"I still can't get out of the chokehold, but Maggie's really good," Genie grinned. "And, she can do a decent knee sweep now too. She knocked Dex on his rump last night."

Grady stood and rubbed my shoulders, easing the tension.

"Did you really think we'd let anything happen to Genie?" Katie asked.

"No, but I didn't expect to see bruises on her either," I snapped.

"I have low iron," Genie pouted.

"Which she's supposed to take supplements for," Maggie said. "But I was there the entire time, and she really didn't get hurt."

"No more skipping your pills, Genie," I ordered, before grabbing a few of the dirty plates and carrying them into the kitchen.

Grady followed me in, carrying another stack.

"Did you notice anything?" Grady asked.

"What?"

"You just carried six plates with your left arm," he grinned, nodding to the plates.

"How's that possible?" I asked, looking down at my hand

"Probably all the great sex helped your shoulder heal," he whispered before leaving me with all the dirty dishes.

Late afternoon, Grady, Bones, Dex, and Tech, dressed in their tuxes, left the townhouse to inspect the banquet hall and ensure the security equipment was functioning properly. After a light dinner, the rest of us dressed and prepared for the charity ball.

I stood facing my reflection in the mirror. The gown I was wearing was Champaign colored and had a light sprinkling of blue rhinestones at the dip of the bodice that looked like real sapphires. I was glad my ring wouldn't look out of place with the gown.

I looked down at the ring and sighed as I moved it back to my right hand.

"I have earrings and a necklace too," Bridget said from the doorway. "Top drawer of Grady's dresser."

"Why are they in Grady's dresser?"

"Because he bought them when he had your ring redesigned with the sapphires," she giggled. "That wasn't even the original dress I bought for you to wear, but after I saw the sapphires, I went shopping again."

"It's a lot of money being spent for just one night," I complained, opening up the velvet jewelry container.

The necklace and earrings both had emerald cut diamonds, surrounded by tiny sapphires. They were beautiful and elegant, and I held my breath as I slipped the necklace around my neck.

"He shouldn't have," I scolded aloud, as I tried to sniff the tears away and clear my emotions.

"He loves you," Bridget shrugged. "Are you okay with the open-back style of the dress? I wasn't sure, but Grady said you'd be fine with it."

"Grady was right," I nodded. "My scars are part of who I am. I won't hide them anymore."

"I'm glad because you look smashing," Rebecca said from the doorway. "And, Bridget, that gown you are wearing is sinfully delicious. My brother is going to be drooling all night."

"Please," Bridget said, rolling her eyes. "I'm his little buddy. He doesn't even notice me that way. But, I'll be damned if I don't turn a few other men's heads tonight."

After turning to check her ass in the red sequined gown, Bridget winked at us and skipped out of the room in five-inch heels.

"Should we tell her?" Rebecca laughed, looking down the hall.

"That Bones is into her? Hell no," I laughed. "It'll be more fun to watch it play out if we don't say anything."

"True," Rebecca laughed. "You ready?"

"I think so," I said, looking in the mirror one more time. "With the rhinestones on the dress, does it look to be a bit much with the sapphires?"

Rebecca didn't respond, so I looked back to see if she was still there. Her face was scrunched in confusion as she stared at me.

"What?" I asked.

"Those aren't rhinestones."

I looked back at the dress and the tiny stones bordering the low draping neckline. "Nooooo. He didn't."

"Oh, yes, he did," Rebecca grinned. "Something about your eyes lighting up when you realized they were real."

What should have been a nice gesture, just royally pissed me off. I threw the now empty velvet box on the bed and grabbed the designer heels that matched the dress, leaning over to strap them on.

"Bumbling idiot," I grumbled, turning to face Rebecca. "Let's go."

"Oh, I see it. Shit," Rebecca laughed, as I glared at her.

Walking past her, I led the way down the stairs where everyone was waiting.

"Her eyes can definitely outshine the sapphires when she's pissed," Rebecca called out as she followed me in.

"Yes, Luv," Alex grinned. "But waving red in front of the angry bull isn't smart. Everyone to the limo."

Alex led Rebecca out by the arm, turning back briefly to wink at me.

"You heard him," Anne said, leading the rest of the party out.

"Why are you so mad?" Katie asked.

"Because he spent a fortune on a gown and the jewelry," I answered, clenching my fists and teeth.

"And, if we thought he couldn't afford it, we would've stopped him," Katie grinned, walking out the door ahead of me.

"What do you mean?" I asked, trying to catch up.

Katie waited for me by the car door, handing me a Champaign colored clutch that matched my dress.

"Did you really think Tech and I wouldn't run a background on anyone you got close to?"

"You what?"

"Don't you dare fake indignation. Running a background would've been the first thing you would have done if the roles were reversed."

I didn't want to admit she was right, but I didn't dare deny it either. I just stood there and continued to glare at her.

"Let's just say that while Grady might not be as wealthy as you, he can easily compete with Rebecca and Dex when it comes to bank accounts," she said before she slid inside the expansive limo.

I slid in after her finding the limo full of smirking faces. I didn't continue the conversation.

"Don't forget to check inside your clutch," Bridget giggled. "I wasn't sure which lipstick to pack."

I rolled my eyes again but looked inside the clutch. Tucked in the small bag was indeed a lipstick case, along with my driver's license, a company credit card, and the tiniest one-shooter gun I'd ever seen.

"Nice lipstick," I grinned, leaning over to show Katie.

"I'm so jealous," Katie giggled.

"You two aren't really talking about lipstick," Anne said, reaching over to drag the top of the bag over so she could see inside it. "I should have known."

Chapter Thirty-Eight

I insisted being the last person to exit the limo in case a sniper was waiting nearby. A full security team escorted everyone inside in small groups, and when they were safely away, I slid to the edge of the seat. Grady grinned down at me, holding a hand out.

"I'm mad at you," I grinned, reaching for his hand.

"I figured you would be," he chuckled, pulling me up and tucking me close to him as he moved us to the entrance. Once we stepped inside, he pulled me even closer and whispered in me ear. "Tonight, when this is over, I want to see you with nothing but the shoes and jewelry."

He didn't give me a chance to recover as he moved my hand into the crook of his arm and escorted me down the extravagant hallway and into the crowded banquet room. As was the plan, everyone scattered in pairs throughout the room so as not to be seen together. Rebecca was instantly surrounded by unfamiliar faces, but as she socialized, Dex kept a watchful eye on anyone approaching.

I spotted Bridget's parents toward the front stage. I glanced around and made eye contact with Bridget. She nodded, acknowledging she saw them too, as she prodded an angry Bones in the opposite direction.

Turning back to face Grady, I was startled by someone touching my arm.

"My apologies, ma'am," a middle-aged gentleman laughed. "I didn't mean to startle you. I just thought you might have an interest in my business card. I couldn't help but notice your back."

Before I had a chance to take the card, Grady took it for me. He barely glanced at it before he ripped it into quarters.

"She doesn't need a plastic surgeon. She's perfect, just the way she is," Grady told him, stuffing the pieces of the card behind the man's pocket square.

I thought it best to tug Grady's arm in the other direction. He grudgingly followed, but placed a hand on the small of my back, against my bare skin. It felt intimate and protective, and the playfulness in his eyes returned when he noticed my reaction to his touch.

"This is going to be a long night if you keep thinking about my hands on your body," Grady whispered.

"Maybe you shouldn't touch me then," I laughed.

"Like I could stop," he said, as he stroked one finger barely under the edge of the dress.

"Behave," I laughed, turning into his body to glare up at him. "We have a job to do, and I haven't spotted Jonathan yet."

"I know where he's at," Grady whispered back. "He's on the other side of the room. Dex and Bones both have eyes on him, and Tech has a visual of the entire room. Jonathan's trying to circulate, but he's being shut out of several conversations."

"Genie?"

"Kierson and Maggie delivered her to Tech, and they have two security guards watching their backs."

"Bridget's parents? I had them in sight, but then I lost them."

"They are still near the front stage, just further to the left. Tech's telling me over the coms that Bridget's grandfather just joined them. Was he expected?"

"Yes," I nodded. "I sent him an invitation along with a note."

"He a good-guy or a bad-guy?"

"My gut is telling me he'll be on Bridget's side, but we shall see," I shrugged.

Grady grinned down at me and shook his head.

"I know," he said in answer to something over the coms.

I spotted Dex chuckling, shaking his head at me.

"Are you two making fun of me?"

"Just appreciating your scheming abilities, my love," Grady grinned.

Someone coughed, and I looked back to see Alex choking on his own laughter.

Grady guided me to the furthest wall away from the stage. "We're being ordered to move toward the back as Jonathan moves toward the center of the room."

I watched Rebecca, as hostess, escorted up the short stairs to the stage. The jazz band playing in the corner neatly ended their melody and let it fade out as she stepped up to the microphone.

"Ladies and gentlemen, thank you for coming. If you could all find your seats, we'll be beginning shortly."

Dex guided her away from the mike and turned to block her view as they discussed something in private. He obviously didn't like her exposed in the center of the stage. And, despite the social smile Rebecca presented on her face, she wasn't giving an inch into his request, as she returned to the mic.

The media invited to the event had set up on the sides of the room and were turning their cameras and lights on Rebecca. I noted one reporter continuously glancing back at me. I wasn't sure who she was, but knew she recognized me. I raised a finger to my lips with a grin on my face. She smiled and nodded in return. If she knew who I was, then she knew she had just walked into the goldmine of stories. She continued to grin as she texted someone on her cell phone, most likely warning the network to hold a spot on the late-night news for her.

Grady chuckled beside me, not missing the exchange.

"Tonight," Rebecca continued. "We are raising money for a very special cause. And, we are fortunate to have two very influential guest speakers with us to explain why this cause is so important to them. Having known the first speaker since boarding school, it gives me great pleasure to introduce Bridget Delano."

A polite round of applause followed as Bones escorted Bridget up the stairs. Her eyes danced with nervousness around the room. Tech and Katie walked out from behind the curtain to stand on one side of Bridget. Bones stood behind her with a hand lightly set on her hip. Anne walked up the far stairway and met her on her other side. Bridget grinned at each of them, tears pooling in her eyes.

Reggie walked into the ballroom with Haley on his arm and walked her up the stairs, where they parted, and Haley walked over and hugged Bridget.

"You're here?" Bridget grinned, tears sliding down her cheeks.

"Dragons spitting fire couldn't keep me away," Haley smiled. "You've got this."

Haley kissed Bridget cheek and then stepped back to her side. Bridget reached out and grabbed Haley's hand for support.

"I've rehearsed my speech a million times, but find I'm overwhelmed by the support of friends and family up on stage with me tonight. Because, you see, I didn't have that growing up. From the earliest years I can remember, I was told to sit still, be quiet, act like a young lady. Little did I know, those would be the happiest days of my childhood, which abruptly ended on my ninth birthday."

Bridget's father made a move to get up but found himself shoved back into his chair by Dex who was now standing over his left shoulder.

"On my ninth birthday, most of the wealthy families in the area were invited to witness my parents gifting me with extravagant presents, including a real live pony. It should have been the best memory of my life. And, it might have been if my father wouldn't have raped me later that night."

The quiet room erupted in shock, turning their attention back and forth between Bridget and her father.

Bridget didn't give them time to react any further before she continued with her story. "The abuse went on for years, and by the time I was thirteen, I was stealing to pay for drugs. I didn't know how to deal with the abuse, so I got high instead. And, when I was finally caught, I was immediately sent off to boarding school."

"She's lying," Bridget's father yelled out.

Bridget wiped away the tear that slipped by and laced her fingers with Haley's. "Boarding school ended up being the sanctuary I needed. For the next three years, I thrived. Making up excuses to stay at the school during the holiday breaks, I was able to stay safely away from my father."

Bridget stood up straighter, taking a deep breath. "I studied as much as possible, educating myself so I could earn a decent wage when I graduated. I made friends that taught me how to laugh. And, in time I stopped looking over my shoulder and cowering when I heard a man raise his voice. I was happy. Until Christmas break when I was sixteen. That was when my father took the liberty of surprising me at the nearly vacant dormitory, where he raped me for the last time."

I watched Bridget, chin up, tears streaming down her face, stare down her father. I wanted to run to her and stand beside her, but Grady held me firmly in place.

"Unhand me," Bridget's father demanded, shoving Dex away. "I'll not listen to any more of this. You're a liar and by your own admission a thief and a drug addict. How dare you say such insulting things? You're nothing but a whore."

Bridget's mother, glaring at Bridget, stood beside her husband.

"Security, throw that whore of a daughter out of this hall immediately," Bridget's father yelled, pointing a finger at Bridget.

"Thank you, Bridget, for sharing such a tragic story with us," Rebecca said, over the microphone. "As I already stated earlier, I went to boarding school with Bridget. I remember when the rest of us returned to school after winter break. I remember seeing the bruises on Bridget. I remember her dorm roommate gathering donations to help Bridget with a secret project. Soon after we all pooled our money, Bridget disappeared. The money was for her freedom, we had discovered. Somehow, someway, she had managed to escape a life of abuse, far away from her father."

Several guests stood and lightly clapped their support.

"Security, please escort both her parents off the grounds. They will no longer be welcome to any venue I attend."

More guests stood and clapped as Bridget's parents were escorted down the long walkway. Bridget's grandfather stepped into the middle of their path, and the guests quieted again. He was in his late seventies and used a cane that seemed to be more of a fashion statement than a walking aide. He didn't say anything. He just glared down at his son. The crowd, including myself, held our breaths.

"You can't possibly believe that whore of a girl," Bridget's father sputtered.

Bridget's grandfather didn't hesitate, slamming his fist into his son's jaw, sending him reeling backward into Dex.

Dex chuckled and shoved the man upright and toward the door.

Bridget's grandfather walked down the aisle to the stage, looking up at Bridget. She had a puzzled look on her face as she looked down at him.

"I was too busy building my wealth when you were a child," he said, shaking his head. "I didn't see it. I saw a quiet child who preferred to keep to herself, so I let you be. But when you ran away, I hired an investigator to find you. He sent me hundreds of pictures of you laughing, surrounded by strangers you adored. I had never seen you so happy." He paused to clear his throat, obviously affected by the story she had told. "I couldn't steal that joy from you. I decided to leave you be, to let you live your life. Now that I know the reason you left, I'll never forgive myself for not protecting you. For not making sure you knew you could have counted on me."

Bridget took a step, stumbling. Tech took one arm and Bones took the other. They helped her walk across the stage and down the stairs. She reached out and placed a hand on top of her grandfather's, the one resting on the cane.

"I forgive you," she grinned.

"And, that's the person your granddaughter became," Bones said calmly, but coldly. "But it won't be that easy. We're her family now. If she chooses to get to know you after all these years, it's on her terms, but she will always have one of us with her."

"Thank you for keeping her safe," her grandfather nodded at Bones, before turning back to Bridget. "I'll deal with your father. He'll never bother you again."

The old man turned and walked down the aisle, nodding at me as he passed. The room went from quiet to the sound of bees buzzing around as everyone whispered rapidly to those around them. Bones and Tech escorted Bridget to the back hall where she would wait with Tech and Genie. Rebecca cleared her throat to get the room's attention.

"Dramatic story, I know," she nodded, wiping a tear of her own away. "But a very real and all too common story. Tonight, we join together to raise money to fight child abuse. To increase funds for children services programs, private investigators and children advocate programs. To start off the donations, my grandfather has generously issued me a check for two-hundred and fifty thousand dollars. I am also matching that donation. But the money we raise will not be spent solely in the Pittsburgh area, though it's desperately needed. It will be going to a national program focused on not only abuse from within a child's home environment but at the hands of human traffickers and pedophiles. Here to tell us more about these dark atrocities, guest speaker, former Miami police officer, and a very influential investor in Barrister Industries, Ms. Kelsey Harrison."

Grady held out his arm and grinned down at me. "What is it that you girls always say?"

"Game on," I grinned up at him as he escorted me toward the front of the room.

Jonathan stood in the center of the room, looking frantically about until he spotted me. His eyes turned cold, and his fists clenched. Grady stiffened beside me, and I rested my other hand on his forearm to keep him from tearing after Jonathan.

"They said you were dead," Jonathan screamed.

Jackie reached up, placing a hand on her husband's arm, but he jerked his arm away.

Rebecca, seeing I wasn't going to make it to the stage for the showdown, handed the microphone off to Dex, who jogged it over to me.

"Oh, who, me? You thought I was dead?" I grinned, speaking into the mike. "Now, Jonathan, you should know by now that it takes a hell of a lot to kill me. Oh wait—you weren't allowed to kill me the first time. Nola ordered you to *break me*."

Grady grinned, kissed me on the cheek and took a seat in a nearby chair, turning it to face me. "Shred him, Babe."

I winked at Grady and turned back to Jonathan.

"I hear you're having a bad week, Jonathan. I'm so sorry."

My tone reeked of sarcasm, and the guests quietly chuckled around me.

"I assure you that when I secretly bought up your companies and turned them against you, I had no idea that we'd be able to steal sixty percent of your clients in under a week. I mean—that has to be a record."

The crowd laughed aloud.

"*You*!!??"

"Oh yes. I'm the one who dared go up against the great Jonathan Vaughn. See, your orders when I was kidnapped and held by Nola were to 'break me'. And, I must admit, you succeeded. I was a wreck when I escaped. I still have nightmares. But like Bridget's story, I had people in my life who protected me. They helped me cope with what you put me through."

I looked at all the loving faces moving closer to surround me. Katie and Anne walked down the stairs to stand beside me. Alex and Reggie moved from the tables in the middle of the room and stood behind Katie and Anne. Bones and Dex stood off to the side with Rebecca. Grady stood and wrapped his arm around my waist, standing behind me.

I turned back to Jonathan and grinned. "And then, they helped me destroy you."

"The FBI raid?" he glared.

Kierson and Maggie moved out from the back wall and stood at the end of the aisle.

"Oh, I might have tipped them off," I nodded. "Of course, let's not forget all the times the media was in the right place at the wrong time this week either."

"Don't forget the personal jet," Mr. Stykes said, standing a few tables away.

"Or faking your death, so he had to pay the hitman," Bones laughed.

"She took all his best employees too," Katie grinned.

"You're insane," Jonathan yelled. "I'll bury you. Do you know what I can do? You'll wish you were never born."

"Been there, done that," I shrugged. "And, believe me, as long as I live, I will never forget what you are capable of."

I turned toward the stage, looking for someone I knew I couldn't see, but who always had my back. "Tech, please start the first slides."

Three large screens on stage lit up, showing the smiling faces of the women Jonathan had murdered.

"Do you remember them, Jonathan? Do you even know their names?"

Jonathan looked at the pictures displayed and started backing up. "You can't prove anything. It's all lies," he yelled, looking frantically around the room, grabbing his wife by the arm to drag her with him.

"Let her go," Bridget yelled, rushing to help Jackie.

Bones and Dex were already in motion to get closer to Bridget.

"Take your hands off her," Bridget glared.

"Let go," Jackie cried, knocking his grip away and huddling toward Bridget. "My kids," she cried.

"They're safe. We have security sitting near your house. He can't get to them," Bridget said, guiding her away from her husband and behind Dex and Bones.

"You weren't leaving, Jonathan, were you?" I grinned. "I never took you for a coward."

Someone brawked like a chicken, and several people laughed.

"And, we have serious things to discuss here. Like Pam Tate," I said, pointing at the first picture. "Twenty-two-year-old college student. Do you remember her? You should. You cut her to pieces right in front of me. You let that poor girl slowly and painfully bleed to death."

"Lies! All of it!"

"How about Karen Pierson?" I said, pointing to the next photo. "You sat in a nearby chair and whistled happy tunes as she screamed for help."

I stepped out of Grady's embrace, needing to face Jonathon alone. My skin was hot with anger as I glared at him.

"No?" I yelled. "You don't remember her? Let's try the third picture. Leslie Davis, eighteen years old and engaged to marry her high school sweetheart. I later found out Leslie had been pregnant. Her parents told me about the pregnancy when I told them that their daughter was savagely murdered. I promised them I would find a way to destroy her murderer. I made that promise to all their loved ones. Including the parents of Alandra. I know you remember Alandra."

All three screens changed to the smiling face of the sweet innocent girl in her fluffy pink party dress. The guests around the room shrieked and swore. Several of the women were openly crying.

"The mental and physical torture you put that little girl through," I said shaking my head, lowering the microphone. I no longer needed it. The crowd listened intently to my every word. "I can't get it out of my head. I hear her screams. I feel her little hands, clutching my leg. I was unable to move! I was unable to fight for her!"

Grady's arms wrapped around me, holding me close, offering me his strength. I wiped my tears and nodded to him that I was okay. He lightly kissed my shoulder.

I turned back to Jonathan.

"Jonathan Vaughn, may you burn in hell for what you did to that little girl."

Jonathan stood silently glaring at me. He moved to step forward, and as one, my friends and family moved closer to me to offer their protection. Jonathan spared them only a brief glance before he turned his glare back to me, his eyes burning black with hate, his lips turned into an evil grin.

Kierson, followed by Maggie, started walking down the aisle toward Jonathan.

"Jonathan Vaughn, you are being taken into FBI custody for questioning in the murders of Pam Tate, Karen Pierson, Leslie Davis and Alandra Jackson," Kierson said as he approached.

Jonathan's grin expanded, and before I had time to warn anyone, he bolted toward the service hallway.

"Security!" Grady yelled, joining Kierson to chase after Jonathan.

I moved my friends and family to the sidewall and assigned security guards to watch over them as the rest of the security team scattered to catch Jonathan. I ordered two FBI agents to accompany Jackie to her house to pick up her children, just as a precaution in case he got away.

The guests, having had enough excitement for one night, quickly vacated the venue, most of them dropping checks or cash into the donation box on their way out the door. You could see the fear in their eyes. They had discovered that the monsters of the world were much closer than they had ever realized.

Chapter Thirty-Nine

It seemed like forever before anyone from the security team returned. The first to return were some of Donovan's men that I recognized, but didn't know personally. Finally, Kierson, Grady, and Bones walked back into the banquet hall.

"No!!" I screamed. "NO!! You have to find him!"

Grady jogged over to me as Katie and Anne wrapped their arms around me. My body shook violently as my knees gave out. Grady held my weight in his arms as I leaned my head into his shoulder.

"Grady," I cried. "He can't have his freedom. He'll hurt someone. He'll come after us."

"We'll catch him," Grady said, stroking my back. "But until we do, we need to move everyone back to the townhouse."

I nodded into his shoulder before pushing away from him. He stepped toward me again and held my face. "Tech and Genie are searching all the videos and trying to get a bead on him. We've already alerted the local police. We'll get him."

I pushed away from him. Katie and Anne both reached for me, but I turned and stepped away. I walked to the center of the room and began pacing back and forth. He had escaped. He had slipped right through our security and was free. He'd come after everyone I cared about. I had put them all in danger.

Grabbing the edge of a round table, rage fueled my muscles as I tipped it up and over, shattering the plates and glasses. The chair remaining upright in front of me taunted me with its presence. Picking it up, I slammed it across the top of the next table. Glasses flew off the table, throwing shards of glass all around me.

I tried to pull a breath as my blood continued to boil and my lungs frosted over. Evil thoughts fueled my rage. I thought of all the things I would do to Jonathan when I tracked him down. Because whether I spent my life in prison or not, I was going to kill Jonathan Vaughn once and for all.

"Stop it," Grady said, pinning my arms to my body with his own. "We'll get him. I promise you, I'll get the bastard."

"Grady—,"

"I know," Grady said, leaning in and forcing me to look at him. "Let's get everyone somewhere safe first."

I stared up at him, my body still fighting the tremors.

"Kelsey, you're not alone. I'm right here. Are you with me?"

I continued to stare at him, unable to speak.

"Your family isn't safe here," Grady yelled inches from my face. "Do you understand?"

I nodded.

Grady was right. I needed to ensure my family's safety first.

"Katie, book flights out immediately. All of you are going straight to the airport. I want everyone in Texas tonight. No arguments. Full lockdown until I track the bastard down."

Katie nodded, tears streaming down her face. She pulled her phone out of her clutch to call, but her hands were shaking too hard. Anne took the phone from her and called the airline.

"I need your com," I ordered one of Donovan's men.

He hesitated for only a split second before he removed it and handed it over.

"Tech, do you have anything?" I asked after placing it in my ear.

I looked around the room. Everyone stood waiting for an action plan. Even Kierson was looking to me to find a way out of this mess.

"No, not yet," Tech said. "We are looking at the footage of the vehicles leaving the area, trying to see if we can spot him driving someone's vehicle or forcing a ride."

"Smart. Jonathan wouldn't hesitate to take a hostage and jack a car," I nodded turning to pace again.

I was mid-step when my body froze, chills racing from head to toe. I turned to look at Kierson. I missed it. How did I not see this? I looked frantically around, hoping I was wrong. But she wasn't there. She never returned to the banquet room.

"Oh, my God." I cried.

"What is it?" Grady asked, looking frantically around while grasping my hand.

"Tech! Find Maggie! I think he took Maggie!"

"Search the premises for Agent Maggie O'Donnell!" Kierson yelled as he ran from the banquet room with several other agents.

"Kelsey," Grady said, stepping into my space. "I'm here."

He gently ran his fingers over my cheek, wiping away my tears.

I stepped back away from Grady. I looked at my friends and family and took another step back.

"Don't you get it?" I laughed humorlessly, shaking my head. "People get hurt when they're near me. None of you are safe because of *me*!!"

Hours later I paced alone in the confines of Dex's townhouse. I had two security guards at the front door and two more in the back yard. It had been deemed too dangerous for me to go looking for Jonathan and Maggie.

My family, still dressed in their gowns and tuxes, boarded a private jet to fly to the safety of Texas. Donovan was flying out with Lisa and Abigail as an extra precaution as well. Carl was moved to the safety of the clubhouse where the Devil's Players would protect him.

Everyone else was out breaking down doors trying to find Maggie. I knew better than anyone, what would happen to her if they failed.

I tried to clear the hatred, the rage blocking my ability to think logically, but it was like a dark fog that I couldn't lift. My pacing only increased in speed as the clock ticked off the seconds, minutes, hours. By the time Grady and

Dex returned to tell me they were running out of leads to follow, I had bitten my nails until they were bloody. I kept pacing.

Grady made me a cup of coffee and passed it to me. I made sure not to touch him when I took the cup. He sighed but didn't push the issue. I had warned him that I couldn't live with the guilt if something happened to someone I cared about. I had warned him of what it would do to me.

I sipped the coffee, not even caring that it tasted bitter on my tongue. I resumed my pacing and made it five more laps across the living room before I realized my mistake.

I turned to Grady as the cup slipped through my hand.

"I'm sorry, Kel," Grady said, running to catch me before I fell. "I can't lose you."

Grady had drugged my coffee.

Chapter Forty

I woke abruptly with a screaming headache, only enhanced by the sound of a gun being shot nearby.

"I'm not fucking around!" Tech yelled. "Stay away from the door!"

Laying on the couch in the den, I sat up to see Tech was holding a gun, pointed at the den door.

"Did you just shoot at someone?" I asked, holding my head in my hands.

"They deserved it," Genie said, slamming away on her keyboard on the other side of the table from Tech. "He's warned them several times. That's the third time he's shot at them. Unfortunately, he's aiming too low."

"Who's out there?"

"Grady, Bones, and Dex," Tech grinned, setting the gun down. "Welcome back. We stocked some thermoses before we kidnapped you and moved you to the den. There's plenty of untainted coffee to help wake you up."

"But do it quick. We need your help," Genie ordered. "I'm down a profiler. The dumbass the FBI sent in is worthless. Help us, Kelsey. You know Jonathan better than anyone."

I stood on wobbly legs and moved to the cups and thermos, pouring myself a cup.

I heard someone at the door, and Tech picked up the gun again. I held a hand to stop him.

"I'm awake, fuckers. And, unlike Tech, I won't be aiming for your damn toes if you try to breach that door. Go find Maggie."

"Are you okay?" Grady yelled.

"I'm fine. Just leave me alone. I mean it, Grady."

I heard three loud sighs before I heard them shuffle away.

"Would you really shoot them?" Tech whispered.

"I have a screaming headache from whatever they used to drug me. I'm likely to shoot anyone who pisses me off at the moment." I went to sip my coffee but looked at it uncertainly.

"It's safe. I've been drinking it for hours," Genie grinned.

"How long have I been out?" I asked, slurping down a healthy dose.

Neither of them answered as they continued working on their laptops.

"I need a timeline. How long has it been since Maggie disappeared?"

"Eighteen hours," Genie answered, wiping the steady stream of tears away as she focused on her work.

"Shit," I said, trying to draw in a ragged breath.

Maggie needed me. I had to focus. I had to work this like any other case.

"Did we get any hits on Maggie's SUV?"

"It was found abandoned outside of the city. It looks like he may have had another car in storage, but we don't know any of the details on the vehicle."

"Tech, pull up a map. I need a visual."

The TV screen lit up with a map showing a line from the banquet hall to the location the SUV was found. Several major highways intersected nearby.

"Expand the map."

I followed the highways with my eyes as Tech continued to expand the map.

"Stop."

"Please tell me you know where she is," Genie begged.

"Did the plantation house get searched?" I asked.

Genie sighed and nodded.

"They turned the place upside down and then stationed Feds down the road. No one has seen anyone coming or going from the house," Tech said.

"They're wrong," I said, barreling out of the room and startling Dex, Bones, and Grady. "Will you trust me?" I asked Grady. "Even if I sound 100% crazy, will you trust me enough to help me?"

"Always," Grady said without hesitation.

"Then gear up. Dex, call Kierson. I need the FBI to fly us to New Orleans. Let him know we'll be armed."

Dex scrambled for his phone as Bones and Grady jogged off to gather our gear.

"Kelsey?" Genie said, from behind me.

"I'll get her back Genie. I'm going to find Maggie," I said, as I held her shoulders and looked at her.

"I believe you," she nodded. "But might I suggest putting on some pants first? The FBI isn't going to appreciate your outfit."

I looked down and realized I was wearing only a t-shirt and underwear. I laughed and jogged up the stairs, to throw on some clothes. When I returned, everyone was ready with our gear, and we moved out to the SUV parked at the curb.

I called Nightcrawler on the way to the airport.

"You still in New Orleans?" I asked when he answered.

"Yes. I heard about Maggie. What do you need?"

"Head out to the plantation house, but keep a low profile. The Feds are sitting down the road. I'll be there in a couple hours."

"You think she's there?"

"I think he has warning systems set up to alert him if someone gets too close. He'll kill her before he flees again. So, don't get too close, hear me?"

"Copy. I'll wait by the crypt," Nightcrawler said before hanging up.

"Is that why you didn't let me tell Kierson anything other than our destination?" Dex asked.

"Jonathan's devious. He has layers upon layers of plans. He knew the layout of the banquet hall and most likely had hired thugs ready to help him escape. He's known his whole life that one day, someone would come after him. He's been ready for the chase for a long time."

"How will you get to her then? Before he kills her?" Genie asked.

"By not setting off any of his traps," I said, shifting closer to Grady so he could help me strap on a shoulder hoist for my Glock.

"What if you're wrong?" Dex asked.

"If you've got another lead to chase down, we can pull over right now and let you out," I said, not bothering to look up as I checked my gun clip.

"We've got nothing," Bones sighed. "Grady's been kicking himself for hours about drugging you. We need you to do your witchy-woo shit and channel this guy."

"Well, Grady and I will be having a serious conversation and setting up a new rule about not drugging each other," I said, glaring over at Grady, "But I have to admit I'm thinking a lot clearer after my mandatory nap."

"It was only supposed to knock you out for an hour or two," Grady sighed.

"I don't react well to sedatives," I glared. "Let's just not experiment again, shall we?"

Grady nodded, trying to hide his smirk.

I shook my head. It was pointless to fight about it. I understood why he did it, but we both know we lost precious time we couldn't afford to lose. "Let's just concentrate on getting inside the house quickly, quietly, and without setting off any of the traps. Maggie's there, I can feel it."

"What's the plan?" Grady asked, transitioning into mission mode which was where both our heads needed to be.

"Tech, Genie, and Kierson will stay in the vehicle on the back side of the property. We won't alert the local Feds we are there. The rest of us will travel by foot to meet up with Nightcrawler. Dex and Bones will stay on the perimeter as lookouts and you, Nightcrawler and I will move in."

"Why Nightcrawler and not one of us?" Bones asked, pointing between him and Dex.

"Because Nightcrawler will follow Kelsey's directions right down to crossing the T," Grady nodded. "You two would actually be a liability because you were trained to move first. If Jonathan has traps rigged for alarms or worse, bombs, every small step is going to matter."

"And Grady is almost as good as I am at sensing traps. Thus he's the other one going in," I nodded.

"Almost?" Grady grinned over at me.

"We'll re-evaluate after this OP," I smirked. "Tech, once we get into position, I need you to switch us off from joint coms with Kierson and his team. You, Genie, and those of us on the ground will be the only ones listening. This won't work if we follow regulations. Genie, to protect yourself, pretend you can't hear us when Tech switches us over."

"Kierson is going to flip," Genie grinned. "But I'm down for whatever works to pull Maggie out. I want my friend safe."

We all nodded as we pulled up to the waiting jet.

"It's a two-and-a-half-hour flight. Prepare best you can, and pray for the rest," I said, before sliding out of the car.

Chapter Forty-One

"It's me, don't shoot," I whispered into the blackness as I approached Nightcrawler.

"About time," Nightcrawler grumbled, stepping away from the crypt and into the tree line. "I haven't heard or seen anything since you called. You sure she's in there?"

"I'm sure. I can't prove it, but I'm sure," I nodded.

Bones handed over a flak jacket and holsters to Nightcrawler and Grady helped him suit up.

"You good with going in with Grady and me? The place will have traps, and I can't promise we'll come out of it alive," I said.

"I've got nothing better to do tonight," Nightcrawler grinned.

"If you take one step without clearing it with Kelsey or me, you could get us killed, and the bad guy will know we're here," Grady said.

"Got it," Nightcrawler said. "Life and death version of Simon Says."

"Dex and Bones, stay inside the tree line," I said. "Let us know if there's any movement, but watch the perimeter. If for some reason, he's not here yet, I don't want him sneaking in behind us."

They both silently moved further into the trees in opposite directions. I handed Nightcrawler a com.

"Tech, switch our coms," Grady ordered.

"Wait—," I heard Kierson argue before a click switched in my ear.

"You're now on unregulated coms," Tech laughed. "Genie's trying to calm Kierson down, but she might have to get her cuffs out."

"Grady, are we ready?"

"Pliers and wire cutters are on your utility belt next to your lock-pick gear. I've got bolt cutters and a leverage bar. Guns loaded, safeties off. Mini-mag lights on both side of everyone's utility belt. What about night-vision goggles?"

"No, too risky," I answered. "We'll need to be able to identify any foreign light and to shoot if we are surprised. The goggles will distort everything and blind us if we walk into a lit room."

"Then we're ready when you are. Nightcrawler, stay focused on our voices over the coms and move silently behind us," Grady ordered stepping out of the tree line.

I led the way diagonally toward the side yard near the back of the house. As I approached, I scouted the ground for anything foreign.

"Bingo," I whispered barely louder than my breathing. "Fake rock straight ahead. Move one step to the right."

"Damn, good eye, Babe," Grady said as we moved around the first trap.

"Grady, I suspect the stairs are wired, but only some of them. He would want to be able to travel up and down them without setting off the alarm."

Grady squatted low and used a small mag lite to shine under the boards.

"First two steps and the top landing are clear. The third step has a sensor."

I moved up the stairs, skipping the third step and approached the door. Sliding a probe under the door, I looked on the screen to see into the room on the other side. Nothing appeared to be directly attached to the door, so I pulled the probe back and passed it to Grady. Taking my lock-pick kit out, I released the throw on the deadbolt.

"Wait," Grady said when I went to open the door. "Could have rusty hinges."

He passed me a mini can of WD-40, and I sprayed the hinges down. I doubted Jonathan would be able to hear the door even if it did squeak, but every precaution we took helped us get closer to Maggie. I passed the spray back and pulled the door open slowly. Glancing in, no one was in sight. The clock on the stove was back-lit but didn't offer enough illumination to see across the room. I didn't have a choice but to turn on a mag light to have a better look before stepping inside.

I moved the flashlight up and down each wall in slow motion around the room. When I had a good visual, I stepped forward.

"Stay on this side of the kitchen. There's a motion sensor at the other end."

Grady and Nightcrawler moved in behind me.

"You want me to try to disarm it or will we crawl under it?" Grady asked.

"Neither," I shook my head grinning as I used my light to search the open pantry shelf beside me. "He didn't realize it when he installed it, but it's a clue. He wouldn't set up sensors in areas of the house he uses. There must be another door hidden behind this pantry shelf."

Grady helped me search the pantry. We found the release, but we continued searching, looking for trip wires or alarms. The release was a manual release, not electronic. We couldn't find any wires attached anywhere.

"It looks clear," Grady shrugged.

"WD40," Nightcrawler whispered.

"Good call, brother," Grady nodded before reaching around and spraying the hinges. "Kelsey, what are we going to find when we open this?"

"I'm guessing stairs leading down. The stairs will be rigged, but we won't be able to look underneath them to see which ones are safe. I'll check the rails and the side risers, and if they look clear, I'll head down first. If I can get to the bottom without setting off an alarm, I'll see if I can identify where the traps are and let you guys know."

"That's the first thing you've said all day I don't like," Grady grumbled.

"It's the safest move," I shrugged. "If it will make you feel better, I'll let you be the one to open the door we are hoping like hell isn't rigged to explode."

Grady quietly snorted and flipped the manual release, pulling the door open.

I searched the doorway, before crouching down and inspecting the rails, risers, and treads. The risers and rails appeared clear, so stepping over the landing, I placed one foot carefully on the angled riser before shifting my weight, so my other foot moved to the other side. I gripped the railing tight, hoping I wouldn't slide downward and that the treads on my shoes would allow me to control my movements.

"Breathe, Babe," Grady whispered. "Nice and steady."

I moved one foot forward a few inches and then the other. I slowly descended into the darkness, not a speck of light to be seen around me, while keeping my feet on the outside risers.

I felt the chilled air, and musty scent of the lower level, before I reached the bottom.

"Grady?" I whispered.

"Yeah, I was afraid of that," Grady sighed. "Just breathe. You're not alone. Nightcrawler and I will jump down the entire stairway if you say the word."

I nodded into the dark before I realized he couldn't see me. "Keep talking," I whispered, stopping myself near the bottom of the stairs, to pull my mag light and look for sensors. "Tripwire on the bottom step. I don't see any other motion sensors, so I'm stepping off onto the floor.

"Just go slow," Grady ordered. "When you step off, stop and re-evaluate again."

I released a huge breath when both feet were firmly on the rough cement flooring. Sweeping my flashlight in a circle around me, I first checked the flooring before moving behind the stairs to inspect the underside of the steps.

"The landing is clear, but the second step and the last step are rigged. Both appear to be only motion sensors."

"Copy," Nightcrawler whispered.

Grady was the first to reach the bottom, and he reached out to tilt my head up. He was making sure I was okay.

"Mission mode," I nodded.

"If being down here starts to bother you, you tell us."

"I've got it contained at the moment."

Nightcrawler joined us at the base of the stairs.

"Now what?" Nightcrawler asked as we used our flashlights to scan the room.

I was inspecting a large woodstove at the bottom of the stairs. It was cold to the touch but large enough to heat an area fifty times the size of this room. I followed the vents, many of them branching off into different directions to the rooms above us. Three more vents split off and led along the ceiling into dark passages on three different sides of the room. I swept my light slowly over each entrance.

"This one," Nightcrawler pointed.

"Nicely done," I told him as I moved over to the door on the north end.

"What did I miss?" Grady asked.

"Cobwebs," Nightcrawler answered. "It's the only entrance without cobwebs streamed across the opening."

I carefully inspected the muddy cement floor, the cold stone walls, and the cobweb covered ceilings as I led us down the passageway.

"Don't touch the walls," Grady warned.

"I hear something," I warned.

We all froze in silence. When the sound came again, I leaned over, trying to force myself to breathe.

"Stay focused. We save her by not letting him see us coming," Grady said, rubbing my back.

"That was Maggie, wasn't it? She was screaming," Nightcrawler whispered. "It sounded so far away."

"I think she's closer than you think," Grady said, shining his light up ahead. "There's a motion sensor up ahead."

I looked up to see where he held his light. He was right, the sensor blocked the path. I turned my light back up to the ceiling to look at the vent running between the stone wall and the ceiling. Leaning into the wall, I looked directly up.

"The vent splits off through the stone. He's heating an area on the other side of this stone wall."

"Another secret door?" Grady asked, inspecting the wall.

"Not a secret for much longer," I answered, no longer whispering. "We move in, guns out, as soon as this door opens. If you have a shot, you take it."

I dropped my mag light to the floor and pulled my Glock. The safety was already off. I counted to three and hit the hidden release.

The door gave, and Grady reached over my shoulder to force it open as I walked through it into the brightly lit room.

"Jonathan, let her go," I shouted across the room, never taking my gun sight off his forehead.

He was standing behind Maggie, leaning over her with a knife to her throat. Using the knife in a choke hold, he wrapped his other arm around her waist and pulled her upright for better coverage.

"Shoot him," Maggie cried, barely able to stand.

"I thought Dex and Bones trained you better, Maggie," I said clearly, still focused on my target.

Maggie pivoted her head toward Jonathan's elbow, and I pulled the trigger.

As Jonathan's body fell heavy to the rough concrete floor, I moved forward, gun still aimed at him even though I knew the head shot had killed him. I stared down, seeing his eyes cloud over into death. Too peaceful, I thought. I fired three more rounds into his chest. I watched, but nothing happened. I felt empty and cold, lost in the moment until Grady reached forward and took my Glock from me.

"He's dead. It's over," Grady nodded. "But we have to help Maggie now."

Nightcrawler had moved past me and gathered Maggie's naked, bruised, cut-up body in his arms. She was unconscious. Grady stripped his flak jacket and removed his shirt. He passed both to Nightcrawler.

"Tech, we need medical," I called out over the coms. "Have them meet us at the crypt."

"Copy. How is she?" he asked.

"The bastard hurt her, Tech. But she's alive."

"Sending in medical," Genie said over the coms, followed by sniffling. "Thank you, Kelsey. I knew you could save her."

"She'd have done the same for any of us, Genie."

Nightcrawler lifted Maggie to carry her out. I took the lead, reminding him where to step and Grady took the rear as we retreated much quicker than we entered.

Chapter Forty-Two

Kierson stepped out of the ICU security doors. We all stood, anxious for an update on Maggie.

"She wants to see Kelsey," Kierson said, placing a hand on my shoulder and leading me past the double doors and down the hall.

Slipping into the room as Kierson remained outside the door, Maggie jerked in fear and pulled the blanket closer to her until she realized it was me. A dark bruise covered one side of her face and her eyes were red from crying. I knew under the blanket she hid the cuts from Jonathan's blade.

"It's not your fault," Maggie said.

"Shit, Maggie. This is all my fault." I placed my hand on top of hers, but when she jerked away, I moved to the end of the bed to give her space. "I should've just killed him."

"You did. When the time was right, you pulled the trigger."

"You know what I mean."

"It wasn't your fault he got away," she said shaking her head. "Your plan went off without a hitch. The security team and the FBI botched covering all the exits. And, then when I saw him, I went after him alone. That's on me."

"He wasn't supposed to hurt anyone else." I raised my hand over my eyes, trying to hide the tears that threatened. "Maggie, I'm so sorry. I know how scared you were because I've been there. I've been in a dark dungeon with that madman."

"I'm not as strong as you, Kelsey. I know now, I couldn't have survived him torturing me for months. Hell, he had me for a day and I feel like crawling out of my own skin." She wiped the tears flowing freely down her cheeks.

"What do you need?" I asked.

"I don't know," Maggie said, shaking her head. "I don't want to see anyone. But, I don't want to be alone either. I'm so damn scared."

"I have a safe house near Atlanta. Nightcrawler took me there after I escaped. I can take you there and stay with you."

"You need to be with your family. And, I need you to take care of Genie. She won't understand why I can't see her."

"Then let Nightcrawler take you. He can keep you safe and help you get on your feet again."

"I can't ask him to do that."

"But I can. And, he'll do it. I know he will."

"Are you sure?"

I nodded. "I'll set it up."

Maggie curled onto her side and pulled the covers up. She cried quietly into her pillow as I slipped out the door.

Grady's arms wrapped around me as soon as I was near the waiting area. I folded into him, absorbing the warmth of his body.

"How is she? Can I see her?" Genie asked.

I shook my head no, pushing away from Grady to talk to her.

"Remember how jumpy I was after what happened to me?"

Genie nodded, her lower lip trembling.

"Physically, she's going to be fine. But mentally she needs some time. She needs some distance."

"But who will take care of her?" Genie asked.

"I'm hoping Nightcrawler will," I answered, turning to look at Nightcrawler.

"For as long as she needs," he nodded. "I'll get her to the safe house as soon as she's discharged."

"Here," Grady said, pulling out a wad of cash from his wallet. "We'll get you more money, but whatever she needs, just let us know."

Nightcrawler took the cash and looked at me.

I nodded, tears slipping past my emotional shields. "Take care of her."

Grady turned me into his chest, burying my face in his shoulder. He moved us to a corner chair in the waiting room. Everyone else followed us in.

"I don't understand why she doesn't want to see me," Genie said, tears streaming down her face.

"She can't," I said. "She can't put on a brave face for everyone right now. Her brain is spinning, and she needs to process what happened. You have to give her time."

"How much time?" Genie asked.

"As much as she needs," I answered, reaching out and grabbing her hand. "She's strong. She's a fighter. And, until she's ready to come home, Nightcrawler will stay with her and keep her safe."

• • •

"She'll never blame you," Genie said, squeezing my hand. "We all botched the OP in Pittsburgh, including Maggie. She shouldn't have chased after him alone. We should've had better surveillance in the parking lot and every exit covered. The mistakes are on all of us."

I nodded at Genie. I knew Maggie would never blame me for what happened, but I blamed myself. I turned to Tech, trying to smile.

"Flight to Texas?" he grinned.

I nodded again. "Genie, what were your plans for your three-week vacation?"

"I didn't have any," she shrugged.

"Come with us," I nudged her.

"You sure? Should you call and ask first?"

"I think it's a little late to ask. I've already moved half of Southwest Michigan to the ranches," I grinned.

"Alright then," she nodded. "Think we'll find me a cute cowboy?"

"I'll text Jackson and see if he can wrangle someone up for you," Tech grinned.

"Kierson? You want to join us?" I asked.

"No," Kierson said shaking his head. "I have to get back to the plantation and tie up some loose ends. I'll call in a couple days and maybe catch up with everyone."

"Have your lab techs check the basement woodstove," I sighed.

"For what?" Kierson asked.

"DNA."

"He cremated the bodies?" Grady asked.

"I think so," I nodded. "The door on the woodstove was unusually large. And it looked like the woodstove had been used regularly even though it's summer."

"It's a good thing you killed that fucker," Kierson grumbled, walking out of the room.

We arrived at the ranches well after dark. Every muscle in my body hurt as I walked up Pops' porch steps. Grady walked beside me looking just as rough. Genie was the only one wide awake, bubbling with energy as she 'oohed' and 'aahed' all the ranch critters and the big veranda porch. I led the way into Pops' house, not entirely surprised to find the house packed.

Everyone silently watched us enter.

"Tech?"

"Yeah."

"Did you forget to tell everyone we rescued Maggie?"

"Oh, shit," he laughed.

Loud cheers went out, and hugs were exchanged. I maneuvered through the affection in the general direction of the couch, finding my son sitting in my favorite spot waiting for me. I landed with a thump beside him and pulled him up onto my lap.

"I missed you," I whispered, kissing his head and hugging him close.

Grady thumped down on the couch beside us, and I leaned into his large frame.

"Aunt Kelsey?" Sara asked, walking over to us.

"Yeah, Little Bug?"

"Is it over?" Sara asked, climbing up onto Grady's lap.

"It's over, Sara," I nodded. "We can go home now."

Even with a packed room of rowdy people, I drifted off to sleep with Grady's arm around me, my own arms wrapped around my son.

I woke to someone trying to crawl over me. I looked up to see Grady was trying to climb out behind me on the couch to get up.

"What time is it?" I asked, pulling the afghan back up over my shoulder.

"Near lunchtime according to my stomach and the smell of whatever Hattie has cooking," Grady grinned, kissing me on the forehead. "We slept half of the day away."

"Where is everyone?"

"Either outside or at Reggie's," Charlie answered for him, as she stormed into the room.

She was livid. I wasn't sure why she was so angry but decided I better sit up and prepare myself. Grady finished standing and stood with his arms crossed and a worried look on his face.

"What the hell is this shit?" Charlie yelled, tossing a pile of folders at me.

I looked down at the scattered documents. They were my files on our grandparents' deaths.

"You snooped in my bags?" Grady snapped, seeming quite pissed off.

"Anne and I were pulling out dirty laundry, and these were at the bottom."

"You need to stay out of my shit," Grady growled, gathering up the documents.

I paused his hands, by placing my own over his. I pulled the documents away and picked up the flash drive that had fallen to the floor.

"Where are the kids?" I asked, stacking everything on the coffee table.

"Out in the barn with Wild Card and Pops," Charlie glared down at me.

I nodded and looked up at Grady.

He was still pissed, but he nodded he understood and went out to keep an eye on them.

"You knew all this time our parents were responsible for the car accident, and you did nothing?" she yelled.

"Oh, I did something," I chuckled humorlessly.

"What the hell does that mean?"

"I used their death to secure your freedom. And, I prostituted myself for your protection," I answered.

I stood, grabbed her hand, turning it over, and set the flash drive in her palm.

"After you are done watching this, I want it destroyed. I'm trusting you to do that. You can do whatever you want with the rest of the information. It's your decision. But the flash drive is a nightmare I can't relive again."

I walked away, down the hall, and out the front door.

Hattie sat in one of the old rocking chairs at the end of the large veranda.

"Mind if I join you?" I asked as I walked toward her.

"That would be lovely, Sunshine," she grinned.

I sat, looking out across the yard where Sara and Nicholas were running in circles, in and around Pops, Whiskey, Wild Card and Grady. Grady looked back at me, crooking an eyebrow. I nodded all was well.

"He's a good man," Hattie grinned.

"Pops? Or, Grady?" I grinned back.

"Both, I suppose," she laughed.

"Did you talk to Henry?"

"I did. He seemed a bit miffed but wished me well before he left."

"Now what?" I asked.

"Nothing," she sighed. "My home is with you and the others. You're my family."

"So, you're not even going to give Pops a chance?"

"What's the point? He lives here, and I belong there."

"Michigan is my home now, I can't deny that," I sighed. "But, I also need Texas. I need to stay connected with my family here too. I want to build a cabin on the land I own so I can come back every winter and stay a month."

"Really? What about the store?"

"I'm not going to keep working at the store. I'll turn it over to Alex, Katie, Anne and Lisa. It will be theirs to run, and they can slowly buy me out."

"What will you do?"

"Anything? Nothing? Who knows," I shrugged. "I'm going to spend some time with my son, and I'll figure the rest out later."

The front screen door opened and Charlie stepped out carrying the folders. She paused but didn't look at me. She dropped the flash drive to the porch floor and stomped on it with the heel of her boot. A tear dripped off her chin. Still not willing to look up at me, she descended the stairs. She went to her SUV, climbed in, and drove away.

"What was that all about?" Hattie asked.

"The last of my secrets," I answered, staring at the smashed flash drive.

After lunch, Grady suggested we all go for a swim. Everyone changed and followed the path to the small lake about a half mile back from the house. Grady held one of my hands while Nicholas held the other on the long walk.

"Mom? Can we stay in Texas?" Nicholas asked.

"No, Nick," I said, shaking my head. "We live in Michigan now. But, we can visit every winter. Can you live with that?"

"Ok," Nicholas sighed. "Is Grady going with us?"

"You couldn't get rid of me if you tried," Grady grinned, releasing my hand so he could swing Nick up onto his shoulders.

Nicholas laughed as he laced his fingers together under Grady's chin so he could hold on. Sara ran over giggling, and grabbed my hand, swinging my arm back and forth.

Hattie had been walking alongside Pops up ahead, and he stopped her and moved her off the main path as we all continued on. She was wringing her hands and glanced over at me. Pops shook his head no at me and then turned in front of Hattie to block her exit.

I knew Pops would never hurt her. Quite the opposite in fact. He'd take a hundred bullets before he allowed her to get hurt. I kept walking, glancing back only once more to see Pops reach up and wipe a tear from her cheek.

"She ok?" Anne asked, jogging up to the other side of Sara.

"They need to talk," I nodded. "Pops will make sure Hattie doesn't leave until everything that needs to be said is said."

"And, what about you?" Anne asked, glancing over at Grady and then back to me.

I laughed and looked over at Grady.

"She's going to marry me, she just doesn't know it yet," Grady chuckled. "Until then, we'll be living in sin at the main house in Michigan."

Anne and Sara both grinned.

"The house is going to be like a Saturday potluck party every day," Sara said.

"It is going to be a bit packed," Anne laughed. "We can move Carl up to Katie's old room, and then Nicholas can have the other downstairs bedroom."

"It will be fine, for a while," I grinned. "We can always build a few more houses on our street so we can branch out a bit as our family grows."

Approaching the edge of the lake, Genie ran past us, tossing her towel in the grass, throwing her heavy dark rimmed spectacles on top of the towel, followed by dropping her cover-up next to the pile. Wearing nothing but a tiny tie-string white bikini set, she splashed her way directly into the water, spraying everyone close by.

"Damn," Wild Card groaned, watching her tight body glide into the water.

Grady set Nicholas on the ground, turning his back to the water.

"It's like lusting over your kid sister," Grady chuckled, shaking his head.

"She's 100% an adult," Wild Card laughed. "Both legally and physically."

Wild Card shucked off his shoes and shirt in record time and joined Genie in the water.

"It's a good thing there's another body I'd rather see," Grady grinned down at me, pulling my long t-shirt up over my head while he kicked off his shoes.

I laughed as I reached up and dragged his t-shirt up over his head, tossing it next to mine.

"I really wish we wouldn't have had everyone come with us," Grady whispered, walking me backward toward the lake.

"Like the kids wouldn't have followed us, anyway?" I laughed, stepping into the cool water.

"True," Grady grinned. "We can come back to the lake tonight after the kids go to sleep."

"Swimsuits optional?"

"The hell with swimsuits."

We swam and played with the kids for hours before Anne and I both decided it was time to get them home. They had been running at full speed since dawn.

Stepping out of the lake and drying off, Pops came charging up to me.

"Kelsey Harrison," Pops said, very formerly.

"Yeah?" I laughed.

"I would like to officially ask for your blessing in marrying Hattie."

"My blessing?" I laughed, turning to look at Hattie. "Hattie, do you want to marry Pops, or not?"

"Yes dear, but you're the head of our family, and therefore I asked Pops to get your blessing," she grinned.

I turned to Anne, and she giggled. I turned to Grady, who was rubbing his forehead, trying not to laugh.

"Ok," I shrugged. "I officially give my blessing. When's the wedding?"

"Saturday," Pops grinned before swooping Hattie up and kissing her.

"Saturday?" Katie asked, stepping up beside me.

"As in this Saturday?" Lisa asked, walking up carrying little Abigail.

"How are we going to plan a wedding so quickly?" Anne asked.

"This is Texas," Reggie grinned. "We can have a hundred people here by Saturday and a big tent wedding. No problem."

"Why the rush?" I called out over to Hattie and Pops.

Pops turned with Hattie still wrapped in his arms. "We decided to live six months in Michigan and six months in Texas every year. But, Hattie won't let me stay in the main house in Michigan until we're married."

"Hattie, you do know that Grady's moving in and I'm not married?"

"You are not married, YET," Grady chuckled, wrapping his arms around me and pulling me into his body.

"Sinners," Hattie giggled, following Pops down the trail to the house.

Anne snorted.

"She meant you too," I laughed, hip bumping her, so she lost her balance.

"Whiskey and I don't live together," Anne said, shaking her head, still laughing.

Everyone turned to her, including Whiskey.

"Oh," she giggled. "I guess you do live with me."

"That's ok, Babe," Whiskey chuckled. "I'll make an honest woman out of you."

"You will?"

"Just tell me when," Whiskey grinned down at her.

Chapter Forty-Three

A few days later, wrapped in a warm blanket sleeping, Nicholas and Sara's giggles woke me. I kept my eyes shut, waiting to see what they were up to.

"Shhh," Nicholas whispered, not so quietly. "You're going to wake her."

I felt my ring being pulled off my right hand. I waited until it was at my last knuckle before I closed my hand into a fist, sat up and yelled loudly. Both of them jumped back, landing on their butts on the floor.

I laughed, pushing the pillows up and leaning against the headboard as I slid the ring back down in its proper place.

"Dang it," Nicholas pouted.

Grady had offered the kids $5 each time they managed to move the ring from my right hand to my left. Sleeping now required staying fully dressed at all times. Sara had succeeded twice in switching the ring. Nicholas was striking out.

"Now that I'm awake, where's my coffee?" I laughed.

"Aunt Katie said you have to come out for coffee this morning," Sara grinned, before skipping out of the room.

Nicholas followed her out to see what trouble they could get into next.

Bummed about not getting coffee in bed this morning, I pulled my ratted hair up into a scrunchy and went to the dining room where Hattie, Pops, Grady, and Donovan sat.

Grady poured me a cup of coffee out of the carafe, and I curled up in the chair next to him.

"Good Morning," I grinned at everyone.

"Good Morning, Sunshine," Hattie smiled, sliding a plate of bagels and cream cheese closer to me.

"Where is everyone?"

"The girls are working with Reggie and Jackson on the final wedding stuff," Hattie shrugged. "I just hope they don't overdo it. The whole point of having a short-notice wedding was so it wouldn't get out of control like Lisa's was."

"Oh, I'm sure they'll overdo it," I laughed.

"Have you talked to Charlie, dear?" Hattie asked.

Grady reached over and placed a hand on my leg. I shook my head at Hattie.

"I called her and invited her back for the wedding, but she said she couldn't make it," Hattie said. "She sounded upset."

"I blindsided her the other day with answers to the questions she's been asking her whole life. It's going to take her a while to adjust to the truth."

"Should she be alone?" Hattie asked.

"No," I said shaking my head.

I reached over and picked up Donovan's phone, using it to call Kierson.

"Donovan, damn it, I was trying to sleep in," Kierson cursed, answering the call.

"It's actually Kelsey," I laughed. "I've got a favor to ask."

"What's wrong?" Kierson sighed.

"Charlie's gone rogue, and I'm not the right person to reach out to her right now. I was wondering if you could go check on her for me?"

"Where is she?"

"I'm sure she's in our hometown," I answered. "She'll be looking for revenge. I don't know what she has planned or if she's going to get herself into trouble."

"I'll track her down. I was going to call you today. The lab confirmed at least a dozen DNA samples found in the woodstove."

"Damn," I sighed, resting my head in my other hand.

"At least the victim's families will have closure."

"I know. It just sucks," I sighed. "Any word from Maggie?"

"I took her statement yesterday. It wasn't easy. She's leaving the hospital today, and Nightcrawler is taking her somewhere quiet. She doesn't want to see anyone yet."

"She'll be ok, Kierson. Nightcrawler will help her."

"I hope so. How's Genie doing?"

"Wild Card noticed that Genie is an adult. It's getting interesting around here," I grinned.

"Shit. Tell Wild Card to stay the hell away from her, or I'll lock his ass up. She's like a little sister," Kierson cursed.

"Later Kierson," I said, disconnecting the line.

"Kierson threaten Wild Card?" Donovan asked.

"Yup," I nodded.

I turned to Hattie who was fiddling with the silk centerpiece arrangement.

"Did you find a wedding dress yet?"

"No. Lisa, Anne, and Reggie dragged me everywhere, but I didn't like anything they found. Alex even ordered a few online and had them shipped overnight, but they don't fit right. And, they're all uncomfortable."

"There's a dress in my closet that might work," I shrugged. "Go take a look."

Hattie looked at me curiously, but then got up and walked down the hall.

"When did you buy a dress?" Pops laughed.

"I went to see Maude Rallins, yesterday. I knew she'd have something Hattie would like," I winked.

Maude was a local seamstress and dressmaker. She didn't do fancy, but she made simple, elegant dresses for all occasions. I found a cream dress that would look lovely on Hattie and fit a backyard wedding theme perfectly.

"What's that?" I asked Donovan, nodding to the rolled floor plans that were leaning against his chair.

"I was showing Grady the blueprints for the new security site. He's agreed to be the new recruit trainer, so he won't have to go out on as many jobs."

"Would you consider hiring me for jobs?" I asked, sipping my coffee.

"No," Donovan grinned. "Not because you wouldn't be good at it, but because Grady had a better idea."

"Please say yes," Tech grinned, walking into the dining room holding Katie's hand.

"Say yes to what?" I asked.

"Running our new investigations unit," Donovan grinned, unrolling the blueprint on the table. "We have a large room we can turn into a War Room. Tech has agreed to be your data analyst if you agree to run the unit. Not only could you work for private citizens, but you could subcontract jobs from police departments and the FBI."

"Seriously?" I asked, leaning over to look at the layout.

"I hope you agree because Tech already ordered all the equipment," Katie laughed.

"So, I'd investigate what, exactly?" I asked.

"Right now, we have bodyguard assignments out on five stalker cases," Donovan said. "You can help us clear those up and then pick and choose what cases you work."

"And, you'd be my boss?" I asked, scrunching up my nose at Donovan.

"I'll try not to be insulted by your facial expression," Donovan laughed. "No, I can offer you a partnership for running the unit. I've also been given permission to tell you and everyone else that Grady is my only other partner."

"What?? But I met your other two partners. On several occasions," I said, looking back and forth between Grady and Donovan.

"They have been pretending they were my partners to keep Grady's ownership a secret," Donovan grinned. "They really just handle some of the management duties for us."

I looked over my shoulder at Grady, but he just grinned as he drank his coffee.

"If I decide to do this, I will insist on part ownership so neither one of you can boss me around," I said.

"We know," Grady grinned. "It will be your unit. You'll work with us only when you need protection on a job."

"What about Nick? He won't understand this," I sighed.

"I'll talk to him if it's what you want to do. And, unlike in the past, there will be a whole pack of people around to keep him safe if a case gets dicey," Grady said. "But, it's your decision."

"Draw up a contract, and I'll take a look," I nodded.

Grady slid a folder down the table to me.

"Really?" I laughed, shaking my head and taking the folder and my coffee down the hall to check on Hattie.

After a quick knock, I opened the door to find Hattie standing in front of a mirror with tears streaming down her face. She was wearing the cream dress, trimmed out in antique lace.

"You don't have to cry about it," I laughed. "We can find a different dress before the wedding."

"You know this dress is perfect," she grinned. "You know me better than anyone."

"And, you know me better than anyone," I grinned, tossing the folder on the bed and sitting on the corner to look up at her.

"What's in the folder, Dear?"

"A job offer," I shrugged. "Donovan and Grady want me to open an investigation unit within the security company. They already have some stalker cases for me to investigate."

"I see," she grinned, sitting carefully on the other corner of the bed. "And, you didn't want to tell them you're afraid."

"They don't think of me that way," I sighed. "They see the woman that can find the bad guy, fix the problem."

"If you think Grady sees you like that, then you're a moron," Hattie chuckled.

"Hattie!" I laughed.

"Well, it's the truth. He sees your fear, but he also sees your passion and your unrelenting drive. Think about it—even after Nicholas was taken, you took in Anne and Lisa knowing bad people were after them. Grady knows it's only a matter of time before you walk right into the middle of a mess again. And, he's scared too. By offering you this opportunity, you and Nicholas would always be protected by the security firm. You'd be on everyone's radar, and you wouldn't feel like you had to battle the bad guys alone."

"What if I can't do it anymore? What if I can't stomach seeing any more evil in this world?"

"Now you're being naïve," Hattie chuckled, standing to unzip the dress. "You can't turn a blind eye and pretend the monsters aren't out there. It's not in your nature to hide from them. You have a unique gift, Sunshine. Don't waste it. The world needs you."

She stepped into the bathroom and around the corner, returning a few minutes later in her normal clothes.

"Thank you for the dress," she said, leaning down to kiss the top of my head.

"You're welcome, Hattie," I grinned.

"Take the job, Sunshine," she giggled, walking back down the hall.

I smiled as I watched her walk away.

I fully intended on taking the job.

Thank you for reading Kelsey's Burden Series! Stay tuned for new novels, both spinoffs from the original gang and new standalone books. And, who knows... there may be more adventures for Kelsey in the future too...

Special thanks to Judy G. and Kathie Z. for your editing and proofreading assistance. You're both marvelous! Thank you.

Novels by Kaylie Hunter:

Kelsey's Burden Series
Layered Lies
Past Haunts
Friends and Foes
Blood and Tears
Love and Rage

Standalone Novels
Coming soon... Slightly Off-Balance

About the Author

My brother was a 'picker'. Not a nose picker! I mean he would relentlessly pick on other kids until someone stopped him. He wasn't a bully. He just thought it was funny and never knew when enough-was-enough. As his younger sibling, I got more than my fair share of this attention. Most days I had to resort to tattling just to survive. It was either tattle or he would continue on with his non-stop pestering until I ran to my room crying. (Yes, I was an emotional child.)

One day, we were out in the yard and he was at it again. I don't even remember why he was picking on me, but I warned him to leave me alone, several times. But, as always, he didn't stop. And like an out-of-body experience, I watched my seven-year-old self grab a shovel that was leaning against the house and with a full batter's wind-up—I slammed the flat side of it into his forehead.

After the vibrations had stopped rattling my little arms, I dropped the shovel to the ground. My brother was laying several feet away from me—silent—for once. Of course, he was unconscious, possibly dead, but he was finally silent.

I stood there a long time, just staring down at him. There wasn't any blood, but I could see his forehead growing at a rapid speed, and he still wasn't moving. Knowing I had no other choice, I ran inside to tell my mother that I knocked my brother out. Guess what—she didn't believe me! It took a lot of convincing, but she finally followed me outside. Once she saw him, she screeched a lot until she managed to get him to wake up.

As he glared at me from his bed in the grass, I remember thinking, he's going to kill me. My mother must have seen the look he gave me too. And, being fast on her feet, she executed an immediate punishment: *I had to be his servant for a week*. That's right, you heard me. The punishment was to wait on my nine-year-old brother and indulge his never-ending whims. And, of course, out of brotherly love, he made the most of every bit of my punishment. I had to get him water, then with more ice, then with less ice. Oh, and that darn TV! This was before remote controls existed, so every five minutes the TV channel either had to be changed or the volume adjusted. He'd wait for me to sit down and then bark a new command. I had to make his bed, do both our chores, and even serve him his meals.

I learned two things from this childhood experience. The first, when you're dealing with children, the most effective punishments are the most creative. The second? Don't rat yourself out when you knock your brother unconscious.

Love you Scoot! But you're still a pain.

Thank you to my readers for your continued support and very appreciated reviews. Until the next book...

Best Wishes to All,
Kaylie Hunter

For updates on new releases, follow my Amazon author page. You may also find me at Facebook: Author Kaylie Hunter, Twitter: @BooksByKaylie, or email: AuthorKaylieHunter@gmail.com